D0428834

Girl in the Afternoon

Girl in the Afternoon

SERENA BURDICK

ST. MARTIN'S PRESS
New York

This is a work of fiction. All of the characters, organizations, and events portrayed in this novel are either products of the author's imagination or are used fictitiously.

For information, address St. Martin's Press, 175 Fifth Avenue, New York, N.Y. 10010.

www.stmartins.com

The Library of Congress Cataloging-in-Publication Data is available upon request.

ISBN 978-1-250-08267-1 (hardcover)
ISBN 978-1-250-10668-1 (e-book)

Our books may be purchased in bulk for promotional, educational, or business use. Please contact your local bookseller or the Macmillan Corporate and Premium Sales Department at 1-800-221-7945, extension 5442, or by e-mail at MacmillanSpecialMarkets@macmillan.com.

First Edition: July 2016

10 9 8 7 6 5 4 3 2 1

For my sister, Lilia

ENGLAND 1878

Sometimes, in this big, cold house, I pretend I am an explorer on an expedition, navigating the long corridors like rivers, the huge rooms like undiscovered islands. I crawl under tables and leap onto sofas. I take my sister's hand, and we run through the rooms together. But the air next to my body is cold because she isn't really there, and when I look at the empty space next to me, my chest hurts. It hurts right where my heart is, so I think that this must be what is meant by a broken heart.

"Why," I ask Maman, "is everything different?"

She puts her hands on my cheeks and looks at me with eyes that are so soft and brown I wish I could touch them.

"You are just a boy," she says. "It is too much for a boy to understand."

PARIS 1870

Chapter 1

Aimée was never told why Henri came to live with them. She was never told anything that mattered. She used to think it was because she was a girl, and only boys got to know the truth about things, but eventually she came to understand that some things are better left unknown.

On that cold December morning when Henri disappeared, Aimée lay on her bed with her face buried in a pillow. In her right hand she held her stone necklace, smoothing her thumb and forefinger over the cool surface.

It was raining the day Henri found the stone. It was the size of a thimble, clear as crystal and flecked with pink. They were children then, and with his head bent against the rain, Henri showed her the perfect hole in its center. Later that night, he strung it on a piece of string and tied it around her neck.

Aimée lifted her face from the pillow and dropped back onto her cheek, covering her nose and mouth with her hand. Even the icy temperature couldn't stem the rank smell of gun smoke and cannon fire. She breathed into her palm, her breath moist and warm, just as Henri's breath had been against her lips last night.

She remembered the surprising taste of his mouth, his salty lips, and the firm groping of his tongue, how the kiss had grown gentler and slower and had made her feel as if her legs wouldn't hold her up.

Tossing off her warm eiderdown quilt, Aimée jumped out of bed, sucking frigid air through clenched teeth, and slipped her feet into icy slippers. She snatched a shawl off the back of a chair and wrapped it over her shoulders. Through the window, a band of sunlight stretched across the room and lit up the doorknobs on her wardrobe like tiny blue flames.

She pulled a sketchbook from her desk, flipping it open to a picture of Henri, his features thin and youthful, but with the awkward beginnings of maturity. There was a look of mischief in his eyes, maybe a touch of fear, and a hesitant half smile on his lips.

It was the sketch she'd done when she was fourteen years old—Henri already a mature sixteen—and she'd insisted he take his shirt off. "Just do it already," she'd said. "It's the only way I'm ever going to paint a nude. You'll get to go to the académie and paint all the nudes you want. I'll be stuck here with the peaches."

Aimée snatched a peach off the table where their instructor, the acclaimed Barbizon painter Monsieur Camentron, had meticulously placed it and sank her teeth into the pink flesh.

"Aimée?" Henri had leaned his long arm on the shiny mahogany and gave a disapproving wag of his finger. "How are we going to finish our paintings with one less peach?"

She shrugged. "We'll scrape one out and insist he only set out two. Camentron's too senile to remember anyway."

Aimée could remember how warm the sun had felt pouring through the high windows, turning everything rich and vibrant. She could remember the sweet taste of the peach as she'd watched

Henri unbutton his shirt and cautiously tug the cuffs over his hands, sliding his lanky arms through the sleeves. She remembered the heat in her cheeks when she'd seen his scrawny, hairless chest, and how she had laughed a stupid laugh.

"Start drawing before someone catches us," Henri had said, and she'd dropped the sticky pit back into the bowl and taken up her box of Conté crayons.

It was Henri who'd taught Aimée to draw when he had first arrived.

"It's an acceptable way to keep to yourself," he'd told her.

They would lie on their stomachs with their drawing boards in front of them, kicking their legs in the air. Very quickly Aimée had found she could copy the objects in front of her with amazing accuracy.

"Exceptional," Henri had said when she'd handed him a drawing of a toy monkey.

Aimée had bitten her bottom lip and looked down at her blue-veined hands, the praise warm in her belly. She was a skinny, pale child with narrow lips and gray eyes. There had never been anything exceptional about her.

When they drew, Henri would tell fantastical stories of faraway places, and Aimée would add pictures reflecting the tale. Later, when they had inched their way into adult bodies and began seriously painting, they spoke very little. It was easier to pretend they were concentrating, when really they had grown shy. There was none of the relaxed carelessness of most siblings, no banter or ridicule. But then, they were not brother and sister, rather companions who had been raised in the same home, and that was the difference.

After a while, the silence became what they needed most. A form of communication more precious than their art, balanced tenderly and cautiously between them. There was an intimacy in it, a suspension of time like the moment right before a kiss. And it was this that they first fell in love with, the ability to be together and alone at the same time.

The day before Henri disappeared, Colette Savaray stood in the parlor smoothing her hands down the front of her dress and staring at the floor where the rug used to be. They'd rolled it up months earlier and removed it with the rest of the First Empire furniture. The wood, where the rug had been, was shinier than the wood around the edge of the room, and Colette realized it would be no easy feat getting that enormous rug placed again.

She looked over the sparse room. There was a velvet sofa marooned in the middle of the floor, stripped of its end tables, facing two walnut chairs taken from the dining room, their red upholstered seats completely out of place against the blue-and-gold paper on the walls. Colette hated the bareness and the way every sound, even the click of her heels, echoed and bounced back at her.

She yanked open the brocade curtains they now kept closed in the daytime. Dust floated like a strip of tulle in the dull light. Colette swirled her arm through it, scattering the motes with her open hand.

A loud crack shot down the hall, and she snapped her arm to her side, imagining a bullet barreling through the doorway.

The sound came again, and she laughed. It was only the front-door knocker.

"Marie?" she called, looking one way and then the other before sitting in one of the chairs. "Marie! There's someone at the door."

They hadn't had a visitor in months. Even with the horrors outside—bloodied soldiers being carried through the streets in omnibuses and all those dead horses—it was knowing that no person could get in or out of Paris that made Colette feel most frantic, like a caged animal. Just hearing the sound of that knocker gave her a sense of hopefulness, despite the state of her house. She reached a hand to her hair and pushed the pins in place, wishing she'd taken more care with her toilet that morning.

Their housekeeper, Marie, the one loyal servant who remained, made her way down the hall. She was a stout, middle-aged woman with shocking red hair that sprang in tight, uncontrollable curls.

"I'm here, madame," she called as she passed the parlor door, and Colette heard Marie's wooden shoes clomping in the vestibule and then the reverberating chink of the outer door's steel handle.

When Édouard Manet stepped into the parlor, Colette rose with a ravishing smile. "My goodness!" she exclaimed, extending a hand. "Any visitor would be cause for celebration, but you, Monsieur Manet, really are a thrill."

"Madame." Édouard took her hand, kissed it, and released it back to her. He looked thinner than usual in his military greatcoat, but his beard was still full, his small, dark eyes authoritative and reassuring. Even in wartime he was impeccably dressed, his coat brushed, his shoes polished and shiny. He was a man who claimed a room, and Colette found this irresistible.

"Do sit down. I want all the news." She gestured to the sofa, easing herself onto her chair.

Édouard sat, unbuttoning the top two buttons of his coat. "It's either smallpox, starvation, shells flying through our windows, or else we'll be buried alive in sandbags," he said with a wry smile. "You should have left with the other families when you had the chance. Stubborn, the lot of you. The Morisot women refused to leave as well."

"You can't blame any of us. Who knew the Prussians would be so fierce and so many?" Colette leaned forward with a hand to her chest. "I, myself, am a liberal Bonapartist, but clearly Gambetta and the new republic were unprepared. We've blown up our own bridges, for goodness' sake, and even that hasn't stopped the Prussians. I heard Bougival and Louveciennes have suffered as much damage as anywhere else. Such carnage and wreckage is beyond me."

Colette was not a frivolous woman, as she often appeared, but rather quite intelligent. Édouard appreciated this about her.

"Losing the battle at Loire has done us in, I'm afraid," he said. "I don't know how much longer we can hold out. We're shooting each other out there now." He jutted his chin in the direction of the window. "No one even knows who's in charge. It'll come to a civil war if there isn't an armistice soon, and that will mean full surrender." He turned up his hands, opening them to the ceiling as if the Prussians were waiting in the rafters.

"At least it would put an end to all of this suffering," Colette said.

"How are you faring for food?"

"We're not starved yet—unrefined bread and cabbage at twenty francs a head. What I wouldn't give for a warm café au lait."

Sitting across from Édouard, Colette could almost feel the warmth of that café au lait slipping down her throat. For the first time in months she felt certain things would normalize. Surrender or no surrender, Paris would survive this war, and her Thursday-night soirées would resume. Her dining room would be full of guests again. There would be music and spirits and laughter.

Édouard cupped his hands to his mouth and blew a puff of air into them. "How is Auguste's wound?"

"What wound?" Colette gave a dismissive flip of her hand. "His foot healed weeks ago. He just refuses to get out of bed."

Édouard smiled. "Warmest place to be. He did his duty. Might as well rest up. Things are only going to get worse before they get better." He stood and gave a slight bow of his head. "Madame, I apologize that I am not able to stay longer. I just wanted to make sure no one was sick or intolerably hungry." Then he said, "I assume the children are well?" which seemed silly to Colette, calling them children. Aimée was eighteen years old, and Henri would be twenty in April.

"They're doing as well as can be expected. Still painting until their supplies run out, as I'm sure you are." She smiled, thinking of the portrait of her Auguste had commissioned Édouard to paint. For three months Édouard's superior eye had been on her, and it had given her a gratifying sense of importance.

After Édouard left, Colette went into her husband's study and stood in front of that painting. It was almost ten years ago now. She looked young and beautiful with her dark hair pulled into a high chignon and her slender hands crossed in the lap of her shimmering green dress.

She had been sure Édouard would seduce her with all those hours alone together. But he had worked silently, bitterly scraping away what dissatisfied him and scrupulously filling in what pleased him. When it was over he'd simply thanked her and said good-bye.

Colette stepped away from the painting and caught the reflection of her older self in the window glass. She ran two fingers along her hairline, pulling at her skin with a restlessness that was not brought on by the war, but by a sense of entrapment in her body. It was amazing what ten years could do to a woman. She would be thirty-nine years old in the spring. As a little girl she'd watched her maman bind her face in raw meat at night to prevent wrinkles. Colette's solution required eggs, rosewater, alum, and sweet oil of almonds, all of which were unattainable in this disastrous war.

Turning away from her reflection, she walked past her husband's meticulously organized desk, thinking of Édouard with a shudder of desire.

The next morning, when the sun rose bright and cruel above the haze of smoke that covered the city, Henri made up his mind to leave. He had only slept a few hours, and he lay with his wrist flung over his eyes, blocking out the sharp light that persisted through the windows.

Last night had the outlines of a dream, its degradation cloaked in uncertainty. But it wasn't a dream, and the shame of it coiled through him, cool and piercing as wire.

The crack of a bullet came from outside, a sharp whine as it sailed through the air, and then silence. Henri pulled his hand from his face and tucked his arm under the quilt, pressing his icy fingertips into his bare stomach. From his pillow he could see the underside of the varnished cherry bedposts, and the blooms on the wallpaper bursting open to the ceiling.

How sweet it would be to roll over, pull his head under the warmth of the quilt, and fall back asleep. But the slant of light through the windows, and the silence in the house told him that it was still early, early enough to slip away undetected.

On a count of three, he tossed the covers off and sat up. The air was so raw the shock of it almost took away the hollow dread in the pit of his stomach.

The fires in the house hadn't been lit in months. Paris had been under siege for one hundred days, and there was nothing left to burn. What peat they had was reserved for cooking, but even that wouldn't last much longer.

Taking short puffs of air into his lungs, Henri snatched his wool stockings from the floor, his linen drawers and undershirt, and hurriedly put them on. From a trunk he took a pair of twill trousers, a shirt, waistcoat, and cravat. His armoire had been removed for safekeeping, and his clothes were badly creased. But that hardly mattered now.

He struggled to tie his cravat, his fingers stiff with cold as he walked to the window, watching a pall of black smoke curl over the rooftops into a clear sky. The street was eerily deserted, the road a sheet of ice. It would be slippery going, he thought, feeling very weak, like a boy again standing at his old bedroom window in England. There had been snow on the ground when he left then too, and he had felt this same sense of dread.

Shells fell outside like cracks of thunder, and Henri pressed his palms over his eyes. He was not a brave man, and yet he wasn't afraid of being hit by a stray bullet or freezing in a gutter. He was afraid of facing the intolerable loneliness he'd known before coming here.

He turned from the window as the sound of footsteps came down the corridor, frantically stepping toward the bed as if he meant to hide under it. He couldn't face Colette, or Auguste, but it was the thought of seeing Aimée's serious eyes and her honest, straightforward face that made him feel sick.

The latch to his bedroom door clicked and lifted, but whoever stood on the other side clearly couldn't face him either, because the latch fell back into place, and the footsteps receded down the hall.

Henri didn't waste any time then. He grabbed his bag, threw in two pairs of stockings, a shirt, trousers, and his black frock coat. Briefly, he fingered his waistcoat embroidered with tulips and edged in silk ribbon, then shoved it back into the trunk.

Pulling on his greatcoat, he hoisted his bag over one shoulder and stepped gingerly into the hallway. He wondered how he was going to retrieve his paint box and portable easel from his studio on the third story where the militiamen were now billeted.

The corridor was empty and quiet. Henri knew he should hurry, and yet he stood looking at the small dent on the floor where, as a child, he'd dropped a large, marble elephant Auguste had given him. The elephant was still on the mantel in his bedroom with a chip in its trunk.

Henri thought of going back for it, but he didn't, and when he finally moved forward, it wasn't courage or any sort of heroic strength that drove him, only simple, undeniable shame.

As Henri crept down the hall, stepping cautiously over the soft sections of floor that moaned with pressure, Colette sat at her dressing table untangling metal curlers from her hair and trying to ignore the gurgling noise coming from her husband's open mouth in the bed behind her. With a hand mirror, she arranged the curls at the back of her neck and then pinned a large amethyst brooch at her throat. After last night, she felt it imperative to look particularly lovely today, no matter the war.

When she finished, she stood over Auguste and watched him sleep. The white coverlet was clutched up to his chin, which had sprouted unruly whiskers. *Lazy whiskers,* Colette called them. He'd been a lot more attractive in his lieutenant's uniform, before he'd suffered the minor wound that forced him to leave the service. She may have been able to find something attractive in him if he'd been in the artillery, fighting heroically, but he'd been posted to the general staff where there was no real danger other than accidentally dropping his bayonet straight through his foot.

It was not that she didn't love him. She was just disgusted with him. What woman wouldn't be? He lay in bed all day complaining even though he could walk perfectly well with a cane.

"What's the point of getting up when there's no meal to go down to?" he grumbled. "Besides, keeping to bed is the only way to stay warm."

He'd tried to get her to join him, tugging at the front of her dress as he pulled her on top of him, and she'd had to slap his hands away from her breasts.

"You're too pathetic an old man to attract my attention anymore," she'd said, struggling to her feet, which had only made him laugh, as if he didn't really believe her.

This had always been their marriage. He would want her, she'd push him away, he'd become inflamed by her flirtatious nature, there would be a passionate fight, and then they'd fling themselves at each other. She held back for Auguste's own good. Marriage was boring. If she gave in easily there'd be no struggle, and men like a struggle.

She'd known this from the beginning. She made Auguste wait three years for her hand in marriage even though he had asked the very night he met her.

"You're magnificent," he'd whispered, pulling her off the dance floor onto a dark balcony. "Marry me."

"I've only just met you!" Colette had cried, her voice pitched with youth and the delight of attention. "Besides, I'd be a fool to marry the first man who asked."

She was only seventeen, after all, and not the type of girl to make things easy on anyone.

After that, she entertained more suitors than was respectable, receiving an outrageous number of proposals even for a woman of her beauty. Most men would have given up. Not Auguste. He didn't bother with the coy formalities of courtship, but worshipped Colette openly, which she rebuked, though secretly adoring his attention. He'd drop conversations the moment she entered a room, rushing to take her hand, holding it firmly as he ran his thumb over the ridge of her knuckles, at first gently, and then with enough pressure to arouse her.

If he'd only touch her like that again, Colette thought.

Auguste groaned and rolled over, one arm falling limply off the edge of the bed. He looked vulnerable in his sleep, and as Colette turned away, the gravity of what she had done sliced through her, sharp as a blade, leaving a deep wound of regret.

Auguste's maman, Madame Savaray, was the only one who saw Henri leave.

Earlier that morning she had been in the kitchen checking on the menial provisions Marie had procured for the day's meals. In normal times, Colette ran the household and had always made it perfectly clear that Madame Savaray was not to interfere. But ever since that first shell fell on Paris, Colette had receded, doing nothing to ensure their survival.

Madame Savaray, on the other hand, knew all about survival. She came from the Nord—a much heartier people than the pampered Parisians—where she'd practically starved as a child. She knew what it was to be hungry, and she knew what it was to sleep on soiled linens. She also knew they should be grateful that, under Marie's vigilant stewardship, there was *something* to eat every day.

They had been fools to stay in Paris. Auguste had wanted to send them to England, but Henri, who was not obligated to fight since he was not a Frenchman, had refused to return to his homeland, something Madame Savaray simply did not understand. Colette had also refused to leave. She'd said, "I don't see why I should be cast out of my own home. These things always sound worse than they are." Of course, Auguste let her do exactly as she pleased. So here they were, stuck in Paris as it crashed and crumbled around them.

Fools, every one of them, Madame Savaray was thinking as she ascended the stairs, stopping at the sight of Henri, bag and easel in hand. He looked sickly. He had always been a thin, weak child, and he had grown into a thin, weak man. His stooped shoulders, his restless blue eyes that never seemed to settle anywhere, and the way he mumbled—as if petrified to speak up—had always made Madame Savaray pity him, as if the simple hardships of life were too much to bear.

Today, he looked particularly troubled, and there was such desperation in his piercing eyes that Madame Savaray stepped forward unwittingly, but he practically ran out the front door. She had the urge to run after him. Where in heaven's name was he going? To paint in the open air? What a ridiculous business this new method of painting outdoors. His hands would freeze. He would get shot. What could he be thinking?

Quickly, she went to the parlor.

Colette had just come in, missing Henri by minutes. She was seated at the far end of the room near a set of double doors that, in warmer months, opened onto a garden. In her hand she held a piece of ecru fabric cinched into an embroidery ring.

Madame Savaray couldn't help noticing how thoughtlessly attractive Colette looked this morning. There was a war on. The woman could at least attempt modesty. It was sacrilegious to sit in her silk dress with a brooch at her throat when people were freezing to death.

Wetting the tip of her finger and knotting the end of her thread, Colette glanced up at Madame Savaray. Her mother-in-law was a formidable woman, taller than most, with wide hips and an abundant chest that, with age, had turned into a hapless mound of flesh. Her face was set hard beneath a black bun, and her dated wool dress swished over the floor. It had always amazed Colette that—given Madame Savaray's age—her hair had never grayed. It was still so black that sunlight could turn it blue.

"Where is Henri going?" Madame Savaray demanded.

Colette's needle hovered over the tiny, yellow bird she was stitching. "Whatever do you mean?"

"He just walked out the front door."

Colette looked as if not quite understanding. Then she dropped her embroidery on the chair and stepped to the window. "He can't have," she said, drawing back the curtain.

"Well, he did!" Exasperated, Madame Savaray left the room. "Aimée?" she called, mounting the stairs to the second story, a muscle in her left leg cramping as it always did in this miserably cold weather, not to mention her hip joints cracking at every step. "Aimée?"

Her *petite-fille* stepped into the corridor, her hair half-up, the rest hanging straight down her back like a slab of dark wood. Aimée still had the figure of a girl, but she had grown into a thoughtful, serious woman with the most unusual eyes. At times, like right now, they were as soft and pale as the morning sky. But they could shift, without warning, to a sharp, unrelenting gray.

Madame Savaray halted in front of her, respiring quickly from the climb, the pain in her left leg worsening as she stood still. "What have you put Henri up to? You might as well tell me the truth. I have not the time, nor the patience, to drag it out of you."

"I haven't the slightest idea what you mean," Aimée said, a

hot rush of fear and excitement expanding through her. Henri must have already told her papa about them.

"He's gone." Madame Savaray's eyes narrowed. "And I suspect you know why."

"I'm certain he's in his room."

"Well, I'm certain he just walked out the front door."

"That's impossible. He can't have."

A puff of air exploded from Madame Savaray's lips. "It's quite possible," she said. "I just saw him leave."

Stunned, Aimée said, "Why would he do that?"

"He had his easel. I imagined you two had come up with some preposterous idea of risking his neck for a painting worthy of the *salon*." She shook her head. "Or some such nonsense."

Aimée flew down the hall. Henri's bedroom was empty, the bed covers tossed aside and the sheets rumpled where Henri's body had been. There was a slight indent on his pillow, a shirt-sleeve hanging over the edge of his trunk like a limp arm. Everything had the look of an impulsive departure, and Aimée felt a sudden lurch in her chest.

In the parlor, Colette was at the window with her fist clenched around the curtain. She did not look at her daughter when Aimée stood beside her. There was a hefty sigh from Madame Savaray as she sank onto the sofa, tucking her foot under her petticoat and flexing it to relieve the cramp in her leg.

Aimée pressed her forehead against the glass, the cold sending a tendril of pain coiling behind her eyes. The rue de Passy was empty. Nothing, save for a lone set of footprints broken through the ice-coated snow.

"Henri wouldn't paint in this weather," she said, peeling her head from the window, a red circle widening across her forehead. Henri would not leave her either. There must be some explanation. "We should tell Papa. He can send someone to find him."

Colette let go of the curtain and stepped carefully away from her daughter. "There's no need to worry your papa." She lifted her embroidery from the chair and sat down. "Monsieur Manet walked through the streets yesterday. Clearly, it's not that dangerous."

There was a pulsing in Aimée's neck, a fast thumping near the ridge of her throat as she watched her maman plunge her needle into the fabric. Her maman was not a cold woman, but she reserved her warmth when it came to Aimée and her papa, dishing it out in small, controlled doses. Where Henri was concerned, however, there was always a kind word, a smile of avowed admiration. Aimée pictured the indentation on Henri's pillow, the mark of his hurried absence, and fear ballooned inside her.

She turned back to the window, the snow outside brilliant and blinding.

"Aimée," Colette spoke sharply, focusing on exactly where to place the bird's outstretched wing in her embroidery. "Come away from that draft. You're struggling to see something that is not there."

If Colette had seen the desperation on her daughter's face, if she had noticed Aimée's hands turned up at her sides and her neck tilted forward in a silent plea for help, things might have turned out differently. But all Colette saw was the silhouette of her stubborn daughter in the window.

"I'm sure Henri just needed to get out of the house for a while," she said. "What I wouldn't give for some air."

Madame Savaray made an audible snort. "From the expression on Henri's face, he was not stepping out for a bit of air."

Colette gripped her needle, her hand dashing up and down. "And what expression was that, exactly?"

The question, in Madame Savaray's opinion, did not deserve an answer. She was no fool. She could see the uncertainty passing over Colette's face, her white knuckles, and her hand quickening its pace.

Seventeen idle years in this house had turned Madame Savaray into a keen observer. She made a game out of it, predicting the meanings behind a look or a gesture. There was so much a person didn't say. It amazed her that others didn't pay more attention to the silences. But then, there were so many things that had amazed her since she'd moved into this house after her husband's death.

She'd come from the town of Roubaix, where her husband had devoted himself to the new opportunities in textiles and made a great fortune. A huge portion of this he had used to finance his son's endeavors in Paris, where Auguste Savaray now ran a successful lace and linen thread business.

Madame Savaray had no idea how it was so successful. Her son, in her opinion, was lazy, and in her day a lazy man did not make a fortune. Her husband had worked fifteen-hour days and never once, in twenty years, took a holiday. She had worked just as hard beside him, controlling the accounts, keeping the books, distributing the raw materials, and inspecting the finished products. Every day, no matter the weather, she opened that factory gate at six in the morning for the workers. Her life was spent in a world of quality control, price fluctuations, and labor problems until her husband died, the business was sold, and she was forced to move in with her son. At the time, she imagined Auguste could use her help. Very quickly she learned that her son did not believe a woman, young or old, knew anything about running a business.

Madame Savaray watched as Colette deftly snipped a thread with a tiny pair of swan-shaped scissors. She did not understand this new generation of women. All they did was sit around in silk dresses planning soirées. She closed her eyes, the cramp in her leg finally easing up. She supposed Colette wasn't to blame for her ways. Men didn't want women to know the value of money anymore. It was just how the world was now.

A shell fell so close it shook the house. Madame Savaray's eyes flew open, and Colette's scissors dropped to the floor. Aimée clutched her skirt, watching the smoke swallow the street, blotting out the last blue strip of sky.

"Henri will be home by dinner," Madame Savaray said. "Aimée, my dear, you must stand away from that glass."

But Aimée couldn't move. She felt weak and brittle, like a withered twig hanging on to an already dead tree. It seemed she'd crack with the slightest movement, shatter, if she so much as bumped against something.

Chapter 2

So Henri did not come home for dinner.

Three weeks went by, and a deeply forlorn sense settled into the Savaray house. They did not celebrate the new year. If Henri had been there they might have found something hopeful to look toward in 1871, but he was not, and it seemed as if the war, their hunger, and the bitter cold would never end.

Now, Auguste hated to be in bed. Even with his aching foot he found it hard to keep still. His restlessness moved him through the house, and he wandered the corridors as if they were the streets of Paris, sharpening his worry over a grindstone of terrible thoughts, imagining Henri. Imagining the worst.

In the dining room one day, deeply exhausted, he dropped into a chair. Slumped over the table with his hands spread before him, he thought of his sons, something he did not let himself do often. He imagined how handsome they'd be if they'd had a chance to grow up, what lovely wives and children they'd have. He closed his eyes and filled the room with the noise of them, set the empty candelabras alight, the fire ablaze, drank his favorite Chambertin, lifted lamb to his mouth, potatoes doused in melted butter and plums swimming in their own, sweet juice.

Very quickly the images dissolved into a wide black hole

behind his eyes, and he opened them, taking in the silent room. If he could just get a whiff of something cooking, a scent of perfume, a flower, even, but the fetid smell of his own body, the stench under his arm and in his unwashed hair, made it impossible to imagine anything other than this dismal room and his immense loneliness. Smells, Auguste thought, held everything. Too much could ruin a perfectly decent woman, not enough, a perfectly decent meal. A smell could bring back the most vivid memory, or, like right now, ruin a delicate fantasy.

The urge to close his eyes again, to shut out the world, was great, but he forced himself not to. He looked out the window where snow fell in thick clumps against the panes. He realized he had no idea what time it was, or what day of the week, and this surprised him, that he'd lost touch with the things in life that grounded a person.

He pictured Henri crouched in a doorway, his boots packed with snow, his arms wrapped around his thin chest.

As a boy, Henri had once slipped his hand inside of Auguste's and said, *I wish you were my real papa.* Auguste had looked down into Henri's wide eyes and said, *Boys don't often love their real papas. Much better this way.*

Two days after Auguste crawled back into bed—deciding he would keep to it until this blasted war was over—Madame Savaray resolved that she must do something. Even with the Sabbath, and the pain in her hip, she needed to bring some semblance of normalcy to the household. Since she did not care one whit about keeping up appearances, she went into the kitchen and took the cook's bloodstained apron from the hook.

Marie came in just as Madame Savaray was cracking the layer

of ice in the water bucket. "Madame," she said reasonably, "you ought not to do that."

Madame Savaray plunged her rag into the freezing sludge at the bottom of the bucket. "I did it before my marriage, and I can do it now," she said.

It hurt more now, that was all, but Madame Savaray could tolerate the ache in her knuckles and her cracking hips. What she could not tolerate was this house. If she could scrub away the self-indulgent filth, she would. Grabbing the bar of lye soap, she swiped it over her wet rag. Then, to Marie's horror, Madame Savaray got down on her hands and knees and began scouring the floor.

Working the rag with her head down and her shoulders hunched, Madame Savaray was reminded of her maman's kitchen on washing day. She remembered the smell of ash, and the moist air that made her hair curl at the temples. For eighteen hours she had stood pouring water through the bucking cloth, over the ashes and potash, collecting it from the tap, reheating it and pouring it through again and again. Despite her wrinkled hands and blistered feet, she had found the work soothing. Nothing soothed her like that anymore.

When the kitchen floor was finished, she rinsed her rag in the bucket. Her knees hurt and her hands were numb, but she found satisfaction in that. Her legs and back had ached at the end of washing day too. Pain was a job well done.

Later that afternoon, Colette found Madame Savaray in Henri and Aimée's studio on her hands and knees, and she thought the old woman had lost her mind.

"God help us! What do you think you're doing?" she cried.

Madame Savaray couldn't be bothered to look up. "Cleaning."

"Why would you do such a thing?"

"It needs to be done, and I'm not proud."

"Well, you ought to be." Colette walked to a table where a stack of books had been arranged next to a sheet of paper, a quill pen, and a bulbous decanter. "You didn't touch anything in here, did you?"

Madame Savaray dropped her rag in the bucket. "Of course I did." She heaved herself up with a grunt, her knees taking a minute to straighten. "I dusted all around those." She nodded at the objects Colette was scrutinizing.

Sunlight settled on the tubes of paint laid out on a console table next to a row of brushes and an empty wooden palette, the neatness sadly expectant.

"He's not coming back," Madame Savaray said, and Colette stiffened. "I knew it when I saw his face before he walked out, but I didn't really believe it until I came in here."

The light from the window cast a glow, and the flecks of gold in Colette's eyes jumped like sparks under the low slant of her lids. She was much too beautiful a woman, Madame Savaray thought. There was always trouble to be found in women who were so beautiful.

"You had better take that thing off by the time this war is over," Colette said, watching Madame Savaray wipe her hands down the front of her apron. "There will be no end to the gossip."

Madame Savaray ignored her. "I suppose if he loves Aimée enough he might come back for her."

Heat leaped into Colette's cheeks, and she tilted her head with a look of subtle confusion. "What, exactly, do you mean?"

"Goodness." Madame Savaray raised a single eyebrow. "You and Auguste are fools if you haven't seen it. Aimée and Henri are quite in love, and you can't blame them. Putting them in such proximity all these years. What did you expect? I thought you'd have had more sense."

Colette's lower jaw bulged as she clenched her teeth. Lifting her shoulders in a graceful but deliberate shrug, she said, "I do believe you've mistaken love for boredom. If Henri cared about any of us, he'd come back. At the very least he would let us know what's become of him. It's the benevolent thing to do, after all we've done for him." She moved to the door, flicking her hand as if shooing a fly. "You'll stop this foolishness soon enough," she said, walking out.

In the corridor, Colette scraped her teeth together as she steadied herself against the wall, the sound reverberating in her head.

Henri simply could not come back. Not now. Not for Aimée, not for any of them.

As her maman made her way down the hallway, Aimée stood at her bedroom window watching a bloody soldier crawl across the street, snow glittering around him in the sunlight. Another soldier leaned against a building smoking a cigarette. Aimée thought the man on his knees was going to ask for help, but he crawled right past as if he had somewhere important to go, as if crawling on one's knees was a perfectly acceptable thing to do.

Aimée dug her nails into her sunken cheeks. She wanted to rip out her hair, to scream, to throw something that would smash and fly apart in a million pieces.

She slammed her fist into the frozen window latch and pushed the window open, letting the cold wash over her. A satisfying line of red blood rode across her knuckle. The soldiers were gone, and a thin cloud cover had swept across the sky, turning it as white as the snow. Holding on to the windowsill, Aimée braced herself against that cold, empty, colorless world.

For weeks, Henri's departure had altered the shape of things. Furniture, windows, rooms. Nothing felt certain, not even solid things like oak chairs. Now, the fragility Aimée had felt since Henri left, the tremor under her skin and the loose detached way she moved through her days, had disappeared. She felt shaken awake.

The extraordinary effort of that soldier crawling along in the bitter cold made the dreadful weight of her own life feel worthless and insignificant. Maybe Henri had felt the same way. Maybe he had left because he needed a way to feel as if he were worth something.

For the first time since Henri's disappearance, Aimée forced herself to picture a life without him. She tried to remember who she had been before he'd arrived on that bleak day in April 1860 when she was just eight years old.

Chapter 3

There was a light spring drizzle the day Aimée was forced to wear her best dress with the too-tight bodice and ruffles.

She had been storming around the house since breakfast while everyone ignored her. No one would tell her why they were getting a grown boy from England instead of another baby brother. She assumed it was because the babies kept dying, but children died at all ages, so she didn't see how this was any guarantee.

The first baby had only lived for two months, and Aimée, who was three at the time, thought she had killed him because she had poked her finger in his mouth and he screamed the most terrific scream. The nurse whisked him away, and the next day her *grand-mère* told her that the baby had died suddenly, and they were not to speak of him again. Her maman wouldn't come out of her room, and her papa went away for a long time, so Aimée assumed they thought it was her fault too.

The second baby boy was born in the middle of the night. When Aimée asked to see him her *grand-mère* looked very grave and told her to *hush up*. There was never any mention of him again.

Then little Léon came. He lived for two whole years, and

Aimée loved him dearly. The first time he slipped his small, fat hand inside of hers, she was startled at how warm and soft he felt. No one ever touched Aimée with that kind of tenderness. Some children were propped on laps, caressed, and kissed. Some held their mamans' hands in the street, hugged their papas good night. Aimée was not that child. Her papa kept a solid distance between them. If he looked at her at all, it was with a confused, startled expression, as if not sure how she'd gotten into the room with him. Sometimes, her *grand-mère* would pat the top of her hair, but all Aimée felt was a rattling sensation in her head. Then there was her maman's bedtime kiss. Colette would swoop in like a bird diving for food and plant a kiss on Aimée's forehead. But Aimée was certain her maman was just kissing the air up there because she never felt a thing.

It was Léon who touched Aimée. He curled in her lap and wrapped his hands around her fingers. He kissed her, tugged on her clothes, and grabbed her hair. She didn't mind the sting of a scratch down her cheek or the accidental poke of an eye. She would pinch Léon's arms and suck on his plump fingers that tasted of sour milk. He never swatted at her or pushed her away, and she would rub his cheeks and stroke his head, feeling that she could never get enough of him.

Then he turned red with fever, and his hands became hot as fire. Long after Léon's face faded from her memory, Aimée could feel the heat of his hand that last time she touched him.

She didn't know that a body grew stiff and cold after it died. When they laid his tiny coffin in the ground, she hated her parents for leaving her soft, warm brother down in the dark earth all alone. She wanted to lie down there with him and hold him and tell him not to be afraid. It was her papa who dragged her out of the graveyard.

Now, some strange boy was coming to live with them. No

one was calling him her brother, and yet everyone was behaving in the same way they did when a new baby was expected. A room was made up for him, new clothes were purchased and laid out in the armoire, an elaborate dinner had been prepared, and Colette was glowing with anticipation.

When Henri arrived, Aimée refused to greet him. Instead, from behind the parlor door, she watched the short, timid boy step into the vestibule. He had hair the color of dirty straw and eyes as blue as the ones on her porcelain doll. An elegant woman wearing a blue traveling dress and an enormous blue hat stepped in behind him. Under the hat, Aimée could see that the lady's hair was the exact color of the boy's.

With one hand held to her mouth, the lady spoke to Aimée's papa. Aimée couldn't hear what she said, but her papa looked very solemn, and he kept shaking his head. Colette wasn't paying any attention. Probably because the woman was exceptionally pretty and her maman didn't pay attention to anyone who was prettier than she was. Colette crouched in front of the boy, smiling widely, her eyes crinkling at the corners as she brushed his hair from his forehead. After a few minutes the woman in the hat turned to leave, and then turned back, placing her gloved hand on top of the boy's head and giving him an uncomfortable little pat before she was gone.

Aimée's parents gazed at Henri as if he had dropped from heaven. Aimée thought he looked rather sickly, although he was richly clothed, and he'd come with a number of large trunks so at least he wasn't from an orphanage. Maybe his real parents would want him back.

At dinner her maman told her to speak English so Henri would feel at home. Aimée spoke clear, beautiful French all through the meal, and Colette gave her an icy look and Auguste ignored her, directing all of his attention to the boy.

Though Aimée promised herself she would stay away, later that night she walked into Henri's room without knocking and sat down at the foot of the bed. Henri was standing in the middle of the room holding a piece of paper, which he quickly tucked into his pocket. His breeches had shiny brass buttons on the cuffs that glinted in the lamplight as he brushed his foot over the rug.

"Well," Aimée said, in English. "You needn't bother to be nice to me because I have already decided I am not going to like you."

Henri smiled. He had a beautiful smile. It made him look like an entirely different boy. "That's all right," he said in poor French. "I'm rather used to not being liked."

Aimée pressed her lips together. She desperately wanted to ask *why* he hadn't been liked, but then it might look as if she wanted to be friends, which she did not, so she said nothing.

Henri sat down next to her. Color had risen to his cheeks. "I studied French, but I haven't had much opportunity to speak it. I'd prefer you *not* speak English to me so I might improve."

Aimée turned her head away. He was annoyingly agreeable.

Sounding very grown-up, he said, "I've never been around other children."

"Well, I've been around far too many." Aimée glanced sideways at him. "Maman loves having guests, so there are always children in the house. The boys are the worst. I have three boy cousins. They're horrid, always running about. I can never wear ribbons in my hair because they pull them out."

The truth was she envied their freedom. She'd tried to run about and had been slapped so many times that, eventually, it hadn't been worth the trouble.

She shifted her whole body so she could look at Henri straight on. "They'll like you more than they like me because you're a boy. They always like the boys more."

Henri wasn't sure if she meant her parents or her cousins.

After a few minutes, Aimée said, "You don't look like a boy who runs about."

"I'm not."

"Or one who pulls ribbons?"

"No."

"Well, that's good." She was starting to think a boy she could actually speak with might not be so bad. "Why were you sent away?"

Henri walked to the other end of the room, gazing up at a large portrait of a great, dead Savaray uncle on the wall. "There was trouble in my family."

"What trouble?" This sounded good.

Henri looked around his new bedroom, his face pale again. "I can't speak of it," he said quietly. For some reason he felt as if he were letting Aimée down. "I'm sorry," he added.

"You can tell me. I won't tell anyone," she pleaded.

Henri felt her watching him intensely. "I don't want to." He clasped his hands behind his back. "Please, don't ask me to."

There was so much sadness in his voice that Aimée, who was persistent and usually got what she wanted, just said, "Well, then, at least make up an interesting lie."

Henri looked so relieved that she never asked him again, and now, ten years later, Aimée stood in front of her window imagining Henri had gone back to where he'd come from. She envisioned him walking away with that lovely woman in the big blue hat, holding her hand.

PARIS 1873

Chapter 4

Postwar Paris flourished under the new republic. Streets were rebuilt, renamed. Picture dealers restyled their shops as galleries. Storefronts expanded, windows widened, displays became lavish, indulgent even. Dresses became sleeker and tighter, necklines lower, sleeves shorter, and gloves longer.

The biggest change for Auguste and Colette Savaray was the birth of their son Jacques, who was born into a house that begged for the distraction of a baby, a boy, a replacement.

The pregnancy surprised everyone. Colette was nearly forty years old. It was Aimée who should be married and having children. All the Savarays had hoped for was a grandson one day. A boy of their own, after all this time, was like being handed a gift too precious and terrifying to open. They held their breath after Jacques's birth. For months no one spoke above a whisper. Everyone tiptoed. Even as the boy grew into a fat, healthy baby, no one could quite trust he wasn't going to disappear.

That first year, Aimée was afraid to touch him. Watching his wrinkled newborn skin fill into lumps of soft flesh made her uncomfortable. His fists flailing in the air, and the sour smell of milk at the corner of his pink mouth, brought memories of Léon, filled with warmth and comfort and sadness.

It was only when Jacques came crawling to her one day that Aimée finally picked him up. At first, he just buried his head into the hem of her dress, then, clutching fistfuls of her skirt, he yanked himself to his feet. Aimée stared down at the boy's crown of fuzzy, blond hair, and waited for him to drop back onto his knees. Instead, he let go, wobbling on unstable legs for the first time. Aimée felt a rush of pride, as if somehow responsible for this triumphant moment. In an instant, Jacques fell backward, and Aimée screamed when his head smacked the wood floor. A scream quickly rivaled by Jacques's own tremendous wail. Swooping down, Aimée lifted him in her arms, rocking him until he quieted.

After that she didn't mind the warmth of his legs wrapped around her middle or his arms around her neck.

When Jacques was two years old Aimée let him into her studio. She sat him on a sheet of paper in the middle of the floor with sticks of pastels that he quickly ground into piles of dust. When Colette came in she found him covered in pale pink powder.

"Good gracious, Aimée," she said, lifting him off the floor and holding him at arm's length. "He will asphyxiate himself."

"Would you rather I give him paints?" Aimée said, and Colette rolled her eyes.

"Crayons would do, a pencil. Why do you have to be so unreasonable?" she said, walking out with Jacques hanging limply in front of her.

Aimée spent most of her time in the studio. Becoming educated and honing her talent were her only options aside from marriage. So she filled her studio in the Savarays' new apartment on the rue l'Ampère with books, splitting her time between reading and painting. She immersed herself in Roman history, French, and Greek, read Livy, Michelet, Aristophanes, Plutarch,

Homer, and Plato. She spent hours at the Louvre copying the old masters, and hours outdoors painting the changing light.

It was only in the silence of painting that she brought Henri back to life. She would listen for his steady breath beside her. Hear the rustle of his shirtsleeve and the shuffle of his shoes. She did not believe he was dead, but she had stopped believing he was coming back for her.

She became obsessed with drawing hands. Touch, she decided, was what made a person real. At night she'd lie in bed and stroke her fingers up her thighs, imagining the hands of whatever model she'd painted that day pressed against the walls of her skin, trying to feel herself into her own life.

After a while, hands did not satisfy her. Nudes were what she wanted. Ripe nipples, plump breasts, muscular thighs, taut arms, and full, rippled stomachs.

She enrolled at the Académie Julian. It was crowded and loud and horribly competitive, but it was the only school open to women, and the only place where she could paint her nudes, turn the bristles of her brush into hundreds of tiny fingers brushing the models to life.

The noise was frightening—all that snickering, coughing, shuffling, sighing, and general chaotic din that comes with a roomful of people. But Aimée had never liked painting alone in the three years since Henri had left. At least at the académie she was surrounded by real artists all struggling for the same end. Which, of course, was to get into the Salon de Paris, the official art exhibit of the Académie des Beaux-Arts.

Aimée's instructor, Rodolphe Julian, told her there was no hope. Her work was too bright. She used far too much blue. *Tone it down,* he would say. But he didn't have the faintest notion of values, so his criticism did not deter her. Aimée spent fourteen hours at a stretch at her canvas, took lessons in anatomy, endured hours of life classes. She started keeping real vertebrae in her bureau drawer next to her perfumed paper and visiting cards, which she'd study in the late hours of the night.

The mistake she made was in thinking that this would be enough, filling her canvases, filling her mind, filling up time. It wasn't. A part of her was restless and unsettled, expectant. Waiting, always, for something to happen.

And then it did. At first, the moment appeared insignificant, a passing encounter, hardly enough to change the course of everything.

It was a mild evening in late November, nothing too cold. The sky was clear with bright flecks of stars and the cool light of a half moon. Already the snow lay thick on the roofs, and the sparrows alighted on the eaves, balancing on twiggy legs.

Colette Savaray was throwing one of her soirées, and everyone appeared in high spirits as they shed their coats and hats, smiling at Colette and Auguste, who stood side by side, opulent as ever.

Aimée hovered behind her maman, self-conscious in her green shot silk dress with its low, round neck. Colette had picked out the fabric, much darker than her own pink and white stripes, but a color that suited Aimée.

A tall man walked through the door, and Colette lowered her chin, keeping her eyes on the man as she whispered to Aimée, "Arnaud Gaudet," whom they all knew as the wealthy owner of a porcelain factory.

Aimée watched the man draw his greatcoat from his shoulders, swing it around, and hand it to the housekeeper with an efficient nod. The man's neck was far too long for his small head. Under all his fine fabric he was certain to have hideous, knobby knees and elbows.

Avoiding an introduction, Aimée hurried over to her cousin

Julia, who had come in behind Monsieur Gaudet. They latched hands and kissed. Aimée glanced over her cousin's shoulder, thinking how strange it still felt to see Julia without her brothers, those rowdy boys who had pulled the ribbons from Aimée's hair so long ago. All three of them had been killed in the war.

Everyone, in some way, had been affected by the war and the revolution, topics that wove their way into conversation at the dinner table, opinions flying over gleaming baroque silver, crystal glasses, truffle salad, and lobster, shelled and drenched in brown butter and vinegar.

France had lost the war, full surrender. They spoke of Napoleon III's deposition and the National Assembly that was formed, a monarchist majority that agreed to all of Prussia's peace terms. And in low, fervent voices, they whispered of the bloody revolution, the massacre, that took place just months after the war ended, when spring was forgotten under a smoldering red cloud of smoke and the streets of Paris filled again with gunfire and lifeless bodies.

Aimée ate silently, listening as everyone blamed the commune—the Parisian workers, the unemployed, men who had fought diligently in the National Guard—for rising up and making demands the government wasn't prepared to meet. Aimée imagined there was only so much a person could take, and she pictured the soldier she'd seen from her bedroom window, his boots dragging behind him, his blood smeared against a palette of snow. For one fleeting moment she thought of Henri, but pushed him from her mind. She couldn't stand to think of him as that soldier, or one of the Communards who had been imprisoned by government troops—forty thousand, Aimée had heard, men and women, wealthy and poor, bound together by their wrists and marched through the streets in a sheet of rain.

It seemed strange that she was sitting here, and others, like her cousins, were simply dead.

She looked at her maman, radiant and lively, her cheeks flushed from wine, her lips parted as she listened to the man on her left. Aimée's papa sat at the opposite end of the table shooting his hand in the air and making declarative statements in support of the new republic with its monarchist leanings.

A memory came back to Aimée, an isolated, childhood memory. She was descending the stairs with her thumb in her mouth, her rag doll—with all its yarn hair pulled out—thumping behind her. Her papa was coming up the stairs, and he halted when he saw her. Because of their positions on the steps, Aimée could see his face clearly. *Papa,* she had asked. *Are you sad?*

It was his unhesitating *yes* that stood vividly in Aimée's mind. She wondered if it was because she had been young and insignificant that he felt he could tell her the truth. He'd never say anything like that to her now. As she listened to him, she wondered if he believed all the things he said, or if he just said them to be liked.

Last week he had ranted about Édouard Manet helping draft a charter for a new society of plein air artists. After being rejected from the Salon de Paris, these radicals had decided to form their own association, with elected members, shares, and partnership. Claiming the Académie des Beaux-Arts refused to recognize progress, they had decided to exhibit independently, doing away with judges, juries, and rewards. *Ridiculous lot of fools,* her papa had called them, outraged at their deliberate attempt to insult the new republic, whose president happened to be the director of fine arts at the académie. And yet, here Édouard was sitting next to his fat wife, Suzanne.

Aimée knew all about the independent exhibition of these plein air artists, but she had said nothing to her papa. Her papa always said that a difference of opinion, especially when it came to politics or art, made for a boisterous evening. It was dull to dine with people of like mind. And yet, Aimée knew this referred to important men, such as Édouard, and not herself.

Three chairs down from Aimée sat Madame Savaray, who hadn't eaten a thing and sat rigid listening to a woman discuss the deportations to New Caledonia in an unreasonably loud voice.

"I'd rather be shot to death than deported," a bold young man declared. Madame Savaray gave him a withering look, thinking him ridiculous. At any other time she would have said so out loud, but the nation's troubles, for now, weren't nearly as concerning as hers.

Two weeks ago, Madame Savaray had been out walking, under a bleak winter sky, when the truth of Henri's leaving hit her, and with such clarity that she stopped right in the middle of the sidewalk. People steered around her, a few knocked into her, but she couldn't move for some time, and when she did it felt as if a boulder had risen in front of her and somehow, dress, shoes, bad knees and all, she had to find a way to climb over it. If she'd been a younger woman, if she hadn't come to understand what people were capable of over the years, it would never have occurred to her. It was unthinkable. It's what desperation looked like. One could argue a war had been going on and they were all desperate. But this went back long before the war to a time when she knew, in her mother's heart, just how dark her son's marriage would turn out to be.

As she sat listening to these people all claiming to know the truth about one thing or another, she felt tremendously lonely holding this secret. When dessert arrived, she excused herself to her room. There was a slight throb in her knee, but she found the pain oddly comforting, familiar and reassuring, a pain she knew how to tolerate and endure.

. . .

After dessert, the guests moved into the parlor. Colette circled the room making sure glasses were full, cigars lit, and conversation steered clear of politics for a while.

Aimée stood listening to her cousin's frivolous account of avoiding being kissed by a man with terrible breath.

"Like rotten eggs." Julia laughed. "And his hair"—she patted the top of her chignon—"shiny as a wax doll's with all that pomade." She leaned in to whisper something more, then snapped her mouth shut, indicating with a tilt of her head that someone was standing behind Aimée.

Turning, Aimée's bare shoulder brushed against the soft velvet of Édouard Manet's frock coat.

"Good evening, Monsieur Manet," Julia said, lowering her chin. "If you'd be so good as to excuse me. I do believe Mademoiselle Beaux is beckoning me." She smiled and skirted away with a pinch to Aimée's arm.

Édouard held the lapels of his frock coat and rocked on his heels, not offering any conversation, and Aimée wasn't sure if she should feel slighted or complimented. It seemed silly to stand beside her if he didn't wish to speak to her.

"Will you be going to the regattas this summer at Argenteuil?" she asked.

"I will, yes." He shifted his arm and the sleeve of his coat slipped away from Aimée's shoulder.

"It's a shame about l'Opéra Le Peletier." Her voice rose with the effort of making conversation. "Burning to the ground, all those costumes and musical scores gone forever. Is it true you were painting it?"

"I was," he said. "The shame is that I wasn't finished."

He made no further attempt to engage her, but he kept his

small, dark eyes on her, and Aimée felt the tips of her ears grow hot. With a tight smile, she said, "It was lovely to see you," and walked away, heat crawling into her cheeks.

It was when she reached the other side of the room that he announced, loudly, as if it had been his intention all along that everyone should hear, "You would be doing me a great service, Mademoiselle Savaray, if you would let me paint your portrait."

The room went silent, and everyone stared at Aimée.

If Édouard had intended to flatter her, it did not work. She felt ashamed, as if suddenly there was something unique about her simply because Édouard Manet declared it so.

Her papa rose from the sofa, and his look of astonishment sent a cool resentment coursing through Aimée. He walked over to Édouard, a feather of smoke spiraling from the end of his cigar.

"It would be an honor, Monsieur Manet, to have you paint my daughter," he said with pride, as if, just now, she had become worth something.

Colette emerged from a group of whispering ladies, their gloved hands held over their lips. "Yes," she said, as if it were entirely their decision. "We would be utterly flattered." But Aimée saw her maman's mouth twitch ever so slightly.

Aimée almost said no. She would have liked to defy her parents. But then she thought of Édouard's painting, *Le Déjeuner sur l'herbe*. It depicted a naked woman staring out, audacious and daring, with the men around her fully dressed, casually enjoying their afternoon in the vast forest of the Fontainebleau.

She was eleven when the painting showed at the Salon des Refusés, having been rejected by the Salon de Paris, and she remembered the gasps, the whispers of obscenity, the scandal the painting brought, disgusting in its ordinariness. Aimée had stared at it, awed, a tingling sensation between her legs, and her maman had clapped a hand over her eyes and turned her away.

Aimée looked from her parents to Édouard, and he looked back at her with amusement and intrigue, as if the suspense of her indecision was even more fun than the asking.

Édouard Manet had broken the rules, endured the assault of ridicule, and he now stood proud and famous, confident in his abilities to do as he pleased.

Aimée gave him a smile and a single nod. She would go, but not because of her parents, or because Édouard found something interesting about her. She would go because of that painting, and the thread of desire it had tugged loose inside her.

Chapter 5

Édouard's studio on the rue de Saint-Pétersbourg was magnificent, vast, and airy. Four enormous windows took in the rue Mosnier on the west side, and the Place de l'Europe on the south. Aimée had walked through the busy plaza to get there, the black trusses of the bridge still covered in a sheen of morning frost, her breath a puff of smoke through her veil.

The concierge, an ugly, long-faced woman, showed Aimée into the studio where Édouard leaned over the divan arranging colorful pillows. "I thought you might change your mind," he said.

"And disappoint my parents?" Aimée stepped into the cool light that poured through the balcony windows.

Édouard lifted a lavender evening gown from the back of the divan and turned to her. "Wouldn't dare disappoint those two," he said, holding out the dress.

Of all colors, lavender was the least flattering against Aimée's skin, but she didn't say a word as she gathered the heavy silk in her arms and walked toward the screen at the far end of the room.

When she stepped out, Édouard was setting pots of paint on the table. He glanced at her and gestured to the divan where he had arranged the pillows.

Aimée lowered herself down. Through the thin soles of her slippers she could feel the tremor from the trains chugging in and out of the Gare Saint-Lazare. Édouard had told her not to wear gloves so her arms were exposed all the way to her wrists and her hands were bare, which made her feel slightly naked.

Édouard plucked a dark object from the console and walked over to her. He smelled of tobacco and of sweet citrus, as if he'd rubbed orange peels on his clothes. Tiny hairs rose on the back of Aimée's neck as he leaned down and pinned a velvet ribbon around her throat.

Reaching down, he smoothed the silk over her knees, draping her skirt first one way and then the other. He placed her hands together, pulled them apart. Lifted the curls off her forehead and let them drop back down. Then he stood and looked at her, tugging on his beard.

"It's your dress. The color's wrong." He sounded irritated, as if this were her fault. "Go change." He dismissed her with a flip of his hand. "I'll have to rent another dress tomorrow."

Those few minutes sitting still, being fussed over, had made Aimée prickle with impatience. Relieved, she said, "I could have told you that when you handed it to me."

Édouard frowned, and a deep line appeared between his eyebrows. "I suppose I should have asked."

"White or black are the only colors I can get away with."

"What shade of white?"

"Pure white. A snow white."

"You looked exceptional in green the other night."

"It was dark green. Very dark."

He gave an efficient nod. "Pure white and shades of the deep ocean then."

Through the scruff of his beard Aimée could see the tip of his tongue and his slightly yellow teeth. His look implied some subtle intimacy, and Aimée felt a loosening in her legs as she ducked behind the screen. She slipped the lavender dress off, now keenly aware of the act of undressing.

When she came out, fastened back into her morning dress, Édouard was at his canvas sketching a pink peony that he had pulled from its vase and tossed onto a sleek table. Within minutes the flower appeared in delicate, vulnerable marks, the petals thin and tender.

Without asking, Aimée took a sheet of paper and pencil and sat at a table under a portrait of a woman sitting with her face completely hidden by a black fan, and one smooth, white ankle extending out from under her black dress. Aimée couldn't see the woman's face, but the daring length of that exposed ankle excited her, and she wondered how it would feel to create something so natural and revealing. Looking down, she drew a single precise mark.

Without breaking the rhythm of his pencil, Édouard said, "I work alone." His voice was not unkind, just decisive and uncompromising.

Aimée had no right to be so bold, but she kept on sketching, and for a moment it seemed he was going to ignore her. Then, a little firmer, he said, "I am not an instructor."

"You taught Eva Gonzalès," she said, continuing to move her pencil across the paper, her confidence growing with every stroke. Aimée did not work from the same obsessed, passionate place as Édouard. Hers was a quiet determination.

"That was different," he said.

From the gossip her maman repeated at the dinner table, Édouard's wife had been unhappy with the arrangement. Maybe he had wanted Eva in his bed, and that was the difference.

Édouard swung around, and Aimée jumped, a line appearing where she had not intended.

"I will paint you as you are now." A smile of satisfaction sprang across his face.

"I'd rather you not," she said truthfully, hoping Édouard did not think her insolent and ungrateful.

But he only looked intrigued. "And why, pray, is that?"

She hesitated, wondering if Édouard was the kind of man you could be honest with. "I fear you will make me look like an amateur. The painting you did of Mademoiselle Gonzalès at her canvas made her appear as if she'd never held a brush in her life. She's a fine painter."

"You forgot to mention that I painted her as the great beauty she is. Which means more to a woman than the way she holds her brush."

"You underestimate some women then."

"Is it you I've underestimated?"

"I'm not a great beauty. I'm not even the slightest bit attractive."

"Then you've underestimated yourself."

Aimée reddened and looked away. Out the window she could see great puffs of steam rising into the blue sky. Édouard's forthright words were flattering, but also a means to get what he wanted.

"I'll have another dress for you tomorrow." He turned back to his canvas. "Come again in the morning."

Determined, Aimée pushed back her chair and stood up. "Monsieur Manet, pardon me for saying it, but I detest sitting for a portrait. I find it impossible to sit still. It makes me itch all over. I only came here because I thought you might have something of value to teach me."

Édouard leaned back in his chair, regarding her without expression. There wasn't a sound other than the dim tapping of his pencil against the wooden armrest. "Tell me," he said, finally, "are you an equally miserable painter?"

"I don't know."

The same look of amused curiosity that Aimée had seen at the soirée came to his face, only now there was something slightly more personal in it.

"Well," he sighed, as if relinquishing a rule he never broke. "I suppose it might be worth finding out."

At that moment, Aimée thought of Henri. It felt like a betrayal, painting privately beside someone else.

Édouard stood and offered his chair. "Draw nothing with the same process." He proffered his pencil. "Forget all your eye has seen before. You must learn to come to the work anew, each and every time."

And so they began.

PARIS 1874

Chapter 6

A cool spring arrived. Buds stayed tight and green, the branches of trees sharp, naked lines against the sky. Thin clouds spread like the inner veins of a feather over Aimée's head as she passed through the Place de Clichy to the steep, narrow streets of Montmartre.

Despite the chill breeze, people moved their chairs out to take in the sun. Aimée was forced to walk in the street, avoiding a man with his legs stuck out and his hat pulled over his eyes. A rat darted across her path, and a horse-drawn cart rattled by, splashing mud up Aimée's stockings. She stepped quickly back onto the sidewalk, slowing her pace as the hill grew steeper. By the time she reached the small, blue-roofed house at the top of the hill, she was hot and short of breath.

"Leonie?" she called, pushing open the front door and moving down the narrow hallway into the kitchen.

It was a small apartment, but decent compared to the others on the street. Instead of one room with a mattress in the corner, there was an actual bedroom in the back where Leonie and her *grand-tante* shared a bed lifted off the floor on a high wooden frame.

The kitchen was stiflingly hot, and Aimée's cheeks tingled.

Old Madame Fiavre stood hunched over the potbellied stove. She glanced at Aimée, and her lips curled in a toothless smile as she waved at the back door. In the small patch of yard, Leonie was pinning wet clothes on the line, the sleeves of her dress pushed up past her round elbows.

"We've done it," Aimée announced.

Leonie dropped the chemise she was holding into the basket and squealed like a child as she threw her arms around Aimée.

"Wait." Leonie pulled away, propping her hands on her hips. "Let me look at you." She smiled, and her dimples sank into her ample cheeks, the gap between her teeth fully exposed. "You've changed."

"Stop it." Aimée laughed.

"Your first salon exhibit? They will award you a medal, and you will be famous." Leonie tucked a strand of fine, brown hair behind her ear and picked up the wet chemise. "Have you told your beloved Édouard? Maybe he didn't get in this year and you did. Wouldn't that be shocking?"

Leonie pinned up the chemise and reached for a pillowcase, giving it a violent shake.

Everything about Leonie was fresh and vivacious. The slightest emotion lit up her cheeks, and her skin was so delicate that when a hand rested against it, red streaks appeared. When Aimée first saw her standing on the corner of the rue Bonaparte with the other models, she reminded Aimée of ripe fruit. She had a full bust, fleshy arms and hips, and an endearing gap between her front teeth, a quirky imperfection that Aimée found irresistible.

"Édouard did a dreadful thing I haven't told you about," Aimée said under her breath.

Leonie turned her soft, brown eyes. "You didn't let him?"

"Not *that*." Aimée slapped Leonie's arm. "Don't be vulgar."

She picked up the end of a sheet, and Leonie picked up the other. "It's just that right before I submitted the painting, he came into my studio and began dabbing away at it."

Pinning her end of the sheet, Leonie handed Aimée a clothespin, watching, bemused, as Aimée clumsily pinned hers. "Who would refuse that? You should see it as your good fortune."

"What if it's the only reason it was accepted? What if it wasn't good enough otherwise?"

Leonie had little tolerance for self-pity. "You're either good enough, or you aren't. A few dashes of someone else's brush won't make the difference." She hoisted the empty basket on her hip. "Besides, it was my lovely complexion that got us in. And, of course, these." She squeezed her shoulders forward so her breasts pushed up over the handkerchief that was tucked into her bodice.

Aimée laughed. She envied Leonie. There was freedom that women in the lower classes of Montmartre had, freedoms she was denied. Working-class women could do what they wanted. Go where they wanted. Lounge in cafés with men, drink absinthe, smoke, dance, with no reputation to uphold, or stop them.

Only once had she said this to Leonie, who was horrified. "I most certainly do have a reputation to uphold," she said. "You've never seen the women with their red lipstick and cheap crinolines." She told Aimée of being apprenticed to a workshop at nine years old. About the stuffy workroom where women swathed in second-rate perfume gossiped over mounds of tawdry dress material. Leonie narrowed her eyes at Aimée. "You're not as smart as I thought if you can't see how free you are. From your bourgeois perch you have no idea what it's like," she said.

Normally, Leonie didn't bother about their class differences. Modeling for Aimée was a job, and a good one, with regular pay, which was hard to come by. Their friendship seemed natural to her. After all, they were both women, with women's problems. No use envying one life over another. It was what it was.

"Come," Leonie said, sidling sideways through the door with the basket propped on her hip. "Have a cup of chocolate with me."

Chapter 7

On the opening day of the Salon de Paris, the Savaray household was full of commotion. Jacques ran from room to room, getting swept out at every turn.

Earlier that week a cart had taken Aimée's painting, and the whole family had stood on the front step and watched the small canvas, crammed in with other paintings, bump down the street like a child being sent out into the world.

Colette ordered new dresses. She even had one made for Madame Savaray, who opened the box, took one look at the drapes and ruffles, and refused to wear it.

But, on the morning of the Salon, Madame Savaray found it carefully laid out on her bed where she couldn't help noticing that, at least, Colette had ordered it in gray. She let her fingers trail over the fine fabric, and decided she'd put it on, for Aimée's sake.

Aimée was so nervous she could hardly button her dress. Never had her work hung in any gallery and now, at this very moment, her painting was on display at the Palais de l'Industrie, the most prestigious art exhibit in Paris. Already people were looking at it.

Struggling with the last button at the base of her neck, she heard the clock chime in the hall and knew they were late.

Instead of hurrying as she should have, she went to her dressing table and slid open the top drawer. Inside a bronze ormolu box lay her stone necklace. She hadn't worn it since Henri left.

She held it up to the window. It pivoted on its string, and the clear stone caught the light and sent an oblong rainbow of color to the opposite wall. Unbuttoning the top buttons of her dress, Aimée slipped the necklace over her head and tucked it into her bodice.

As she took her best gloves from their box and wiggled her fingers into the soft leather, she felt the weight of the stone pulling at her, along with the familiar longing for Henri, barely perceptible, yet still very much alive.

Auguste waited in the parlor for the ladies to come down.

He stood over the chess table, twirling a white pawn between his fingers and remembering the first time Henri beat him at a game of chess. The checkmate had come out of nowhere, and Auguste shot his head up and looked at his son with genuine admiration. Henri had looked mortified, and Auguste, understanding the confusion it causes when a boy discovers he can beat his papa, had given Henri a smile and said, "Well done, my boy. Well done." Still, Henri had hung his head and apologized.

The apology had angered Auguste. He wanted Henri to be more competitive, have more sportsmanship, so he forced the boy to play another game, making sure he beat him that time. Auguste remembered how he'd gloated, showing Henri how it was done.

Flipping the pawn upright, Auguste tucked it back on its square. He reached for a black pawn, moved it forward two spaces, and drew his bishop out at a diagonal. He would teach

Jacques chess in a few years, and he'd let his son win every game if that's what it took to build up the boy's confidence.

The clock struck the hour. They were late. Auguste looked into the empty hall, and considered calling for Colette to hurry up. But that would anger her, and the thought of her anger—even now, after a decent night's sleep—felt exhausting.

Auguste considered himself a judicious, levelheaded man, fair, good with people. Only when it came to Colette did a sort of insanity rise up in him, or at least that's how he saw it. And these days she was taking everything out of him. Their arguments escalated, and they weren't followed, anymore, by stormy lovemaking. Early in their marriage, the arguments were a harmless game, each trying to one-up the other until someone gave in and they collapsed into each other's arms. But after Léon died, Colette wouldn't let him touch her, not until the day they fought like they'd never fought before. Over what Auguste couldn't remember. It wouldn't have mattered. They needed the fight. Colette smashed a mirror with her pearl brush, and Auguste put his fist through the wall. It ended with Colette on her knees in tears, Auguste sinking to the floor to comfort her.

After that, only a passionate fight could arouse them.

Only now, when Colette started in, Auguste just felt overwhelmed and incredibly tired.

The first time he retreated midargument, Colette threw a teacup that shattered on the back of his head. He almost grabbed her, but that was exactly what she wanted, so he forced himself to walk straight out of the room, cutting off her shrill scream with a decisive, satisfying click of the door. In spite of the blood trickling down his neck, he had felt delighted that he hadn't given in, which made him realize how much power he'd handed her all these years.

Auguste reached across the chessboard and picked up the black king, balancing the hefty piece in his hand. He had no idea of the crippling events that would unfold over the next few months, and he couldn't have predicted his part in them. But he would think back to the moment he stood waiting, unable to call up to his wife, seeing his powerlessness so plainly, like the king in a chess game who can only move one hopeless space at a time.

Colette had always had a temper, but the rage inside her now was different. In some dark corner of her mind, she knew it had started the moment she saw Henri kissing Aimée the night before he left. Her daughter's back had been pressed up against the wall, and her hand clutched Henri's as he bent over her in a kiss that reminded Colette of what it was to be desired. They were tender, but desperate, and Colette felt a surge of anger—*How dare they*—and then a deep longing, and something she refused to acknowledge as jealousy.

The morning Colette dressed for the Salon de Paris, she pondered how lucky Aimée was to be supported in her art. Colette's papa would never have done such a thing. When she was seven years old, her papa made her play the piano for a roomful of people. She'd stared at her sheet music in terror, forgetting everything she'd learned. The room was silent, everyone waiting. Even though she knew she'd get a beating afterward, she began banging away nonsensically on the keys, tears streaming down her face. More than anything, she wanted her papa to stop her. But he only watched until she'd exhausted herself, turning to the room when she was finished and crying, "Utterly talentless!" then, laughing, "It's a good thing she's pretty. Otherwise we'll never get rid of her."

If he could see her now. Colette craned her neck to view the back of her dress, pleased with this new look. It was the latest fashion, teal silk with brown stripes, long fitted sleeves and a boned jacket bodice. Finally the cumbersome crinolettes had gone out of style, and a woman could walk into a room without popping through the doorway like a cork, Colette thought, tilting her hat.

She turned from the mirror as Jacques came running into the room. "Maman!" He grabbed the bottom of her dress, and she almost scolded him for pulling at it, but stopped herself.

Jacques, precious, little Jacques, was the only part of Colette's life that felt sweet and good, the only part where her anger softened. If he were naughty, she'd forgive him instantly, taking him in her arms and kissing him all over his soft face. If it weren't for Marie and Madame Savaray, the boy would be quite spoiled.

"My darling, little love." Colette picked him up. "Where is Marie? Are you running about the house all by yourself?"

The boy giggled and pointed to the door.

"Well, then, let's go see if we can find her," Colette said, and walked out as Jacques pulled a satin streamer on her hat and sent it trailing to the floor.

Chapter 8

The Salon de Paris was unthinkably crowded, and the unpleasant smell of warm bodies mingled with the sting of varnish in the central hall as the crowd moved like a single body up the grand staircase.

It took the Savarays two hours to locate Aimée's painting. The rooms opened one into the other, and they kept going in the wrong direction, having to loop back and start again. Of course they stopped to view the most talked about pieces, and every few feet they ran into someone they knew. By the time they found the *S* section, Aimée was high strung and agitated.

The small canvas was not hung well. It was positioned high on the wall and overpowered by a neighboring canvas full of bloody horses and muscular men. Looking at Leonie perched sideways at a table with her strange smile, Aimée's enthusiasm, all the buildup for this moment, dropped out from under her. It was pathetically commonplace, her technique precise and formulaic. There was nothing original about the painting other than the light-color scale she'd used, and that would only draw criticism from this crowd if anyone even bothered to stop and study it.

The disconcerting voice inside Aimée's head, the doubtful,

skeptical one, had been right all along. Her art had become her self-worth, and it wasn't very good.

"Not the best placement," Colette said to Madame Savaray, who stood with a tight-lipped scowl, arms pulled to her sides trying to brace herself against the inevitable stranger who might, at any moment, bump into her.

"Well, at least it's not up there." Auguste pointed to the paintings crammed near the high ceiling.

Colette brushed her hands together as if shaking off any responsibility for her daughter's mediocre work. "It's uncomfortably bright, and there's far too much color. I don't know why I didn't notice that before."

Aimée bristled. Her parents were so boringly conventional. "Better to be noticed for originality than not noticed at all," she said. "Édouard would understand."

Colette rolled her eyes. "Édouard, Édouard," she laughed, hooking her arm through Auguste's.

Madame Savaray thought it a fine painting. Although—and she did hate to agree with Colette—it was much too bright for her taste. Regardless, she was no art critic, and she didn't see that her opinion on color held any importance.

"Fine work, my dear," she said, but all Aimée heard was obligatory praise. "Come along now." She took Aimée's hand and drew her away from Auguste and Colette, who had moved on to a painting of a half-naked woman in repose. "There's more to see, and I, for one, don't know how much more of this stuffy place I can take."

Five rooms later, after looking at a sickly depiction of a dead fish, Madame Savaray excused herself and sat down on a green circular sofa in the middle of the room, insisting Aimée go on without her.

Pushing through throngs of people, Aimée made her way

down the stairs to the *M* section. Édouard was standing in front of his painting, *Gare Saint-Lazare,* gesticulating with grand gestures as onlookers pressed closer. When he saw Aimée he tipped his hat and smiled.

Leaving his audience, he came through the crowd to her, looking very grand in his top hat and white double cravat.

"My dear." He pressed his lips to the top of her glove. "Congratulations. You've made it into this madness." He rested his arm lightly on her waist. "It's criticism as usual," he whispered, guiding her past walls of paintings neither one of them had any interest in viewing. "The Salon rejected two of my paintings this year. And this after the success of *Le Bon Bock*! The ill-mannered lot of jurors infuriates me as much as anyone." He grinned at her. "But, here we are, giving our blood in hopes of a medal. I suppose the reviews can't get as bad as they were for the Salon des Refusés, poor devils. I told Monsieur Renoir they'd be in for it, undermining the values of the académie, shoving antiestablishment down the jury's throats."

Aimée paid no attention to the critics. The paintings at the Salon des Refusés had awed her: Berthe Morisot's *The Cradle,* Edgar Degas's *The Laundress,* and Monet's *Impression, Sunrise.* Those artists captured air, rhythm, truth, and simplicity. They were on the edge of something exciting, something reckless.

"The jurors are the same lot who ran screaming from Wagner as if the music had stung them," she said, the warmth of Édouard's hand a small fire on her hip. "They're not looking to be excited or intrigued, certainly not shocked. They're looking for tradition and stability. It makes them feel safe."

"Like yourself?" Édouard said.

Aimée glanced at him, not sure if he'd meant it as an insult, or a challenge, but Edouard kept his gazc straight ahead and only gave a squeeze to her hip that made her feel certain it was a challenge.

. . .

After a short rest, Madame Savaray left the upstairs rooms and went down to the lower level.

When she first saw the painting, she didn't think much of it. A little village dashed off in rather sloppy brushstrokes. It was the girl who caught her attention. She sat idle in the grass, staring straight out at Madame Savaray, who gave a small gasp when she leaned in. Straining her eyes, she read the title *Girl in the Afternoon*.

Her chest heaved. It was not a moment she could have predicted, and yet it came as one anticipated, dreaded. She should have been prepared, with a plan, but she stared at the painting with no idea what to do.

"*Grand-mère?*"

Madame Savaray whipped around to see Aimée and Monsieur Manet standing directly behind her.

Stepping quickly in front of the painting, she cried, "Oh, here you are!" Her voice strained and unnaturally cheerful.

Édouard tipped his hat. "Madame Savaray, you're looking magnificent. That dress suits you admirably."

She gave a tight smile, her eyes darting around Édouard's shoulders and over Aimée's head. Viewers who had looked eager earlier, now appeared tired and disinterested, not to mention wilted, which was exactly how she felt. That, and stricken.

"Are you quite all right?" Aimée asked.

Madame Savaray noticed Édouard's hand linger over Aimée's for just a moment. "Perfectly," she said. "Where are your parents?"

"I haven't any idea."

"We were just making our way to the garden," Édouard said. "You look as if you could use a bit of air yourself."

Madame Savaray nodded. "I most certainly could."

"Ah, there's Monsieur Lerolle." Édouard shot his hand in the air. "I must go say hello. Let us meet up in the sculpture garden, yes?" he said, and disappeared into the dust that rose from the thousands of feet shifting over the cast-iron floors.

Aimée looked suspiciously at her *grand-mère,* who had not moved from the painting. "It can't be all that bad," she joked, taking a short step around Madame Savaray who was forced to step aside.

Aimée had gotten it into her head that Leonie must be modeling for someone else and that her *grand-mère* somehow thought this was a betrayal. It took her a few moments before she recognized the figure sitting on a lawn in front of a church, the curved line of the girl's nose, her slight frown, and the tilt of her chin as she lifted her gaze, her expression confrontational, as if challenging the viewer. It was her, but it was her in a place she'd never seen, in a place she'd never been. And it was this she stood trying to make sense of, feeling strangely displaced. When she finally understood, a flush of heat surged through her, and there was a fierce ringing in her ears. The room seemed to tilt and slide away as her *grand-mère*'s hands anchored onto her shoulders and pulled her away.

Outside the sun was glaring, the sky a blinding sheet of white. Aimée stood blinking, the people around her shapeless, inhuman forms. Voices swarmed like hundreds of insects, and her skin tingled.

Madame Savaray popped open her sunshade and walked them briskly down the sanded pathway, past lush greenery and rows of sculptures, the milky busts and thighs formless mounds of white behind Aimée's blurred eyes.

She forgot about Édouard, she forgot about her parents, she forgot about Leonie, who she was supposed to meet at three o'clock in the buffet. If it weren't for her *grand-mère*'s firm grip on her arm, Aimée would have forgotten about her as well.

Swept up in the herd of bodies pouring out from the Palais de l'Industrie, they dropped onto the Champs-Elysées and found themselves suddenly free, walking swiftly away from the silk and satin and feathers and ribbons and all that sickening perfume.

"What we need is something to eat," Madame Savaray said. "Not here. The restaurants will be much too crowded."

Madame Savaray slowed their pace, welcoming the shade of the chestnut trees that lined the boulevard. After being packed in like animals, she was grateful for the fresh air. These events took more out of her than she cared to admit, and in spite of the confusing emotions tumbling inside of her, she found herself thinking how a row of chestnuts were more valuable to her than all the art in the world.

By the time they found a respectable café, Madame Savaray's knee ached, and she was grateful to sit down. Aimée wasn't hungry, but Madame Savaray—who hadn't eaten since breakfast—ate heartily: onion soup, grilled herring with mushrooms and asparagus, which was always her favorite this time of year, followed by a large scoop of praline ice cream. After which she ordered them each a glass of champagne.

"We're celebrating, after all." Madame Savaray held up the delicate flute, and Aimée followed. "To your first of many successes, my dear."

Aimée drank the toast stiffly. Drawing the glass from her lips, she asked, "Do you think he was there today?"

Madame Savaray set her glass down and pushed her empty ice cream dish to the edge of the table. "I haven't the slightest idea." She looked around for the waiter.

"You couldn't have hidden it from me," Aimée said. "I look every year."

Madame Savaray sighed heavily. "You know, I never realized it until today, but I believe I've been looking too."

Aimée took another sip of champagne. It tasted yeasty and sour. "Why did he do it?"

Madame Savaray shook her head. She really didn't know.

"I'm not grateful or pleased." Aimée swirled her drink into a small whirlpool. "I'm furious he had the audacity to paint me. Is that silly?"

"No, my dear, there is nothing silly about it. He left you. He left all of us. He never came back, and now here he is, brazenly displaying you in his art." *Brazen wasn't the half of it,* Madame Savaray thought. *Diffident Henri had turned out bolder than anyone could imagine.* Leaning forward, she tapped a long, gloved forefinger on the table. "Anger is appropriate, but useless. Men have reasons for doing things they'll never reveal." She only prayed Henri would never reveal them.

Aimée finished the champagne, liking how light and careless it made her feel.

Madame Savaray paid for their meal, and they left the café. They were both dizzy from the champagne, and it took considerable effort getting into the cab.

"I beg you not to mention a word of this to my parents," Aimée said, holding on to her seat as the horses leaped forward. She pressed her hand to the stone hidden against the soft skin between her breasts, feeling, alongside her anger, a sense of anticipation. Henri was still in Paris.

"We will not speak of it," Madame Savaray said. "Unless, of course, your parents saw the painting, in which case we should prepare ourselves."

Aimée did not answer. Madame Savaray noted the rise of color in her *petite-fille*'s cheeks and the flash in her gray eyes. Aimée was not going to leave this alone.

. . .

It was after dark by the time Colette and Auguste returned home. From her bedroom window Madame Savaray watched them stumble up the path. Colette tripped and caught Auguste's arm, her laugh stabbing the air as they disappeared into the house.

The white thread of a new moon crested the horizon, and Madame Savaray lifted her gaze. She wondered how it was God allowed that shimmering strand so many chances to grow fat, and then thin and new again. She would have liked that chance for herself. No one would think it to look at her now, but she'd once had a fine figure. What she wouldn't give to feel herself in that body again. She laughed out loud, a sound pinched off by something dangerously close to a sob. It was too late for any of them to begin again; she knew that.

Bowing her head, she clasped her hands and prayed that Henri not be found.

Aimée sat alone in the parlor, the fire burned down to a bed of coals. Her parents startled her out of a deep quiet. They tumbled into the room laughing, full of whatever they'd had to drink, clearly unaware of her presence. Her papa pressed her maman up against the tapestry wall and kissed her hard, their hands entwined. Aimée watched. This was what she knew of passion, this dark intensity laced with a kind of danger. Whether they were actually in love was questionable, but not impossible. At times Aimée thought she saw something of it between them, before it clouded over.

Auguste pulled away, watching his wife wipe her slightly parted lips with the back of her hand. She hadn't given in to him in a long time, and he'd never force her. He waited for times like these, when it seemed she might almost desire him again. He took her hand and turned away, intending to lead her from the room when he saw his daughter, sitting, white faced, on the sofa.

"Aimée?" He dropped Colette's hand and stepped forward. After all he'd had to drink, he could be seeing things, and Aimée looked so ghostly.

"Yes, Papa?"

"What are you doing up?"

"It is early yet."

"Is it?" He looked over at Colette.

"I wouldn't know." Colette peeled herself from the wall and headed for the door, her movements languid and sloppy. "I'm going to check on Jacques, and then retire for the evening." She kept her eyes on Auguste. He knew that look. She'd consumed more spirits than usual. He'd follow, quickly, before she changed her mind.

"Yes, yes, me too, I'm all in." He glanced at Aimée. "Everything all right?"

"Perfectly," she said.

It was in the doorway when Auguste thought to turn and say to his daughter, "Well done today."

Aimée did not answer.

It was not because Colette had had too much to drink that she let Auguste sleep with her that night; it was because she'd seen the painting, Henri's depiction of Aimée, and it threatened the order of things. It made her feel as if Henri was lurking on the outskirts of their lives, about to take up residence in Auguste's heart again, about to take away what was rightfully hers.

Chapter 9

Kneeling on aching knees with hands latched over a fat brush, Leonie scrubbed the hearth with all her weight, waiting for Aimée—who hovered above her—to say whatever it was she'd come to say.

Leonie had not heard from Aimée in a week, and since Aimée had not met her at the Salon de Paris as planned, Leonie assumed Aimée was unhappy with the painting and as a result came to sack her as a model, artists being exceedingly fickle and endlessly unsatisfied.

But Aimée's thoughts were far from painting.

"What's got your face all twisted?" Leonie said while scrubbing rhythmically. "Might as well have out with it."

A breeze came through the open window and made the hairs rise on Aimée's arms. She looked around the damp, fireless room. Moisture collected on the walls, and she watched a single pearl of water run down the whitewash. She thought it would be easy to tell her friend the truth about Henri, to describe the submerged remorse and longing that consumed her. But now she found it impossible to speak.

"I have a brother," she finally said, taking a seat at the table with her elbows propped on the clean gingham tablecloth. "Not Jacques, an older brother. One who left years ago."

In a voice soft with emotion, Aimée told Leonie that her brother left during the war. He had a falling out with her papa, she said, and they had not heard from him in three years. For some reason she didn't try to explain that he wasn't her real brother. Perhaps she thought it seemed more urgent, if there was actual blood between them, and it was this simple omission that she would return to, later on, as her undoing.

Leonie rose to her feet and stood listening with the scrub brush held in the air.

A lost brother sounded wonderfully exciting. Leonie had no siblings. Her papa ran off when she was a baby, and her maman died three years later beneath the hoofs of a mad horse. Leonie's *grand-tante* raised her, a hardworking tavern maid who'd made the firm decision to remain unmarried and childless. "No need to sacrifice my life for a man who'll drink every penny I earn away," she'd said.

Except for the three months when Madame Fiavre fell ill from white pox—and Leonie was sent to the workshop in order to put food on the table—her *grand-tante* had worked every day, making sure Leonie stayed in school until she was sixteen. By the time Madame Fiavre was too old to work in the brasserie, she had a nice stash of money tucked away on the highest shelf of the larder. "It's the simple things that make for a decent life," she'd always told Leonie. "Don't go looking for more, and God will reward you for your humbleness."

Leonie had her doubts, but she never said a contradictory word. She'd seen children thrown into the street when there was no one to pay the rent. Drunken mamans stumbling after them, beaten by raging papas and in turn beating their own, sorry children whose starved, swollen faces haunted the avenues of Montmartre.

No one needed to tell Leonie how lucky she was, and she did everything she could to repay her *grand-tante*. She took in mending from the washhouse when there was no modeling work, read scripture aloud by firelight, and bought her *grand-tante*'s favorite sweets and the best cuts of meat, pounding the meat into a mushy pulp since her *grand-tante*'s last two molars had crumbled from her mouth.

And yet, deep down, Leonie's life utterly bored her. She listened to Aimée now like a child to a fairy tale, grasping this bit of Savaray drama with relish, thinking how romantic it would be to have a long-lost brother, especially one clever enough to send a message through a painting.

When Aimée finished, Leonie tossed the scrub brush into the bucket and wiped her hands over the front of her apron, two black smudges appearing down her middle.

"His name is Henri," Aimée said. Leonie could hear Aimée's love for him in the tender way she said it.

Leonie scurried over, swept her skirt aside, and sat next to Aimée.

"The question is, how, exactly, are we going to find him?"

Leonie's unquestioning support made something swell in Aimée's throat. She gripped Leonie's hand. "I don't know."

"You should ask Monsieur Manet. Isn't he on the salon committee? They'll know where to find him."

Aimée shook her head. "He'd tell Papa."

"You don't want your parents to know?"

"I don't think Henri would want it. I'm not sure he even wants me to go digging things up."

"Digging *him* up, you mean. What was the falling out?"

"I don't know."

Years ago Aimée had stopped working the events over in her mind, but now she thought of how she had stopped Henri in the corridor that night before he left. In one breath she had told him she loved him, that she'd loved him for years. First a look of confusion, or disbelief, had passed over Henri's face, and then an embarrassed smile followed by a fervent kiss. With his hand clutched over hers, Henri had leaned down, brushed his lips over her ear, and whispered, *I've loved you for years too.*

Leonie pitched forward, her breasts bulging. "I know lots of models. One of them must have heard of this Henri Savaray. Cafés would be the best place to start, assuming he's still a bachelor. Surely he frequents the usual ones?"

"It's not likely," Aimée said. "Otherwise, Papa would have heard."

Leonie squeezed Aimée's hand. "If your brother's in Paris," she said with a determined smile, "we'll find him."

It was mid-May when Leonie came to the door, wet from the rain and short of breath. Aimée met her in the vestibule where they clasped hands and nearly ran down the hall and up the stairs.

They did not notice Colette watching through the open parlor door, her white-knuckled hand latched to the doorframe. Those girls were getting much too familiar with one another. It was one thing for Leonie to model, another entirely to strike up a friendship. It would not do to have Aimée running around with a girl of that class, becoming the topic of hushed intrigue.

Colette turned to Madame Savaray, who sat with a book splayed open in her lap. "What do you think those girls are up to?"

The old woman's chin was tilted so far down it looked as if her spectacles would slip right off the end of her nose.

"How should I know?" Madame Savaray turned a page, deliberate and absorbed. She had her ideas, but she wasn't about to share them with Colette.

Watching Madame Savaray, Colette wished her *belle-mère* were one of those gossiping old ladies who spoke in low, disapproving voices, inciting scandal with raised eyebrows and knowing nods. Then they could discuss what might be taking place upstairs, why those girls were so giddy and secretive.

"What?" Madame Savaray snapped. "What are you staring at?"

"Nothing." Colette sighed and left the room. Her *belle-mère* would never be anything but cold and pragmatic, and far too reasonable for gossip.

Upstairs, Jacques woke from his nap. Hearing Aimée, he jumped out of bed and barreled into the hall, running smack into Leonie. For a moment he clung to her. Then he realized his mistake, and darted to Aimée.

"Hello, dearest," Leonie said.

Jacques rolled himself into Aimée's skirt and buried his face.

"Not now, Jacques." Aimée unwound him so abruptly that Jacques backed away and squeezed his eyes shut, wrinkling up his face. Worried he was going to throw a fit Aimée crouched in front of him and softened her voice. "Are you hungry?" she said, brushing sweaty strands of hair off his forehead.

Jacques nodded and stuck his thumb in his mouth, glancing suspiciously at Leonie.

"Be a good boy, and go down to the kitchen. Tell Marie I said you could have a whole spoonful of currant jelly."

Jacques pulled his thumb from his mouth. "Two."

"Very well, two spoonfuls."

"Three."

"No, two. Now go." Aimée planted a kiss on his forehead and turned him toward the stairs. "Hold the rail," she called, and his small hand shot out and slid along the shiny banister.

Safely behind the closed studio door, Aimée helped Leonie out of her wet coat and hung it on a hook next to her smock.

Leonie whispered, "I've found him," smiling triumphantly.

A cool sensation ran along the ridge of Aimée's collarbone. "Where?"

"I went to Café Guerbois, and Café de la Nouvelle Athènes, just to be sure, but you were right, no one knew him."

Aimée studied the painting she was working on of a young girl swinging open a garden gate. Until now, Henri had remained her ghost, undisturbed beside her. She wasn't sure she was ready for him to be real again.

Leonie began unlacing her boots. "I was hoping," she said, "at the very least, someone might have heard of him and would know where to direct me, but no one had. I met a writer—grim, serious fellow—who suggested a few places." She pulled her boots off and peeled her wet stockings over her feet. "I went to all of them, but there was no Henri Savaray to be found." She stood up and laid the stockings on the back of her chair.

Aimée picked up a palette knife and began scraping off the girl's hands.

"I went all over the city. Places I'd never been before, and then, wouldn't you know it, last night I stopped in a café right off the Place de Clichy, just to get something to eat, and I asked this girl if she'd heard of him—lovely red-haired thing drinking all by herself—'I have,' she says in one of those husky, untrustworthy sort of voices. 'He owe you money too?' she says." Leonie stood next to Aimée, watching her scrape away all her hard work.

Aimée moved from the hands to the girl's head, wishing she was alone in her bedroom. She would have liked to bury her head in her arms and weep.

"She told me he dined there nightly," Leonie went on, excited. "I stayed just to get a look at him. I had no intention of speaking with him, but when he walked through the door that girl went right up to him, demanded her money, and then pointed to me and said, 'She wants her money too.'"

Aimée put down her knife and studied the mutilated girl, her head gone, her hands cut off at the wrists.

Leonie had expected excitement, delight, or at the very least, gratitude from Aimée. A look of shock would have sufficed, tears, something. But Aimée just backed away from her canvas and sat down, her expression maddeningly unaffected.

"Can you believe all this time and he was right there?" Leonie raised her voice as if speaking to her *grand-tante*. "I must have walked by that café a hundred times."

"You spoke to him?" Aimée asked.

"Yes."

"What did he say?"

"Nothing at first. He just looked at me, bemused, and then told the girl he'd have her money next week, which was not what she wanted to hear. She practically took the door off its hinges on her way out."

Leonie noticed the color had drained from Aimée's face. There was something unsettling in her expression. "Your brother's nice enough," she said as if his niceness was what was at stake. "He came over directly and said he was sorry he'd forgotten such a lovely face." Leonie smiled. "I told him he didn't owe me a sous, that that girl had confused me for someone else. He offered to buy me a drink, said it was the least he could do."

"Did he?" Aimée tried to picture the Henri she remembered drinking spirits with Leonie, or the redheaded model. She couldn't.

"I had one glass and told him I had to get on home. He said he'd walk me, but I insisted on going alone."

"What was he like? I feel he must have changed a great deal."

Leonie shrugged. "Gentlemanly, but sober. He didn't talk much. I had to fill in all those blank spaces that are so uncomfortable when conversing with someone you don't know."

Aimée got up and walked to the window. "Do you know where he lives?"

"No, I couldn't think how to ask." Leonie went to Aimée. From behind, she put her steady arms around her. "Don't worry, love. We know where to find him now."

The Place de Clichy was busy with foot traffic. Steam rose from the damp pavement under Aimée's feet. The rain had stopped, but the wind picked up and pushed massive gray clouds across the sky. They made Aimée dizzy. Everything felt too close, the clouds, the people bumping her on all sides, her dress, her hat, her shoes, even her skin seemed to be suffocating her. Earlier, she'd stepped right into traffic and was nearly run over.

It was a relief to see Leonie standing on the corner of the rue de Clichy.

"This wind is ferocious!" Leonie shouted, holding on to her hat strings. "Come, it's this way."

She linked arms with Aimée and steered her down a boulevard lined with gateways that led into dark, narrow courtyards.

They stepped around the *marchand de fruits,* past the draper's shop and the herbalist, both holding tight to each other, Leonie out of excitement, Aimée for sheer stability.

She'd dropped her spoon at breakfast, then had considerable trouble with the pins in her hair, and couldn't seem to fasten her boots. It was ridiculous, her flustered insecurity, this giddy, feverish anticipation.

Eventually, the large, glass shop windows gave way to smaller, darker ones. The street grew narrower, the buildings tight together. They stopped in front of a small café with a sign above the door that read *Café Gravois.* Aimée glanced through the densely paned window and immediately snapped around.

"I can't go in there," she said.

"Of course you can't." Leonie pulled her into a dark doorway. Far away a clock bell tolled the hour. "But, I can." She righted Aimée's hat, which had blown sideways. "That redhead said he dines here nightly. If he's not here already, he'll be here shortly. Wait for me. I'll tell him there's someone who wants to see him and bring him out."

Aimée shook her head. "I can't do this. Not here."

She stood frozen with misgiving. All day she'd been nervous, but also thrilled. What she felt now was cold dread, a fear that her love would be dug up from where she'd buried it, brushed off and shown for what it really was: a lonely, one-sided affair. A fatuous, silly girl's fantasy.

"Here's as good a place as any. He's your brother. I don't know the circumstances of his parting, but if I had me a brother, I would want to see him and set things right," Leonie said with hands on her sturdy hips.

Aimée wished that none of this was happening. What if he didn't want to see her? What if he walked away?

"Ask to sit for him," Aimée said impulsively.

"What?"

"Tell him you need work. Ask to model for him."

Leonie dropped her hands. "He doesn't pay," she said flatly.

"I'll pay you."

Both girls were silent.

Aimée lowered her head. "I'm afraid he won't want to see me."

It upset Leonie, seeing Aimée so unraveled. Usually, her friend was as strong as she, and Leonie preferred a strong woman to a weak one. Aimée was not someone she was prepared to take care of.

"I don't see what good will come of my sitting for him," she said.

"You can see what he's like, tell me about him. I just need more time."

Something felt amiss to Leonie, but she agreed.

Aimée took her friend's hand and kissed it. "Thank you," she said.

Leonie shrugged, and together they stepped back into the wind.

Chapter 10

While Leonie modeled for Henri, Aimée spent her days at the Académie Julian, and in the garden of a rich client of Édouard's who hired her to do a portrait of his wife. Édouard had arranged it before he went to Argenteuil, and Aimée was grateful for the distraction, even if her mind was always in that café.

At dusk on an evening in June, Aimée left Monsieur Chevalier's verdant summer garden, where she'd spent all afternoon failing to please the man. Somehow he thought it was possible for his hideous wife to look pretty in pastel, which it was not. Agitated, Aimée sent her supplies home in the carriage and left on foot.

It was a warm, clear evening. All day she had felt an aching restlessness. She walked toward the rue de Clichy, and this time, when she came to the Café Gravois, she did not duck into a doorway. She stood right in front of the café window feeling impulsive, as if she might do, or say, anything. The stone necklace felt weighty against her skin. She knew it was superstitious, but she hadn't taken it off since she found Henri's painting.

It only took a minute to spot him. He wore the same collarless waistcoat he'd worn years ago, and she'd recognize the stoop of his shoulders anywhere.

Everything fell away then, sounds, smells, even the pitiful moan of a drunk slumped over in a nearby doorway. Through the streaked window, Aimée could see Henri's hands. They were unusually small, especially compared to her papa's, but that place that flared out between his wrist and thumb, wide and strong, had always gotten to her. One of his hands rested on the table, while the other gripped the spoon he dipped into his soup. His head was bent over his bowl so she couldn't see his face, but his hair was the same pale brown, although longer and curlier than she remembered.

She stood in full view, conscious of the tavern maid clearing empty dishes and the filthy cigar ends that littered the tables, but she looked only at Henri.

Then he looked up, right at her, and she quickly backed away, not sure if he'd seen her, and if he had, not sure he recognized her. She was halfway down the block when she heard her name, low and questioning. "Aimée?"

When she turned, he was only a few yards away. He wore no frock coat or hat, but his shirt was starched and his waistcoat buttoned up.

"Aimée?" he said again, as if still unsure.

"Hello, Henri." A nervous, twitchy smile spread across her face. This simple greeting seemed, somehow, ridiculous.

"I was wondering when you'd come," he said, his voice smooth, its seriousness achingly familiar.

"Oh?" Aimée dug her nails into her palms.

"Yes, ever since I first met Leonie."

Aimée dropped her eyes to the cobblestones between them.

"Do your parents know?" he asked, and she looked up, hurt that he'd question her loyalty.

"No."

They stood in silence, each wondering what to say as the sun slipped away and the sky became a blanket of purple, smooth as velvet, one bright star appearing in its depths.

All those years together during their childhoods, all those hours painting in each other's silence, didn't make this any easier.

Finally, Aimée turned, slightly, as if she meant to leave, then turned back. "How did you know, when you met Leonie?" she asked.

Henri smiled, and it reminded her of that first time she'd seen his smile, how it transformed his face into something dear and lovable.

"I saw your painting." He sounded amused at the obviousness of this. "At the salon."

Aimée gave a short laugh. "Of course. That never occurred to me."

"I wondered if it was a coincidence. But when Leonie asked if I was looking for a model, I was certain you were behind it."

"Then why did you say yes?"

A lightness had sprung between them, a familiarity they'd slipped back into.

"Because she's a find. I was shocked you were willing to give her up, when you could have easily come yourself."

They moved closer as they spoke. Aimée could smell the wine on Henri's breath and the slight scent of resin that came from his clothes. She glanced around the dark street. The gas lamps were being lit, breaking the night shadows into isolated pools of light.

"We've moved," she said. "We had to leave Passy during the attack of the Communards. A shell exploded on the Madeleine. Shattered all our windows, took down every curtain and picture, covered everything in heaps of plaster."

Henri slipped his hands into his high waistcoat pockets and tucked his elbows in like a bird tucking in its wings. "I went past the house a few years back," he said, adding quickly, "I just wanted to see it again," implying that he had not gone to see her.

"Why?" Aimée could hear her anger. "Why would you want to see it again?" *When you didn't want to see any of us.*

The ease between them slipped away as quickly as it had arrived. Henri shrugged and looked down, the soft pouch of skin under his left eye fluttering. Aimée watched the small freckle near his cheekbone tremble and jump like a fly. It used to bother her, that leaping freckle, but now she hungered to press her finger against it, to still his nervousness, and feel how warm and real he was.

Henri glanced at the café door. "I should get back. The proprietress will think I've run off on the bill."

"Yes, of course," Aimée said, that small space between them vast and impassable.

Henri did not offer to see her home. "It's getting dark," he said. "You should get a cab."

She nodded. "I will, thank you."

He turned to go, and Aimée pressed her hands to her sides to keep them from flying out and hanging on to him. "May I come to your studio?" she asked. "I would like to see what you're working on."

Henri hesitated, and that hesitation cut straight into Aimée's heart. "Leonie has the address," he said.

In the doorway he turned. "I hate to ask you to be dishonest on my account"—he wouldn't look at her—"but I would be immensely grateful if you did not mention this to your parents."

Aimée tried to reply, but her throat was dry, and she couldn't find her voice. All she could manage was a nod.

. . .

It was midmorning, and already the sun was scorching.

Aimée stepped off the rue de Calais into a small courtyard, pressing a gloved hand to her nose to block the nauseating stench of manure. The concierge stood in an open doorway fanning her apron and gazing at a flock of swallows rising from the rooftops.

"Pardon me," Aimée said, and the woman pulled her gaze down, looking as if Aimée had spoiled the one peaceful moment she was likely to have all day. "I'm looking for Henri Savaray."

The concierge wiped the sweat from her upper lip and flapped her apron at Aimée. "Three flights up."

Aimée thanked her and headed for the stairs.

It had been a week since she'd seen Henri outside the café, a week in which she'd hardly slept or eaten. At times she wondered if the ghost of her imagination had become spectacularly real, that her desire had gotten the better of her mind, and Henri did not exist at all. She jumped slightly when he opened the door.

"This heat is going to do us in today, I'm afraid," he said cheerfully.

Aimée smiled. Henri was certainly real. He was right in front of her. If she reached out, she could touch him. "Yes," she said, stepping into the apartment. "It most certainly is."

They were both deferential and reserved, as if she were a patron coming to view his work. Henri took care to move aside as Aimée looked at the paintings on the wall, and Aimée made sure her hand did not so much as brush up against his.

The paintings were mostly landscapes, the Fontainebleau, the Seine. Some were good, Aimée noted, but nothing exceptional. *Girl in the Afternoon* was there, so even that hadn't sold. But Aimée was glad it hadn't. It reminded her that Henri had been breathing her to life next to him too.

Behind her, she heard his shallow breath and the rustle of his trousers as he shifted his feet. The silence she used to hold so precious between them made her nervous now.

"How did you capture my likeness?" she asked, turning to Henri who stood directly behind her. His face was no longer soft and round as Aimée remembered, but thin, with stubble gracing his upper lip and chin. She wondered what it would feel like to kiss him now.

"I spent half my life with you. It's not likely I'd forget," he said.

His cheeks were red with heat, and his eye fluttered, his small freckle leaping uncontrollably. There was something clumsy about his smile, as if he hadn't quite committed to it, but his fierce blue eyes held hers steadily.

Aimée looked away, pretending interest in his small apartment as she wrestled with the ache in her chest. There was a single iron bed, a larder, a table of art supplies, three chairs, and a black stove with last winter's ashes still piled in front of it.

She had been so sure Henri had gone back to England, to the mysterious family and wealth that he'd come from. But he'd been here all along, in the back of a building on the rue de Calais, having no luck with dealers and, according to Leonie, reduced to painting potboilers and portraits in this one crammed room.

"Stifling in here," Henri said, struggling to prop the window open with a long stick. "Thing slams down without it. Might slam down anyway, but we'll give it a try."

The breeze felt good. Aimée was perspiring under her dress, and a trickle of sweat rolled down the middle of her forehead. Henri had taken the apartment for its windows and high ceilings. Light was abundant where space was not, which meant, on a summer day such as this one, the room was as hot as a furnace.

Aimée dabbed the sweat from her forehead as she walked to an easel. "May I?" she asked, pulling back the draped cloth before he could answer. Propped on the easel was an unfinished painting of Leonie. Naked. Completely naked. Full breasts, pink nipples, round stomach, plump thighs. One arm draped discreetly over the dark place between her legs. Aimée turned away, not sure why this upset her so much.

A light tap came at the door.

It was Leonie, wearing a white blouse tucked into a pale blue skirt. Her face flushed under her hat. She halted at the sight of Aimée. "I thought you were coming tomorrow," she said.

"I'm engaged tomorrow," Aimée lied. The truth was she hadn't been able to wait.

Leonie put her hand on Henri's arm and leaned in. "Isn't she a wicked thing?" she said delightedly, "not letting me have the triumphant moment of reacquainting the two of you." She untied her hat strings and handed her hat to Henri. Thin strands of hair stuck to her neck and forehead. "She could have at least let me witness the reunion."

"Aimée does what she likes," Henri said, and it was not an insult. He said it because he knew her, because he'd watched her defy her maman as a child. Because her papa's rules had never stopped her.

"A trait I admire." Leonie took Aimée by the shoulders and planted a firm kiss on her cheek. "There now, I've forgiven you."

Aimée wrapped her arm around Leonie and drew her to the end of the room where the chamber pot and washbasin were visible behind the screen at the foot of the bed. "You didn't tell me he was painting you nude," she whispered.

They pretended to look at a sketch tacked on the wall while

Henri carefully ignored them as he gathered his brushes, pushing aside scattered ends of charcoal and nubs of pastels.

Leonie pressed closer to Aimée and whispered, "I've posed nude lots of times. I never thought to mention it." Aimée could smell the orange water and jasmine Leonie splashed her face with every morning, insisting her delicate complexion couldn't do without it. "Are you upset because he's your brother? Is that indecent or something?"

"No," Aimée said. "I don't see why it would be." There were nude studies all over the walls. It should not bother her that he was painting Leonie nude, and yet it did.

Aimée released her hand from Leonie's waist and pressed it to the back of her neck as she watched Henri squirt paint onto his palette.

Dropping her whisper, she said, "I'm only terribly disappointed that you've never posed nude for me."

Henri looked up from his color preparation, and Aimée wondered if he was remembering how she'd asked him to take his shirt off for her all those years ago.

"You never asked me to." Leonie stepped behind the screen, her forehead appearing over the top. "If I did, your parents would run me out of the house. You, my dear," she called, slipping off her skirt and rolling down her gray lisle stockings, "are only allowed to paint a nude in a roomful of overeager students with a stodgy, pockmarked art instructor breathing down your neck."

"If it weren't for the Académie Julian, I would never have had a chance to paint a nude," Aimée said, looking straight at Henri, who snapped his head back down.

What he remembered was how Aimée always wanted him to conspire, to break the rules. He could hear the confidence in her voice now, and see the daring in her eyes. Her daring used to excite him, and he thought how innocent she still was, how ignorant. She had no idea what it meant to really break the rules, how much damage could be done.

Leonie stepped out, stripped of all her clothing. "Paint me now," she said. "You're paying. Might as well get your money's worth." She dropped onto a chair. "Although, you two are getting a bargain. I won't charge double as long as I get supper."

"I told you I'd pay you," Henri said, with a sort of desperate humility.

Leonie shrugged, everything about her sensual and gratifying. "Might as well let Aimée pay. She can." This was just practical, no need to be prideful. Henri could hardly afford this miserably small apartment as it was.

Leonie's nudity made Aimée surprisingly self-conscious. She stayed on the other side of the room, watching Leonie wipe the perspiration from under her full breasts as Henri filled his brush with the rose pink tint of her nipples and touched it to the canvas.

Chapter 11

Without any further discussion, Aimée began showing up at Henri's apartment with her portable easel and paint box.

She told her parents she was off to the académie every day. She'd never lied quite so boldly, but it felt inevitable, their relationship primed for just this kind of deception.

Aimée would stop for a baguette on her way over, buy a hunk of firm, ripe cheese, sausage, a jar of jelly, fresh plums, or a basket of figs. Often she brought an extra canvas or two, a new brush she'd leave behind, tubes of paint. She didn't make a show of it, but the supplies were helpful, and because Henri never said a word she knew he was grateful.

It was strange, what was going on inside Aimée. It wasn't happiness, but a kind of thrilling anticipation. Lying to her parents felt unexpectedly satisfying, telling them nothing of Henri.

She started arriving at the apartment earlier than usual, hoping for a few private moments before Leonie showed up. She would hang her hat and set up her easel with a show of competence and ease. Having familiarized herself with the tiny cups and the one pot that hung on the wall, she'd grate chocolate into a saucepan of milk, pour their drinks, and rinse the pot immediately so it wouldn't crust over. She'd scold Henri for his paltry breakfast, telling him he couldn't work all morning on a hunk of bread.

Henri was tolerant of all of this feminine influence, even appreciative, but he made it very clear, without words, that he wanted nothing of their old relationship. He wanted nothing of their past. He never spoke of it or her parents. He did not ask Aimée a single question about herself, and in turn she never asked how he survived the war, where he'd gone, who had helped him. Desperately she wanted to know why he left. It was the most obvious question to ask, and also the most obvious to avoid. This hole in his past was like a specter, haunting every corner of that room.

Aimée tried to convince herself that at least they had their silence. But even that had changed. The intimacy was gone, the effortlessness of being in each other's company. The silence made them uncomfortable now. Aimée's stomach tensed every time Henri was near enough to smell the mix of cigar and resin that came from his clothes. When he brushed against her, her breath seized in her chest. Once, when she went to put his teacup down, he'd unintentionally put his hand over hers and they'd both pulled away, the cup shattering on the ground.

And yet, there was something undeniable between them. Love might be too much to hope for, but something had kept Henri away all these years, an emotion worth running away from, and this was what Aimée clung to.

No mention of Henri came up in the Savaray household, so after a while Colette stopped worrying. She dropped Auguste as quickly as she'd picked him back up. The summer was progressing, and it was too hot to have him smother her at night, plus she needed her sleep. Her Thursday-night soirées had become a social event of note, and they took the entire week to plan.

She also got it fixed in her mind that Aimée had to marry. There had been no buyer for the salon painting, and it was obvious that the client Édouard sent Aimée's way was merely charity, and not generous charity at that. Monsieur Chevalier made Aimée scrape off his wife's face four times before he was satisfied. Then he only paid two hundred francs for the portrait when he'd originally agreed to three. Aimée, stubborn as ever, vowed she wouldn't paint another portrait, claiming it was commercial art. "I'm not going to paint what someone tells me to," she'd said with a haughty jut of her chin.

Colette told her she was being senseless. Portraits were a respectable way for an artist to make a living, but Aimée seemed to think she had some inimitable talent that made her exempt. Édouard probably put that thought in her head; he was much too complimentary. Now Aimée spent all of her time at that académie, honing her skills, running up bills for supplies with no more commissions in sight.

Colette, for one, was tired of it, and there was Jacques to think about.

Auguste was just grateful Colette's screaming, and the blows to the back of his head, had stopped. Of course he wanted her physical attention, even when it was reluctant. He never considered if there were tactical calculations behind Colette's behavior. He took what he could get when he could get it. He knew she'd inevitably cool again.

Lately, all the women in his household seemed annoyed with him. Just this morning he'd asked Aimée to see her work, and she'd rushed from the table, exasperated, saying that she was going to be late for class. His maman looked as if he'd insulted her as well, setting down her fork and leaving the table without so much as a word. Colette, in turn, offered a raised eyebrow as she spooned sugar into her coffee.

"How am I supposed to know what's going on around here if no one tells me?" Auguste shouted, slamming his fist on the table.

All the silverware jumped, but Colette didn't flinch.

Auguste stormed out of the room. A decent breakfast ruined by unpredictable women.

It was her son's inability to question anything but the most obvious and superficial that angered Madame Savaray.

She had taken to eating pastries in the kitchen in order to avoid him and the rest of the household, settling in with the iron pots, black bottomed with soot, and the shelves of spices, knives, choppers, ladles, and crockery. The servants, as they came and went, gave her weary looks, but for the most part, ignored her. She found the bustle and clutter almost as comforting as the pastry she sank her teeth into, the sweet, chocolate icing breaking away to a slightly crunchy, buttery crust, and then onto the gooey custard center. It was a satisfaction worth the thickening of her middle.

Little else satisfied her these days. For a month, at least, Colette had stopped raging, but Madame Savaray knew that wouldn't last long. Colette preferred to be wildly unhappy. Tidy emotions did not suit her. Her most recent attempt to rein them in only confirmed Madame Savaray's suspicion that Colette had seen Henri's painting.

If the truth came out, Colette had more to lose than any of them, and even though Madame Savaray swore she'd take the secret to her grave, watching her son lured in by Colette's petty show of domestic normalcy was infuriating. If Auguste would just open his eyes he'd see exactly how manipulative his wife was being. And if he paid any attention at all to his daughter, he would see that Aimée was hiding something too. The girl's serious face had given way to a lingering smile, and Aimée practically skipped off to class in the mornings. Whatever it was, Henri was at the heart of it, of that Madame Savaray was certain.

One particular morning Madame Savaray sat in the kitchen feeling worse than usual. It was hot, and she had no appetite. The cook was out getting provisions for the evening meal, and the kitchen was distressingly quiet, and unusually tidy. As if things weren't troublesome enough, she managed to catch the lace cuff of her dress on a rough piece of wood along the arm of the chair.

"Bother," she said, turning the cuff over in order to pull the snag through to the other side. The more she pulled, the worse it got, and in an instant she saw her whole life in that lace, the delicacy of it, how easily it snagged, how totally out of her control it all was.

She let the thread go, feeling the fragility of her family in every shrinking, aged bone in her body, and the sense that they were careening toward an unforgivable end.

Once the truth came out—and she was certain now that it would—there would be nothing she could do to hold this family together.

Chapter 12

Le Boulevard Malesherbes was unusually crowded as Aimée walked toward the académie, the great dome of the l'Église Saint-Augustin like an overturned bowl in the sky, the rosette window an enormous, watchful eye at the street's divide.

She had finished her painting of Leonie, and with no specific reason to go to Henri's, she'd spent the last week painting at the académie.

The two-way traffic rumbled down the wide boulevard, shiny carriage panels flashing in the sunlight. Aimée felt a quiet dread at being packed into the studio with all those ambitious students and an instructor who gave her exasperated looks and little instruction. Already the city was a white haze of heat, and the studio would be miserably hot.

Aimée decided to change direction, making a left on the rue de Naples, heading toward the rue de Calais. She needed to see Henri.

Two weeks ago she had been standing at his table, arranging her paints, feeling slightly disoriented, as she always did when coming out of six continuous hours of painting. Leonie had left, and Henri was standing next to Aimée reading the newspaper. As she shut the lid of her paint box, her hand brushed the edge of his. Without thinking, she reached out and touched that tender place above Henri's wrist. He flinched, just slightly, but didn't pull away. Then he turned his hand over, and Aimée slipped hers, palm up, inside of his. There was no clutching or embrace, just their oil-stained hands cupped together, Henri's fingers curled over the tops of hers, his hand clammy and warm.

Without a word, Henri pulled away, folded the newspaper, and moved it to the sideboard. Aimée—heart pounding furiously—lifted her paint box, nodded good-bye, and slipped out the door.

Now, walking down the street, Aimée imagined Henri in his apartment quietly waiting for her: sleeves rolled to his elbows, the top of his shirt unbuttoned, sweat beading along his hairline.

Not wanting to arrive empty-handed, Aimée stopped at the butcher's. The woman behind the counter was as plump and pink as the meat she slapped onto the scale, the lace on her crisp white apron standing at attention over her shoulders. With dimpled hands she wrapped a pound of preserved sausage meat, aggressively suggested a slice of larded veal, and, then, a half a pound of ham.

Aimée bought all of it. It was early yet for food, hardly past breakfast, but Henri would have to ask her to stay. At first they'd discuss getting another model together, or taking a trip to Fontainebleau and painting out of doors before the summer was over. Eventually, when they were comfortably settled in each other's company, she'd ask him directly why he left, because it seemed to Aimée that the past, as much as they wanted to ignore it, was the very thing standing in their way.

Henri held the door open. His lips were red and moist, hair damp at the temples, shirt untucked. His cuff links were removed, and the ends of his sleeves flapped helplessly around his wrists. Aimée could smell his sweat, and almost feel the heat pulsing off his body. His eyes rounded and filled with pity.

Before she could register Henri's expression, she noticed Leonie, sitting on the bed with bare feet, the strings of her blouse undone, her face tellingly flushed. No easel. No brushes. No paints anywhere in sight.

A tingling sensation ran up the sides of Aimée's face, and her jaw tightened as if she'd bitten into something sour. It was all she could do not to let out a wail, collapse on her knees, and beg them not to do this to her.

Flicking his eyes away from Aimée's stricken face, Henri focused on a dark stain on the wall. He could feel the flutter under his left eye start up, a rapid fire of nerves. A hot breeze blew in, and the stench of the courtyard hit him, the smell of manure sharp and pungent. His head began to throb, and he had the urge to cover his face and block it all out.

He hadn't meant for this to happen. Leonie was just a fresh, fun distraction. She was always arriving late, in a whirl of apology. "Hotter than blazes out there," she would say, and happy to shed her clothes, flash her brazen, gap-toothed smile, uninhibited and endearing, as if she were letting him in on a secret. And, unlike other women, she asked nothing of his past. Said the past was meant to be forgotten.

Aimée's gray eyes were fixed on him, fierce like her maman's. Henri looked down, his hand shaking as he brushed an invisible speck of dirt from his trousers. He wished he had the strength to tell her that he painted *Girl in the Afternoon* because he missed her, but that he never intended to be found. He didn't want to be reminded of the Savarays, of what they had given, and what they had taken away.

When Leonie saw who was at the door she jumped from the

bed and rushed over, giving Aimée a fervent kiss as she would have on any other occasion.

"We've been found out," she said, her lips bowed in a guilty smile. She squeezed Henri's hand. "We were going to tell you, but Henri wanted to wait." She looked at Aimée's stunned expression, dropped Henri's hand, and clasped Aimée's instead. "You look dreadful. It's really not that bad." She glanced at Henri. "Is it?" Then back at Aimée. "Are you upset? I don't want you to be upset. I was going to tell you all along, but Henri insisted I wait."

It felt as if a swarm of moths had flown into Aimée's mouth. There were a hundred sticky wings trapped in her throat, beating their way down to her stomach.

She pulled her hand away from Leonie's. "I was just bringing this by," she gasped, shoving the packages of meat at her.

"Stay." Leonie grabbed her arm.

"I'm due at Édouard's." Aimée yanked her arm away. "I've agreed to sit for him." She wasn't sure why she chose that particular lie. To make Henri jealous? To show him she was worth looking at?

At that she left, surprised at the overwhelming effort it took to put one foot in front of the other. She had wanted so desperately for there to be something secret between her and Henri, some promise of intimacy, that she had ignored what was right in front of her. *Girl in the Afternoon* meant nothing. He had not been sending her a message. It was just a painting. If he had ever loved her, he did not anymore. He had chosen someone else.

Without any real intention, Aimée found herself at Édouard's. His studio concierge said he wasn't in, so she waited outside, standing in the doorway under the brilliant sun.

Sparks were going off inside her, as shrill and sharp as the train wheels screeching on the tie-rods, the sound racketing through her body as she watched the steam from their funnels billow into an unforgiving sky. Something in Aimée had been set alight by the flush in Leonie's face and those marks on her neck. It wasn't passion, or even pleasure. It struck deeper, more of a wounded, furious desire.

By the time Édouard arrived, the sun was high in the sky and Aimée had wilted in the doorway. When she looked up the buildings tilted sideways.

"Goodness!" he exclaimed, grasping her arm as he fiddled with his key in the lock. "You're as red as a beet."

"Well, that's good." Aimée laughed. "Usually it takes a good many slaps to get any color in my cheeks."

Édouard guided her down the cool, dark hall into the bright studio where he sat her on the divan.

Between the heat, lack of food, and smoke from the trains, she'd become increasingly light-headed. Édouard could see this and with deft fingers undid the buttons down the front of her jacket bodice. He reached around, unhooked her dress, and turned his gaze away as he pulled at the strings of her corset.

"Breathe," he said, and Aimée felt a rush of air into her lungs.

Before Édouard could draw his hand away, Aimée closed her eyes and laid her head on the inside of his arm, the muscle beneath his starched white shirt taut and fibrous against her cheek. Édouard's hand stayed firmly pressed against the outside of her corset. No man's hand had ever been on that particular place on her body. Not even close.

Her breath came quickly. Édouard was older, practically her papa's age. Forty maybe? That was no matter. Young women frequently married men of his age. They certainly had affairs with them.

That was not Aimée's intention when she laid her head on Édouard's arm. She had not done it with any intention at all. But as the rage and pain of Henri's rejection dissipated with the warmth under her cheek, a deep pulsing between her legs made it perfectly clear that this was what she wanted.

Chapter 13

The atelier that Colette entered at the Académie Julian was humid and airless and choked with students. She hung back, away from the men and women crammed in beside one another as they slapped muddy hands over mounds of wet clay. Buckets of cloudy water and encrusted rags littered the floor.

Colette had never been inside an atelier before. There was a sensual, earthy smell, as if the clay had just been dug up from the river, and an exciting indecency in the sexes mixed in such close quarters, all those hands slipping over the malleable masses in front of them.

Lifting her skirt, she picked her way across the room to the *massier* who was kind enough to tell her where she might find Aimée.

She walked into a smaller room, with a skylight directly over a long oak table where a male model stood, nude, save for a cloth covering his male parts. The sun beat down on his head, and Colette wondered how any of them, students or model, could stand to be shut up in such a place.

A stately, white-haired man with thick spectacles made his way over. "May I help you?"

"I am looking for Aimée Savaray."

The man shook his head. "Not in attendance today."

"No?" Colette sounded surprised, but she was not. "When was she last in attendance?"

"Yesterday."

For some reason, Colette didn't quite believe him. "In that case, I'd be grateful if you'd show me what she's been working on."

"And who, madame, might you be?"

"Madame Savaray," Colette answered, with unmasked annoyance.

The man grimaced. "Very well. Right this way."

Colette followed him to a wall at the back of the room stacked with canvases. He pulled one out and handed it to her. It was a half-sketched-in picture of the model on the table.

"What else?" Colette demanded.

Pulling a handkerchief from his pocket, the instructor wiped the sweat from his brow. "Nothing else."

"What do you mean, *nothing else*?" Colette pressed her own handkerchief to the bridge of her nose, blocking the smell of body odor and turpentine.

"One cannot expect to accomplish much in a single week." The man walked a few paces to peer over the shoulder of a young, female student. "Aimée is skilled, but not committed." He took the charcoal from the girl's hand and with a great flourish sketched in the shadow of a chin. Wordlessly he handed the charcoal back and turned to Colette. "The greatest painters only became great after a dozen or more years of study. I, myself, exhibited nothing for seven years. Seven years!" He spat the words through a mist of saliva. "Your daughter, at the very least, must show up."

"Has she not been here the entire summer?"

The instructor raised his thick, white brows. "No, madame. She's not been here at all. Not until a week ago."

Colette turned from the man and waved her handkerchief over her shoulder. "Thank you," she called, making her way out of the room, momentarily blinded as she groped her way down the dark stairwell to the clear outdoors.

She strolled up the Passage des Panoramas, curious where Aimée was this very minute. To be lied to did not please her, but to know Aimée was not to be trusted, somehow did. Her daughter's inimitable work ethic, her solitary relationship with her painting, had always made Colette feel inferior. To know that Aimée was capable of disloyalty, that her daughter might be driven by the same reckless emotions that ruled Colette, was a relief.

She slowed in front of the window displays—the fans and silks, leather and chocolate—her thin-heeled boots clicking on the flagstones. She went into one particularly extravagant perfume shop, amber and musk drawing her, and bought an exotic perfume in a crystal bottle with gold leaves pressed into the glass.

If Colette had gone straight home, she would not have discovered anything. As it happened, she stopped in a lace shop and spent almost an hour debating over the Mechlin and the black Chantilly, which put her outside the shop just as Madame Morisot's plump figure stepped out of her carriage.

"Madame Savaray!" Madame Morisot cried, her black silk rustling as she scurried over. "Have you heard? My darling Berthe is engaged to Eugène Manet!" Her round face beamed.

"Really?" Colette tried to picture the lovely, brooding Morisot girl Édouard Manet was so enamored with marrying his brother. "I suppose congratulations are in order." She couldn't resist adding, "Is Monsieur Édouard Manet back in Paris? He must be thrilled for them."

Colette had intended to fluster Madame Morisot, who just looked puzzled.

"I presumed you knew he was," Madame Morisot said. "Aimée was in the doorway of his studio not two hours ago when I rode past."

It was Colette who was flustered. She sucked in a breath, recovered herself, and said, "Of course. How silly of me to forget."

"It's the heat." Madame Morisot patted her arm. "Send my regards to Monsieur Savaray," she said, retreating into the lace shop.

Colette quickly got in a cab. "Rue Saint-Pétersbourg," she ordered, clutching the packages in her lap as the carriage lurched forward.

It happened much slower than Aimée could have imagined, but Édouard knew how to make love to a woman.

There was something in the mix of humility and arousal, in the move from guarded friendship to shameful intimacy that made for a hesitant, uncertain beginning. There was no frenzied discarding of clothes or desperate groping, just tentative, cautious movements that allowed for the shedding of a waistcoat, a cravat, the dropping of a skirt and the peeling away of a corset.

When Édouard kissed her it was not with a rapid, probing tongue like her first kiss with Henri, but a slow, slippery wetness that moved from her mouth to her breasts, his firm, sure lips leaving her nipples distended and misshapen, making their way along her belly, then farther down, his beard scratchy and strangely sensual.

More than anything else it was the surprise of her own body, the unearthly sensations that sprang up and then fell away as he touched her in places she'd never dared touch herself. There was a moment of stunning embarrassment when he gently pressed her knees open, moving his hand between her legs, and she felt her vulnerability slipping away under the expert pressure of his fingertips. When he finally lowered himself on top of her, there was a moment of pain, and then an inexpressible expansiveness.

At times she thought she might faint, engulfed in the noise of the trains, the rumble of the room, the heat, and the smell of Édouard that was distinct and indescribable, a mix of smoke and citrus and turpentine, but also something pungent and all his own. Then the raw strangeness of his body, of this receiving and giving over, would bring her back as intensely as if someone had pressed smelling salts to her nose.

The tenderness, the delicacy of it, almost brought her to tears.

Aimée didn't open her eyes until it was over. Édouard's body lay relaxed and heavy on top of hers, his breath quick and hot on her neck. Slowly, the ceiling came into focus, the narrow beams, the gilt molding, and the roofed gallery with its open arches. *Olympia* hung on the wall opposite them, just above Édouard's shoulder, and it seemed to Aimée that the nude model was smirking at her.

Édouard rolled off of her, right off the divan, and lay on his back breathing heavily. Aimée realized how exposed she was, stretched out in this sunny room, but she didn't try to cover herself.

If she had done it for love it might have been worth it, but she wasn't sure why she'd done it at all. The worst of it was she had taken immense physical pleasure in the act. To think one could find that sort of pleasure without love seemed to make it more sinful, so she lay there trying to stir up a sense of remorse, when what she really felt was languid satisfaction.

She heard Édouard rise off the floor and begin to move around the studio. Eventually, she smelled burning tobacco.

When she sat up, he was fully dressed, sitting in a chair a few feet away with a drawing board across his knees, a pipe held between his teeth, and a pencil in his hand. He smiled at her with such lighthearted kindness it made Aimée think that what should have been a shocking situation, was really very simple and uncomplicated. This was just what it looked like. There was nothing more, or less, to it. And the way Édouard was looking at her told her that he knew this too, that it would never be anything more, or less, than what it was right now.

He took his pipe out of his mouth and let a puff of smoke curl from his lips. "Don't worry," he said. "We'll attach no importance to this." Which she took as his chivalrous way of saying it need not be mentioned to anyone. "Even though it was eye-opening, yes?" He spoke as if about a painting.

Aimée diverted her eyes.

"Thought I'd catch you in a rare, restful moment." He tapped his pencil against the edge of the drawing board. "But if you'd rather not, I won't. I know how much you detest sitting still."

"It's quite all right. I would like to sit for you."

Édouard grinned. "What would people say? Aimée Savaray in the nude? You'd never be able to step out in society again. Not to mention you're an awful model. Unless, of course, you can prove the contrary?"

"The nude you'll have to dispose of." Aimée was surprised at how calm she sounded. More surprising was how calm she felt, how settled. "But I would like to try sitting for you again."

Édouard set his drawing board on the table. He tipped his pipe over a ceramic dish, emptying the spent tobacco before walking over to Aimée and cupping her chin in his palm.

"I suppose I don't need to ask your parents' permission this time," he said, running his thumb softly along her jawbone.

"I suppose not."

"Will this be my only chance at a nude then?" He lifted her face and looked as if he might kiss her again.

"No," she said without hesitation.

Édouard did not kiss her. Instead he reached for her stone necklace where it lay on top of her discarded dress. It was clear from the deliberate way he picked it up that he had been the one to remove it, and Aimée couldn't believe she hadn't noticed. Édouard slipped it over her head, went back to his chair, and picked up his drawing board.

"The last time we tried this I squandered an unfortunate amount of money on a dress rental," he said. "It never occurred to me to have you simply take it off. But you wouldn't have back then, would you?"

She shook her head. *I wouldn't have yesterday,* she thought.

"How do I know you'll sit still and not drive me to frustration?"

It would be different this time, she told him, and he saw in her face that it would. There was something that had not been there before, a melancholy, but also a spark, and he liked this new version. It gave her complexity.

Chapter 14

Colette ordered the carriage to stop directly across the street from Édouard's.

On the ride over she'd been trying to work out why Aimée would lie about going to his studio. She'd allowed Aimée to sit for him precisely because Aimée wasn't the full model he preferred. Although, come to think of it, he'd painted an awful lot of the Morisot girl, and she was skinny as a twig. Regardless, Colette was certain Aimée was not in danger of attracting Édouard's attention. If he had not seduced *her, Colette,* ten years ago, when she was at her most beautiful, there was no chance for Aimée.

Then why had Aimée deceived them all summer about being at the académie? Colette drew the carriage window closed, leaving a small crack through which to peer, her curiosity setting off a tremor of excitement as she waited in the sweltering heat.

It seemed hours before the studio door opened and Aimée stepped out, her hat shielding her face. Édouard stood in the doorway, and Colette noticed immediately that he was not wearing his cravat, or waistcoat, and that the top button of his shirt was undone.

Furious, she wriggled in her seat, straining to see around a carriage passing in front of her. How dare Édouard seduce her daughter. How dare Aimée let him. How dare they lie. By the time Colette's view was unobstructed, Aimée was halfway down the block and Édouard stood watching her go. Colette reached forward and slid open the carriage window. "Drive on," she ordered, envy blistering through her. As the carriage started down the street she changed her mind. "No, turn around. Go back."

The carriage made a swift turn down a side street and back around to the rue Saint-Pétersbourg.

The door to Édouard's studio was shut.

"Slow down!" Colette cried, and the driver pulled the horses to a walk, the great beasts tugging at their bits and tossing their heads with impatience. Within a few minutes she spotted her daughter's hat. "Stop!" She rapped the end of her sunshade on the edge of the open window. "Let me out."

Colette hurried, following Aimée as she turned off the rue Saint-Pétersbourg onto the Place de Clichy, a woman with a handcart full of cabbages nearly knocking her into the street as she rounded the corner. Up ahead she could see her daughter's shiny satin dress slipping through the crowds like the scales of a fish. It was not often Colette got a chance to observe her daughter unnoticed. People reveal all sorts of things when they don't think anyone is looking.

She followed at a distance, ready to duck into a doorway if Aimée turned around. But Aimée never turned. She strode with determination, weaving through the foot traffic, not stopping for anything, and Colette found this reassuring. A girl in love wandered, strolled with her thoughts. There was nothing dreamy or languid about Aimée's movements, and this put Colette's mind at ease. She should not have jumped to such dramatic conclusions. This heat was enough to make any man discard his waistcoat and cravat.

In front of a gray stone building on the rue de Calais, Aimée came to an abrupt stop. Colette shrank back, watching Aimée stare at a series of high windows. Colette couldn't see her daughter's expression, but she noticed the unyielding way Aimée held her body, her shoulders pulled forward, her hands pressed together as if compacting herself down to a smaller size. Aimée took a step toward the open carriage entrance, and then, as if suddenly changing her mind, turned swiftly and continued down the street.

Curious as ever, Colette watched until Aimée was out of sight and then walked briskly to the building, stepping through the entrance into a dank, narrow courtyard. There were apartments on all sides, windows in three directions, but the windows Aimée had been staring at were straight ahead. Cautiously, Colette moved up the flight of stairs at the back of the building.

This was where she expected to find Aimée's lover, some destitute, sorry artist. Maybe he was very old, or very young. The idea of her daughter having a secret lover delighted Colette. Aimée must have hidden him because she knew Auguste would never consent to this sort of marriage. Of course she'd pretend to be shocked; she'd tell Aimée this must never get out. They'd both agree not to tell Auguste, certainly not Madame Savaray. Aimée would need to be married off quickly now, if it wasn't already too late.

Colette was, in no way, prepared for Henri. He never even came to her mind. Which, later, she decided was foolish—she should have known, suspected at least.

Conversely, Henri was certainly not prepared for Colette. After Leonie left he'd fallen asleep in the bright sunshine with his pants rolled to his knees, his sleeves to his elbows, and his shirt open.

The knock woke him. He stumbled to the door, wiping drool from his cheek, not fully awake, dreading that it might be Aimée, but also hoping for her.

Henri and Colette stared at each other, both with looks of incredulity. Henri buttoned his shirt and rolled his sleeves down, glancing behind him for his cuff links.

After a terrible silence, Colette said, "So, here you've been." When Henri didn't answer she extended her hand, slack at the wrist, and said, "Aren't you going to invite me in?"

Without taking her hand, Henri stepped aside and held the door open.

Colette dropped the rejected hand to her side, gave him a light smile, and handed him her sunshade. Her guard was down, and her guard was rarely down. She did not remove her hat. She would stay for a minute, make some excuse, and go.

She looked around, grateful, at least, to see that Henri was a grown man in a real apartment, however modest. Sometimes in her memory he was still a little boy, and that disturbed her.

She pretended to take an interest in his work, but she had never been good at subtlety. "Where did you go? How did you survive?" she said, staring at a landscape without really seeing it.

"Here and there. I got by." Henri stayed near the door, a tremor of anger beating through him as he imagined Aimée betraying him to Colette.

"And Aimée found you? Or did you find her?" Colette turned to him.

Henri's eyes darted to the floor where the edge of Colette's dress, scattered with pale flowers, met the cool, dark wood. "She found me," he said quietly. "I didn't want to make trouble. I meant to leave it alone."

"And yet, you stayed in Paris?" Colette picked up a small

canvas from the table and set it back down. "Well, then," she said. "What do we do with you now?"

Henri kept his eyes on the floor.

Colette walked over to him. At the very least, he could look at her. "Auguste will find out you're here, eventually. Especially if Aimée keeps coming around."

"I don't think she'll come around anymore," Henri said. *Meek and pathetic,* Colette thought.

"You've hurt her again, have you? Let me guess." Colette pointed to the nude propped on the easel, her own jealousy rising at the image of that bold, beautiful woman. "It was with her." She recognized Leonie immediately.

Henri didn't answer. His heart was beating very fast. Colette was right. He had hurt Aimée again. She had every right to be furious with him, to betray him to her parents. She owed him nothing.

Colette reached around Henri for her sunshade. Since the atelier, a kind of frenzy had been rising in her. She felt completely out of sorts. This was a dangerous situation. How she proceeded mattered very much. Henri was here now, and had to be dealt with. Best that she be the one to bring him back to Auguste.

"Dine with us tomorrow night," she said. "We'll surprise Auguste. It will be fun." She walked to the door, tapping the ivory tip of her sunshade on the floor. "What do you say?"

The room was hot, the air thick as sludge as Henri moved in front of her, blocking the door. Sweat dripped into his eyes, and he wiped it away with the back of his hand. "I will not do that to him," he said, angrily. "*You* will not do that to him."

Colette sucked her breath through her teeth and gave a derisive smile. "Very well," she said, stepping around Henri, careful not to touch him.

. . .

Henri could hear the tap of her sunshade against the wooden planks along the corridor, then down the stairs, until the sound faded away. Shaking, he shut the door, poured a drink, and sat down.

He'd kept to himself these past four years, making sure not to frequent popular cafés where he might be known. His work had stalled because he hadn't dared go to any of the reputable studios. By some miracle he'd gotten into the Salon de Paris this year, but his art was uninspired, his living from it meager. He didn't mind his poverty. He preferred it actually. It felt genuine and honest. His life as an artist had been insular, but not as lonely as he had expected.

When he left the Savaray household, he had prepared himself for a world of weary, hardened people. Instead, he discovered beneficent comrades, people willing to help him for no self-serving purpose at all. He was taken in, fed, clothed. It gave him a new view of humanity, a view he hadn't been able to see from his dark, miserable home in England as a child, or the tumultuous home of the Savarays. He made loyal friends, ones as poor as he was, who gave him what they could when they had it, food, money, and he learned to do the same. There had been a few women, not many, but they were all good ones, like Leonie.

He should have known it would come to this. Henri took a drink. The liquor was cheap and bitter. He wasn't sure why he'd bothered pretending he was a decent, honest man all these years. He was his father's son. They could change his name, but not his blood. Eventually, he would have to pay for what he had done.

Chapter 15

When Aimée left Édouard's, she had been determined to go to Henri and tell him the truth about her feelings. Shedding her clothes and giving her body away had heightened a sense of carelessness in her, and she didn't have much else to hide. But as she walked, the reality of what she'd done began to sink in, and the calmness she'd felt at Édouard's was replaced with staggering embarrassment, and then unequivocal remorse.

By the time she stood outside Henri's apartment—imagining him and Leonie together, even more painful now—she couldn't go in. What she had done changed everything. Giving herself to another man removed her from Henri completely.

Hurrying away from the building, she reached inside her dress, yanked off the stone necklace, and with a swift toss, hurled it into the dusty street. The stone bounced over some dry, packed dung and disappeared under hooves and creaking wheels.

With her head high, her eyes fixed on nothing, Aimée walked to the académie. She spent the remainder of the afternoon drawing in the crowded studio with furious concentration. As she sketched, her thoughts hovered just out of reach. She could make herself numb, hold everything at a distance: the exhausting bodies of students, the familiar smells of paint and sweat and turpentine, the ticking clock and scratching pencils. Slowly, she felt her regret shift to anger, and her anger fuel a defiant confidence. By the time she arrived home a new, raw energy pulsed through her.

At first, Aimée did not see her maman at the far end of her bedroom. It was when she removed her shoes that she noticed Colette step forward into the pale dusk coming from the window.

"Where have you been?" her maman said, just the slightest hint of accusation in her voice.

"At the académie." Aimée pulled one boot off and began unlacing the other.

"You're lying."

Aimée struggled with her boot. She could hear the satisfaction in her maman's voice. "No," she said, yanking her foot free. "I'm not." It seemed a lucky chance she wasn't lying this time.

"I've been to see Henri."

Aimée set her boot on the floor, surprise touching off her anger, crouched low in her belly like an animal waiting to spring. "Oh?"

With mild scorn, Colette said, "He told me he's seen you."

Aimée straightened, squaring her shoulders. Colette wore an expectant, self-righteous expression as if waiting for Aimée to confess everything.

The rigid line of Aimée's shoulders, the daring look in her daughter's eyes made Colette's skin tingle. "Why would you keep this from me?" she asked. "You know how much I've worried. It is an unkindness I hadn't thought you capable of."

After today, Aimée thought, she was capable of more than anyone knew. The ache between her legs and the memory of Édouard made her smile, a strange half smile that Colette took as smug. It was a moment when Colette might have slapped Aimée for her impudence. Instead she took a precautionary step backward, smoothing over her anger as she had learned to do with Jacques.

"We absolutely must not tell your papa," she said. "There is no need to bring it all up again. It will only upset him."

Aimée could see how tactful her maman was being. She also sensed a shift in the power between them.

"Which would mean that you're not to see Henri again," Colette said, with no touch of motherly advice, just a warning.

"I agree," Aimée replied, only it wasn't to be agreeable; she had already made this decision. "No need to upset Papa."

Colette looked hard at her daughter. It didn't seem likely that Aimée would give up Henri so easily. She might be lying—clearly she was capable of it—but it was impossible to tell anything from Aimée's look of cold indifference.

"It's settled then." Colette gave a short nod, calculating just what kind of an eye she'd have to keep on Aimée now.

"It seems we've finally agreed on something," Aimée said, her undertone a confirmation of their differences.

The next morning Aimée lay in bed as Marie yanked back the red brocade curtains, and a rectangular patch of light hit the floorboards.

"Leave them, please." Aimée rolled onto her side and pulled the sheet over her head. Yesterday's adrenaline had disappeared, and her grief had condensed, overnight, into a sharp, clear ache in her chest.

It was hot under the sheet, and Aimée threw it off, watching Marie lift a jug of water and pour it into the washbasin.

"Best be getting up, mademoiselle." Marie placed a new bar of soap in the dish and a clean, folded towel in the top drawer of the washstand. "It's a lovely day." She patted the top of Aimée's foot as she walked past the bed, the empty jug held by her side. "You've already missed breakfast."

"I'm not hungry." Aimée swung her legs to the floor.

Marie gave a small *humph,* pulled the jug to her hip, and left the room.

Aimée went to the washbasin and slipped her hands into the cool water. The day ahead seemed bleak and endless. She would not be going to Henri's—she splashed her face—she would not be trudging up the hill to Leonie's apartment in Montmartre. She felt for the towel in the drawer and rubbed it hard down her forehead to her chin. It seemed impossible to think she would never tell Leonie about her afternoon on Édouard's divan, or that she and Leonie might never again sit together in the cool light of Aimée's studio, or at the square oaken table in Leonie's kitchen. More impossible was the reality that Henri was gone, again, despoiling her of all anticipation and hope, leaving her with only a vast, cavernous loneliness.

She wondered what it would be like to keep Édouard as her lover, if there was something other than love that could satisfy her. But when she went back to his studio two days later, it was obvious there was nothing between them. All tender desire from their previous meeting had faded. It was as if the heat, or her near fainting, had put them in an altered state. Whatever it had been, it was gone. Édouard Manet greeted her warmly, as a family friend, a mentor and teacher, nothing more.

And yet, Aimée wasn't willing to completely give up what had happened between them. Not because she felt anything real for Édouard, because she did not. A sensual side of her had been exposed, and since she was not in love with him, she felt empowered instead of vulnerable. Empowered enough to discard the silk mother-of-pearl dress Édouard had rented for her portrait. Empowered enough to deliberately remove the one she was wearing as he watched, bemused and intrigued. She stepped out of her wire bustle, unhooked her corset, and let her chemise fall to the floor.

There was a bottomless feeling in her stomach as she stood, stripped naked under Édouard's watchful eyes. She turned her gaze to the table behind him, focusing on the candles burned to nubs in their silver holders, a plate of cold sausage, an open bottle of wine, and an empty glass with a red-rimmed stain on the bottom.

Searching for the ease she'd seen in Leonie, and in the models that stood under the skylight at the académie, Aimée walked to the divan, the air as heavy and warm as bathwater over her bare skin. She sat on the end of the velvet seat with her back to Édouard, her face turned away. Her dark hair was pulled into a high chignon, and she lifted her hand, resting it lightly on the back of her exposed neck.

"That's all you get," she said. "You will not paint my face."

He called it *Jeune Femme,* and it was the only painting Édouard ever did of Aimée.

Colette was grateful Édouard was keeping Aimée busy. It was foolish to think there was anything between them. Édouard attended every one of her soirées with his wife, whom he clearly adored. Not once had Colette witnessed the slightest intimate glance between him and Aimée. These things were palpable. If there were something there, Colette would sense it. Besides, she had much greater things to worry about.

For two weeks she had the coachman follow Aimée, and he reported that she went straight to Édouard's and came straight home afterward. Colette was relieved Aimée was keeping her word and staying away from Henri, and things might have gone on as they were if Colette had been able to stay away too. As it was, she could not.

She told Henri she was worried about him. He looked thin. Did he have all he needed? Could she bring him food? Painting supplies? She didn't mind, really; it was the least she could do.

Henri insisted he didn't need anything, but Colette brought things anyway.

For a while Henri tolerated it, until the tension and the fear of being exposed got the better of him. He told her it would be best if she did not come anymore.

She scoffed, "It's bad enough I'm keeping you a secret. If Auguste found out I wasn't doing all I could for you, he'd be furious."

But it was her guilt that kept her coming, the idea that she could make up for what she'd done.

The one time Colette came, and Leonie was there, Henri did not open the door. He told Leonie it was a model he'd seen in the street looking for work. "I told her I didn't have any money," he said, the lie coming easily. "Don't answer it. She'll go away."

But he did have money now. Colette brought it to him. The first time she tried to hand him a ten-franc note he flatly refused. After that, she started hiding the money in a pot, or a cup, slipping it under his pillow, or sneaking it under his palette.

Once, Leonie found three twenty-franc notes stuffed inside an empty coffee tin. Henri told her he'd sold a painting, nothing worth mentioning.

After that he made sure to search the apartment when Colette left, furious, as he dug around, for participating in her little game. He believed Colette would tire of it. When it was played out, she'd go away.

He was wrong.

. . .

As Colette's visits became more frequent, Henri became increasingly anxious. The visits were always the same. She would arrive just after Leonie had gone, which made Henri think she was lurking outside. She'd push her way through the door, hand her hat to Henri, remove her gloves, and walk around the room slapping them against the palm of her hand.

She'd make a show of inspecting his work, which was all very fatuous because Henri hadn't painted anything new in months. She'd lean into a tiny landscape as if she'd never seen it before, stopping pointedly to inspect the nude of Leonie, cocking her head, never saying a word. Then she'd sit at the table and look at Henri, who remained by the door.

"Aren't you going to offer me a drink?"

The same thing, every time, and he'd take down a bottle of whatever he had and pour them each a glass. He could buy nicer spirits now, with the money Colette left, but he hadn't spent a single sou.

Colette would take a sip, cough, make a face, and ask why he insisted on buying such horrid spirits. He couldn't possibly like it. "But, then again," she'd say, leaning in. "How would I know what you like and don't like anymore."

She made no pretense of politeness, not to put Henri off, but rather as a way of winning his trust. Asking personal questions about Leonie. How were they getting on, and did he intend to marry her? If so, how did he intend to support her? That sort of thing.

Henri would shift in his chair, try not to look her in the eye, and answer most questions with a shrug. Colette would rise first, and Henri would stand with her, meeting her at the door with her hat. She'd draw out the process of putting everything on, fiddling with her gloves and fussing with hat strings. Then she would raise both hands to the sides of Henri's face and kiss him. Nothing too personal, just a delicate press of her lips over his. And then she'd be gone.

Her visits left Henri sick to his stomach. Not even Leonie could cheer him, nor the lovely autumn days, full of bright sunshine that he hid from inside his apartment.

He worried if he went out with Leonie that he'd find Colette standing in the courtyard, or around the corner of the building. Then he'd have to tell Leonie something of his relationship with the Savarays, and that would mean telling her something of his childhood, which, as much as he pretended was lost to him, haunted him as much as Colette did these days. All those horrible, cold weeks in England when the authorities kept coming, when everyone spoke in hushed tones over his head, and no one would tell him where his mother was.

Henri wasn't prepared to talk about it, and he was grateful Leonie never pushed questions when she saw he was reluctant to answer. She was much kinder than he deserved, and cheerful in the face of his gloom. She said it was her disposition. She'd seen hardship. No sense falling into it if you could just as easily pull yourself out.

It was only when Aimée refused to see Leonie that Henri saw a glimmer of melancholy. Leonie had come to his apartment in tears, but even these hadn't lasted long. She'd gulped down her sobs, brushed her wet cheeks, and smiled, sure they'd sort things out over time. Aimée couldn't stay away from them forever.

But Henri was sure that she could. Like Colette, when Aimée made her mind up, she did not waver. It was the one thing they had in common.

. . .

It was Madame Savaray who noticed the change in Aimée. The girl's lightheartedness had slipped away with the warmth of summer and was replaced with the cool reserve of autumn.

She tried to speak with her, but Aimée kept her distance. She hardly spoke to any of them, shutting herself in her studio, or hurrying away to Édouard's. The only member of the family Aimée showed any compassion for was Jacques. Still patting him on the head in the hallway and kissing him good-bye in the mornings before she left, scooping him up in her arms and nuzzling his face.

It was when Leonie came to the door one day, and Aimée refused to see her, that Madame Savaray guessed what had happened. Of course, she thought, sitting in her requisite kitchen chair, Henri's affections were engaged elsewhere. These things always went that way. Leonie was a decent girl, but much too full of everything, and that's what got men's attention—all that fullness.

This roused Madame Savaray, gave her a bit of hope. If Henri had taken up with Leonie, there was a chance he would slip quietly out of their lives again.

What Madame Savaray failed to notice—later, she would be shocked by her lack of perception—was the change in Colette.

Auguste knew something was going on; he just couldn't figure out what.

Colette hadn't let him touch her in months, which wasn't all that unusual, but she barely looked at him anymore. She'd walk out of a room while he was in midsentence, which he found infuriating. The strangest thing was that she no longer argued with him. This had never happened. Not one raised voice, not a single confrontation.

And yet Auguste could see a ferocity seething under his wife's reserve, a flash in her eyes, a restless look. Something was getting to her. It just wasn't him anymore.

Colette was not in the house the day Auguste came home early from the factory. It was damp and cold, and his foot ached where the bayonet had pierced it—as it always did in this weather.

He called for Colette. Looked for her in the bedroom and dining room and parlor, but she was not home. He sat in his study with the door open so he could listen for her return, fiddling with his pocket watch, wrapping and unwrapping his fingers, suspicion rising with alarming force.

At half past four he heard the carriage pull up, the rattle of the front door handle, and then the click of his wife's boots on the vestibule tiles. He was standing in the hall when she opened the door.

"Heavens!" Colette threw a hand to her chest, her black-gloved fingers shiny as ink. "You startled me. What are you doing home?"

"My foot ached."

"Why aren't you lying down then?"

"I wanted to see you."

She tilted her head and smiled. "Whatever for?" she said, stepping around him and walking down the hall.

Auguste trailed after her, wondering why that particular tilt of her head simultaneously infuriated and weakened him. "I have tickets for the ballet tonight," he said. It sounded more like a challenge than an invitation.

"Which one?"

"*La Source*."

"We saw that in '72. It was no good."

"It was a huge success."

"Who's dancing?"

"I don't know."

They reached the end of the hall, and Colette stopped at the foot of the stairs. "I'd rather stay in."

"I already purchased the tickets."

"Take Aimée," she said, one hand resting on the rail, the other hanging loosely, close enough for Auguste to touch.

"You never refuse the ballet." He took a step toward her, and Colette moved quickly out of range.

Heading up the stairs, she said, "I didn't enjoy *La Source* the first time. I have no desire to see a revival."

Fueled by her dismissal, Auguste jumped up the stairs, wincing at the pain in his foot, and shouted, "I am still speaking with you!"

Colette halted, her heavy dress trailing behind her. "I apologize," she said smoothly, twisting her torso to look down at him. "Is there something more?"

Her eyes were dark, her skin pale, her lips a deep red as if she'd been biting them.

"Where have you been all afternoon?" Auguste's heart was racing.

"Calling on Madame Telfair. She was ill last week. I loaned her a book I wanted returned."

His wife wore an innocent, questioning look, and a tender smile that made Auguste feel foolish and irrational. He stepped backward off the stairs. Where had he thought she was?

Colette lifted a hand to the brim of her hat. "Are you quite through? I'd like to change if you'll allow it?" she asked with a smirk. Dropping her hand and gathering up her skirt, she mounted the stairs without waiting for an answer.

"We leave for the ballet at seven!" he called, but there was no reply, just the swish of fabric and a flash of purple silk as she disappeared.

Later, Auguste would remember that she'd had no book in her hand.

It surprised them all how the two events of the next week collided.

Chapter 16

It was late October and unseasonably cold. Colette stayed longer than usual at Henri's that day. She arrived drenched in a new perfume, wearing a heavy maroon coat, her cheeks flushed from the walk.

"Here." She handed Henri a bottle of vintage claret she'd had the cook dig up that morning.

Wrapping his hand around the delicate neck of the bottle, Henri set the wine on the table, the glass cool and smooth under his fingers. He imagined squeezing hard enough to break it, snapping off the top and pouring the wine through the sharp, jagged glass with bloody fingers, shards glinting in their drinks.

All the memories, the guilt and remorse he'd kept tamped down, had stirred into something palpable, something alive and out of his control.

He should have told Colette to go. Firmly. Demanded it. Instead, he took a knife from the drawer and stuck it in the top of the cork, yanking it out with a sharp twist of his hand. He poured them each a glass. The wine smelled rich and spicy. Sitting across from Colette, he remembered when he was a child and she would kiss his forehead, his cheeks, smooth his hair, envelop him in hugs. It had made him happy then, her intemperate affection that seemed so lavish and excessive.

They drank in silence, tension growing between them. Eventually, Colette walked over to the larder, throwing open the doors and peering at the empty tins and jars.

"How is it you do not have a morsel of food?" she said, walking directly behind Henri. Gingerly, she rested her hands on his shoulders. Henri could feel the curve of her palms and the gentle pressure of her fingers through his thin cotton shirt. "Mademoiselle Leonie Fiavre doesn't seem to be taking very good care of you." She laughed, kissed the top of his head, and moved away. "Go." She swept her hand at him. "Get us something to eat." She went to his bed and sat down, pulling her legs up and stretching out on her side, the thin mattress heaving and creaking under her as she kicked her slippers off—one, then the other, hitting the floor with a soft thump. "Go on then," she said, propping her hands under her cheek, her eyes closing.

Once outside, the biting cold and bright sun began to clear Henri's head. He thought he might go to Leonie's, but really, it was Aimée he wanted to see, to look into her shifting gray eyes and hear her speak in her clear, decisive manner. He could convince himself he hadn't wanted to be found, and yet he was the one who followed Aimée that night when he saw her through the café window. He allowed her into his apartment. Allowed her to paint beside him. He hadn't known how much he would miss her until she was gone. When he'd left four years ago, survival made it easy to forget. Now, he thought of her all the time, and he wasn't ready to lose her again.

Only, he couldn't go to Aimée with Colette on his bed, splayed out with her ankles indecently exposed. He knew she wouldn't leave until he returned, and he had to get rid of her before he did anything senseless, irreparable.

He went to the baker's. The bread warmed his hands through the paper as he trudged back to his apartment, aware of the blue, cloudless sky, of how the light bounced off the hard surfaces of the city, everything looking rapturous and satisfied the way things do in perfect weather. But he recognized it from a distance, from a place so far down inside himself he wasn't sure he would ever enjoy that kind of beauty again.

Colette was awake when he opened the door, sitting on his bed with a small piece of paper in hand. At first Henri didn't know what she held, then he saw the tin box next to her, and anger ripped through him.

"What are you doing?" He dropped the bread on the table and sprang to the edge of the bed.

"Looking for a new place to hide your money." She waved the piece of paper in front of him. "Who wrote this?"

Henri reached for it, but Colette yanked her arm back and held it out of reach.

"You have no right to read that." He took a step backward, resisting the urge to lunge at her. Memories from his childhood were pouring in, the rage he felt for his father, for his mother, for the powerless, meek boy he had been. His temples pulsed, and his head throbbed, and in that moment he hated Colette.

She stood up. "So, it is a love poem then." She looked down as if she meant to read it out loud. "It's quite eloquent. And from the tattered edges it appears as if you've carried it around for some time."

Hard sunlight filled the room. Henri put his hand out, palm up. "Give it to me."

Colette dropped the poem on the bed and stepped up to him—her perfume overwhelming. "You're no fun at all." She took his outstretched hand and pressed it to the side of her neck, his palm damp against her skin. "Tell me you left us for the woman who wrote this poem. Tell me you were never in love with Aimée. Tell me you didn't leave because of me. That it was something else, entirely." Colette rose up on her toes. "I've hated to think it was because of me."

She leaned in then, and kissed him. Henri could feel the thin, sinewy muscles of her neck tense under his hand, and he gripped harder, disgusted with his arousal, with how much he wanted the taste of her wet tongue, and to reach under her dress for that warm, wet place between her legs.

Colette was the first to pull away, calculating the fragility of the moment, along with its urgency. She pressed her body against his, moving her hand to the top of his trousers, easing her fingers under his belt.

Henri shoved her, hard, with both hands, and she stumbled backward catching herself on the edge of the bed. A black rush of humiliation shot through Colette. Henri's gentle nature was what appealed to her, his tenderness. But anger was familiar territory, and she straightened, breathing heavily, her chest heaving against the bodice of her velvet dress as she unfastened the buttons.

Henri watched, increasingly humiliated with each layer Colette shed. He wanted her, but in a frenzied, hungry, grief-stricken way, with a lifetime of longing welling up in him. To be touched. To be loved. To be told he was good.

He ran from the room.

It was half past three when he arrived at the front door of the Savarays. If Auguste had been out, Henri would have left, and never gone back. As it was, Auguste had arrived home half an hour earlier.

He was at his desk, moving his unruly eyebrows up and down and silently mouthing the numbers he was working in his head. Marie was out, and the young housemaid told him there was a man at the door who had not given his name. Auguste said to show him in, assuming it was the messenger boy with the post, or the young accountant he'd hired last week come to help him sort out his financial mess. It appeared that he had been overzealous about an investment and was now feeling the repercussions.

Henri watched from the open study doorway, unable to speak, held motionless by what he was about to do. He knew he didn't have to go through with it. He could simply step backward and retreat. But that wouldn't change anything, and it wouldn't make any of it go away.

With incredible effort, his mouth salivating at the corners, anger and fear and confusion rattling through him, Henri spoke Auguste's name.

For that split second before Auguste looked up, he felt a quiet dread at the hushed sound of his name.

Cautiously, Auguste raised his head, scanning the face of the young man for what felt, to both of them, a very long time before fully registering that it was Henri. Finally, he stumbled from behind the desk.

The men stood silently facing each other. Auguste's large body had gone soft, his shoulders limp, his hands heavy at his sides. He could see how guarded Henri was, how frightened.

"Henri, my boy, please come in. Sit down."

"No, thank you." Henri shook his head. His eyes roamed the room: the huge desk, a leather book open on top, an empty glass, an inkwell, a cigar on an end table, flames leaping in the bright, warm fireplace, and Colette, staring from the painting on the wall. "I came because I must tell you why I left."

Auguste clasped his hands behind his back. "That's very pragmatic of you. Why bother with petty formalities? Much better to get to it right away."

He believed Henri had come to declare his love for Aimée. Possibly admit to improprieties with his daughter. For years,

Auguste had convinced himself that this was the reason for Henri's departure.

"The night before I left, Colette and I spent the night together. She came into my room, and I let her in my bed." It was devastating to say out loud. A hot grip wrung Henri's gut, and he stood as if stripped naked, knowing there was no tenable thing he could say in his defense.

He wanted to explain that he had not meant for it to happen. That he'd never even thought about it before that night. He wanted to say how dark and confused he was at first, how good it felt, how cold the house and how warm her body. He wanted to say, *You were always good to me, but you weren't my real family and I was always lonely, deeply lonely. And for a moment, that night, the loneliness went away.*

But from the look on Auguste's face, it wouldn't have mattered. It was a betrayal of such magnitude that Auguste felt crushed by a blow that came at him from all sides. Instead of lunging at Henri, as he would have liked, he stepped away and sank into his chair, suddenly old, and very, very tired.

Quietly, his voice not sounding like his own, he said, "Get out of my house," but the thought of Henri leaving after just this brief, pitiful moment together, was as devastating as Henri's admission.

What Auguste wanted was for the boy he loved to drop to his knees and beg his forgiveness, crawl to him weeping. He wanted to hear all the justifications Henri wasn't able to give. He wanted to hear Henri say it was just because he loved them all too much.

When Henri left, and his boy was gone, Auguste couldn't get up. He sat thinking that when someone disappears, when there are no explanations, there is at least hope, but when someone turns his back and walks away, there is nothing.

Chapter 17

Colette didn't know it was Auguste who grabbed her. He clapped a hand over her mouth and pinned her arms from behind, her wrists pinched beneath his hard fingers. She heard the bedroom door kicked shut, and then Auguste let go, spun her around, and shoved her so hard she stumbled, tripping backward onto the bed.

"Good gracious, what are you doing?" Colette struggled to get up, only to have Auguste push her back down, his hands landing just above her breasts, making the skin tingle. If it weren't for the terrifying look on Auguste's face, she might have thought this some new, licentious game.

For the last two hours, Auguste had been staring into the empty room imagining his wife with Henri, and now, all the rage Colette had thrown at him over the years, all the rage he'd let bounce off his head, off his heart, rose up like a roaring, blinding wave.

His wife had taken their son into her bed like a common whore. Whore wasn't even a vile enough word for it. But *whore* was what he shouted, coming at her with a raised hand, shaking, his eyes blurred, and ears ringing with the swell of anger. He was going to teach her a lesson.

Colette lay on the bed where he'd shoved her, one arm flung over her head, the other across her stomach. She did not make any attempt to rise. A hot flush covered her neck and face, and her breath came in quick, short bursts.

Auguste dropped his hand. He couldn't do it. He couldn't hit her, and as he stared down at her his heart broke. He knew he couldn't love her anymore. It made him feel as if he'd lost everything.

With alarming familiarity, his anger melted into desire. Intense desire. Instead of striking her he got down on his knees, reached his hands under her dress, and pulled down her drawers.

It was over quickly. Auguste held a clump of her hair in one hand and gripped her chin with his other, his fingers digging into her jawbone. When he was through he let go and rolled onto his back.

Colette closed her eyes. Her scalp hurt, and her face felt tender and bruised. Reaching down, she pulled her dress back over her legs. Her bustle was crushed beneath her, and she wondered if it was ruined, if she'd have to replace the whole thing, or if the steel might be reshaped. It reminded her of the first time a man had taken her to bed. It happened very much this way, and she'd lain just like this thinking of the most ordinary things. That man had stood above her, pulling his trousers back on, saying that he couldn't help himself because she was simply too beautiful. And wasn't it kind of him to show her how special she was?

She now realized it was in this same twisted way that she'd tried to show Henri how special he was, how much she loved him. That was all. She had not meant to hurt him, or anyone else for that matter.

Auguste lay next to her breathing heavily, his fury spent, sweat pooling at the hollow in his neck as he stared at the motif on the bed curtain. It was a repeating pattern of blue flowers circling a white buck being attacked by three white dogs. The absurdity of this, of covering their entire bedroom—curtains, coverlet, upholstered divan, and two upholstered chairs—in this grotesque scene made him laugh out loud, a sharp bark that cracked the silence.

He took a breath, and it was as if the teeth of those dogs were sinking into his own flesh when he asked, "Jacques is not mine, is he?"

Neither of them moved. There was no fire, and the room had grown cold. Colette thought of resting her hand on some part of Auguste, but couldn't.

"No," she said, "he is not."

They lay until the room grew dark, until not even the blue toile canopy was visible anymore. Eventually, Auguste sat up, grateful that Colette appeared only as a shimmering lump of white fabric. He could not have looked her in the face.

"Where does Henri live?" He stood up, pulled on his drawers and trousers, and straightened the frock coat, which he had not bothered to take off.

"Will you hurt him?" she asked.

"Of course not."

Their voices were oddly kind, as if they knew what sorrows lay ahead, as if they both, in their own way, were sorry.

"Number 18, on the rue de Calais," she whispered.

Auguste stepped into his shoes and stood over the bed. It hurt to breathe, as if the truth had cracked every rib in his chest. Colette had not moved other than to pull her dress down. She looked almost peaceful, lying still, her hair spread around her shoulders, dark as the night that had crept in on them.

"Have Marie make up a room for you," Auguste said.

Colette didn't respond, but he could hear her breathing in the dark, a sound so soft and familiar it felt like a part of his own body.

He turned and left, imagining he'd spend the rest of his life listening for that sound.

Henri sat at his table with the empty bottle of wine and the poem Colette had found spread in front of him. He had not read it since he was a boy, and he was surprised to find his mother's words familiar and comforting, not painful, like he imagined. It reminded him that things were not always as they seemed, and that love was slippery and changeable.

The knock startled him. It was late, and he wasn't up for seeing anyone, not even Leonie, but the lamp glowed brightly, and whoever it was knew perfectly well he was at home, so Henri answered the door.

It was the boy he noticed first. A pair of short, chunky legs and a head of pale hair dropped forward; he was sound asleep on Auguste's shoulder.

Jacques had fallen asleep in the carriage, and Auguste had been very careful not to stroke his hair, or hold his hand. That would have been too much. It was hard enough having the boy's warm body wrapped around his middle.

"Take him," Auguste said, lifting Jacques through the air, the boy's limp head rolling back as he was clumsily transferred into Henri's arms. "This is Jacques. He's your son."

Jacques's soft leather shoes bumped Henri's thighs as he hoisted the boy up, awkwardly, staring at Auguste, shock and confusion quickly turning to panic as the weight of this very real child settled on him.

Auguste cleared his throat, the emptiness in his arms a physical pain in his body. "You must give him your name, your real name. A man must know who he is; otherwise he has no place in the world."

He could not look at Henri, or Jacques. He just shoved listless hands in his pockets, bent his head, and hurried back down the stairs.

As the driver slapped the reins on the horses' backs, Auguste smashed his fists into the carriage seat. He was an imbecile. It was freezing out, and he hadn't even remembered the boy's coat. He looked back at the window of the apartment, hoping Henri knew enough to cover the child properly in his sleep. He'd have Jacques's things sent over first thing in the morning—and currant jelly; Henri wouldn't know that the boy's favorite treat was currant jelly.

Auguste remembered driving away from his son Léon's grave, Colette sitting across from him, irreparable pain on her face. He remembered Aimée's screams, and how he'd had to hold her in his lap for fear she might leap out of the carriage window.

He wondered how many children a man could lose in a lifetime before he no longer wanted to go on living. And as he drove away from Jacques, the river of sadness, which for years Auguste had kept underground, burst to the surface and turned into an insurmountable flood of grief. A grief that he would never, not even as a very old man, manage to overcome.

Chapter 18

No one had any idea Auguste had taken the boy.

As far as Marie was concerned Jacques was tucked in his bed where she'd left him. She had been too preoccupied with making up the guest room to tell him a bedtime story that night.

"You might as well know," Colette had told her. "I've been banished from my husband's room. Strip the bed in the guest room and put on the linen sheets I like. You can take them off Auguste's bed. He won't know the difference."

All Colette wanted was to lie down and shut her eyes. Normally, she would have gone into Jacques's room and kissed him good night, but after the day she'd had, she just wanted to sleep.

So the boy's absence was not discovered until the next morning.

At breakfast, all eyes were heavy. No one had slept well, and no one felt like eating, or speaking. Only the sound of a spoon clinking in a cup, the scrape of a knife against a plate, or the crunch of toast passed between them.

Aimée was not feeling well, and she took cautious bites of bread, thinking she might send Édouard a message postponing their session for the day. She didn't notice the shadows under her papa's eyes, or the small bruise on her maman's jawbone.

Sipping her black tea, unable to eat a thing, Madame Savaray looked from Auguste's creased brow to Colette's hard face, the silence between them so rigid an axe wouldn't split it.

The previous night, Madame Savaray had heard the bedroom door slam. Then, when no one came down to dinner, her stomach had done a quick flop, and she'd pushed her food away. She'd seen Henri duck out their front door earlier that day, and been filled with dread. Auguste was not a violent man, but she knew that men could be pushed to violence. It was not her place to interfere, and yet it took all the willpower she had not to burst into her son's bedroom. Willpower and a tall glass of brandy in the parlor with the door cracked so she could listen for sounds upstairs.

Now, looking at his exhausted face, she feared the worst had happened.

A light tap came at the door. "Come in," Auguste said, roughly.

Marie stepped into the room, eyes wide and frantic under her crop of red bangs. "Pardon me for disturbing your breakfast," she said, her voice trembling, "but I cannot find Jacques."

Colette shot up from the table, and her napkin fluttered to the floor like a wounded bird. "What do you mean?"

"He wasn't in the nursery when I went to fetch him." Marie was in a state of panic. Despite the family's loyalty, she'd lose her position if the boy managed to get himself lost in the streets.

Madame Savaray set her teacup in its saucer. "Did you look under the beds?" she snapped, warding off the truth, telling herself that this was not the first time Jacques had hidden. If Marie had a bit of sense she would have found the boy before telling anyone.

"He's probably in the pantry." Aimée set her toast down and

brushed the crumbs from her fingers. "Cook found him there a few days ago licking the last of the quince jelly from the jar."

Marie nodded, wringing her hands. "That was the first place I checked. I've looked in the wardrobes, under every bed. I called and called." Tears rolled down her swollen cheeks. "I looked under the stairwell, in the parlor, and the garden."

"The boy is fine." Auguste kept his eyes on his plate, his forearms on the table, his knife and fork held in each hand. "He is with his papa."

Aimée looked at her papa, certain she'd misheard him. Madame Savaray rocked forward with a hand to her chest. Colette clutched the back of her chair, the room vibrating with an unnatural light, while blackness crept in at the edges of her vision.

Setting down his cutlery, Auguste pushed back his chair and stood up. "I brought him to Henri," he said, avoiding everyone's eyes.

Colette couldn't breathe. The black ring was closing in, clamping down around her windpipe.

Auguste turned to Marie who stood frozen in the doorway. "Pack Jacques's things," he said. "I'll have the coachman take them."

With rising hysteria Colette screamed, "You can't do this!" and lunged at Auguste.

He sprang out of her way, knocking his chair to the floor. Colette stumbled over it and fell to her knees. "You can't do this!" she screamed again, untangling herself from the chair and crawling toward him, her protest savage and harrowing, her face twisted.

Madame Savaray rose from the table. "Colette, get up." But Colette stayed on her knees, violently swinging her head as if she meant to shake it from her neck.

Aimée did not move. Everything seemed very far away as the information shifted into place. This was why Henri had left. It was not because he'd kissed her that night in the corridor, or because he'd told her he loved her. It has nothing to do with her at all. Aimée's stomach lurched into her throat. She put her head in her hands, closing her eyes against the cheerful mockery of sunlight that sprang through the windows. She remembered standing in her bedroom on that bitter, cold day when she'd watched the bloody soldier, when she'd felt her anguish like a wide, impassible sea, when Henri's leaving had been her fault.

The gravity of her maman's sin, the shocking truth of what Colette had done, what she had taken from Aimée and what she had taken from Henri, from all of them, scorched through Aimée like a quick fire, leaving a gaping hole in the center of her heart.

Colette stayed on her knees, her face a mask of torment and rage.

Madame Savaray stood above her. "Colette," she said, crouching down, a cool pain spreading through her knee. "You must get up, my dear." Her voice was soothing. "The only thing to do is to get up." She hooked her arms firmly under Colette's and pulled her to her feet.

Auguste backed all the way to the wall like a cornered animal. He wanted to claw his way out of the room, out of himself. He couldn't look at Colette. This was her fault. He had to make this her fault, or else how could he do it? He would never again touch Jacques's soft cheeks, or hear his small voice, or see the joy in his full, innocent smile. Auguste's pain, upon waking that morning, wasn't the resigned pain of loss he'd felt when his sons died, but a repentant, tortured pain. It was his hand, not the hand of God, who had taken his son this time. And the truth of that threatened to destroy him.

He would have preferred Colette throw something at him, smash a plate to the floor, scream for them both, but her outrage turned to deep despair so quickly that all she could do was sway back and forth with closed eyes, head hanging forward.

Madame Savaray looked at Marie, who stood speechless in the doorway. "Help me," she said, and Marie hurried over and took Colette's arm.

The two of them led her out of the room, guiding her upstairs and into bed where she lay on her side with one arm thrown over her eyes.

Colette heard voices murmuring and the clink of the wooden curtain rings against the rods. She felt her slippers being pulled from her feet, a blanket draped over her legs, a warm hand on her forehead, then cool air against her skin as the hand slipped away. Eventually, the bedroom door clicked shut, and the room went silent.

She pulled her arm from her face and dropped it to her side. She felt detached from her body, cold and heavy as stone, and she imagined herself carved into the bed, a permanent, immovable fixture. A braver woman would find her son, run away with him, risk everything for her child. Colette thought she was that kind of a woman. She'd always imagined herself to be, but here she lay, not running anywhere, feeling the same scooped-out emptiness she experienced after birthing a child. Once the babies struggled their way out of her body, they were no longer hers. The world took them, drew them out into the disease-ridden air and gave them back to God before she even had a chance to kiss them good-bye.

A single streak of sun escaped from a crack in the curtain and fell across the bed, splitting Colette down the middle like a bolt of lightning. God striking her down, she thought, holding out her arm, binding her wrist in that band of light.

For the first time in her life, when it actually mattered most, there was no fight left in her. This was not Auguste's fault. Jacques was her sin. And God, in his own way, had taken him back.

Aimée needed to walk. She needed to be outside, reminded of the sky and the air, things that were sharp and cold and real.

The revelation of Jacques as both Henri's son and her brother was staggering. The idea of her maman and Henri together made her feel as if she could touch the charred edges of her anger, run her hand along the wounded lip of that hole in her heart.

It was nearly impossible to see her way to Édouard's. Inside his studio, the sun was too bright, the windows too large, the ceilings too high and airy and exposed. Normally, she undressed in front of Édouard, aroused just to have his eyes on her. Today, she slipped her clothes off behind the screen, shaking as she stepped out. She felt dirty, her nudity an affront, an affirmation of her own, sinful nature.

A shudder went through her when she sat on the edge of the divan.

"Are you cold?" Édouard asked.

"I'm fine," she answered, but he shoved more coal in the stove anyway, distracted, crouching in front of the open door with his back to her.

"Do you believe Lemercier effaced seven stones of *Polichinelle*? I brought them thirty sheets of the finest Japanese paper to print those lithographs. I never instructed them to efface the stones, which of course I didn't even find out until I'd lined up a buyer. Infuriating." He dropped the coal shovel in the bucket with a clatter that made Aimée jump.

He crossed to his canvas, and Aimée lifted her arm and held her pose. The heat, beating in her face, made her nauseous and it was all she could do to sit still.

Édouard picked up his brush, noticing only the pink flush in Aimée's pale skin.

A light tap came at the door. "Come in," he said, and Aimée turned as a stout girl stepped into the room, her brown hair pulled into a knot at the nape of her neck. She stared at Aimée and then darted her eyes to the floor.

Édouard looked up, irritated. "What are you doing here?"

"Weren't the instructions eleven o'clock, monsieur?"

"Next week." Édouard shook his head, and the girl dropped her ardent expression. "Go on then." He turned from her and dipped his brush.

"Gracious, I don't know how I got it wrong! I'm so very, very sorry." The pitch of the girl's voice escalated, and Édouard raised his hand.

"Go. Go away." He motioned dismissively. "I'm working."

"Of course, Monsieur Manet, my sincerest apologies. I promise to get it right next time." She lowered her head and nearly tripped on her way out the door.

"New models." Édouard grimaced. "So fervent as to be annoying." He looked at Aimée, who had not returned to her pose. "Shall we postpone our session for another day?" Édouard asked.

"Why would we?" Aimée lifted her arm.

"You're looking a bit unwell. We'll stop."

She let her arm fall, and it smacked against her bare side. "I apologize," she said.

"No need for apologies." Édouard took her hand and helped her from the divan. "Go change. I'm almost finished. A few more days and your skin's your own again." He smiled at her, and Aimée stepped behind the screen feeling weak and vulnerable, with an intense desire to lie down with Édouard again.

But the moment she felt the urge, her stomach lurched, and she dressed quickly, wishing Édouard a good day and hurrying from his studio.

She went home on foot, her nausea increasing with every step until she became too sick and light-headed to continue. Stopping in the middle of the sidewalk, she took a slow breath and rested her eyes on the farthest point in the sky. The clouds moved dizzyingly. The shutters of a nearby window were open, and inside she could hear the grating voice of an angry woman, a woman fed up. Aimée swayed. She lurched at the scent of cooking meat in a nearby apartment, leaned forward, and vomited all over the sidewalk.

Chapter 19

The next day the Savaray house was silent. Colette wouldn't leave her room, and Marie brought her a tray of food, which went uneaten. Only Auguste and Madame Savaray ate in the dining room. Not a word passed between them. Aimée had her dinner sent to the studio, where she was working on a meticulously rendered still life: a stack of books, one fallen open on the table, an inkwell, and a quill pen. It had a punctilious level of detail. The precision kept her concentration hard as a rock, isolating her as she painted for hours at a time. She thought of going to see Jacques—no one had forbidden it, not that that would have stopped her—but she couldn't face Henri, not now. Not even for Jacques. So she kept her mind fixed on color and shadow and lines, fighting off the image of Henri in bed with her maman and the reality of Jacques's silent, empty room below her.

What she couldn't keep away was the low hum inside her, the subtle buzz and empty nausea. It was the moment she stood on the sidewalk smelling that cooking meat. The moment when the sky shifted and the earth dropped out from under her that she understood; she knew she was pregnant.

An older gentleman helped her from the sidewalk, avoiding any mention of her vomit at his feet. He put her into a cab and told the driver to take her straight home. But when the carriage turned onto the rue l'Ampère, Aimée told the driver to keep going, anywhere, just for a little while longer.

Five days later Aimée was sitting on the divan at Édouard's listening to the resonant tick of the enormous clock on the wall, waiting for the bell to toll the hour that released her from her pose. She had worked in her mind how she was going to tell him. What exactly she would say. He would have to help her. He had to. She had no one else to turn to. She couldn't tell anyone in her family.

Édouard was not in a good mood. The painting was almost finished, and the end always bothered him. Rarely was he satisfied, and he had little sympathy for Aimée's pale color and trembling arm. It was throwing everything off. But she'd been this way for days, and he didn't think her color was going to improve.

As he glanced at the clock, thinking he might quit early, the studio door flew open. Startled, he dropped his brush, and a streak of paint shot down the front of his pants.

Aimée turned so quickly her vision blurred, and in a disoriented haze she flung an arm over her bare breasts. Her papa was coming toward her.

His eyes were fierce and narrow as he stood above her, thumping the top of his thighs with clenched fists. "Put your clothes on," he said, his voice choked.

Aimée jumped up, fully exposed, and her papa's face deepened in color. She turned, trembling, and darted to the screen, the air splintered and brittle against her bare skin.

During the time it took to pull on her drawers and chemise, hook her corset, step into her bustle, pull on her petticoats and dress, clasp and button everything up, the room was completely silent, nothing other than the maddening tick of the clock.

When Aimée stepped out, Édouard was quietly dipping a brush into a jar of soap while her papa stood with his arms folded tightly across his chest, staring at the painting.

Auguste couldn't help but notice how good it was. It had a natural authenticity that would excite him if it were a painting of a classless, working woman, a girl meant for this sort of thing. Why wasn't it enough to paint his daughter in a sumptuous dress with a coy look? Capture her creamy complexion? Reveal the toe of a slipper? Auguste turned away, repulsed. No bourgeois woman showed the curve of her naked back or her bare neck, and certainly not the seductive lingering of her fingers across her own skin.

"You." Auguste shook his fist at Édouard. "How dare you?" He pointed to the painting. "You will get rid of that filth immediately. I will not have it displayed. Do you hear me?"

Over his initial shock, Édouard stood calmly wiping the tip of his brush with a torn piece of muslin. "I have the utmost respect for your family, Monsieur Savaray," he said evenly. "I would never reveal your daughter's identity." He set the brush down and nodded at the painting. "Her face is hidden."

"It's not her face that concerns me!" Auguste shouted, thumping over to Aimée, his fingers digging into the soft flesh of her upper arm as he marched her to the door.

"Monsieur," Édouard said. "Your daughter sat willingly. It was, in fact, her idea."

Aimée stared at Édouard, furious. It was her idea, yes, but by saying it, he made her completely responsible, cleared him of all wrongdoing. Looking at him she suddenly realized how old he was. Old like her papa. She was the naïve one, the one made accountable. Women, apparently, were the only ones made to pay for their sins.

There was a bitter taste in Aimée's mouth, and with overwhelming clarity she realized that her pregnancy would also be seen as her wrongdoing. Édouard would never be held responsible. He would not come to her rescue, nor would he defend her. He had a reputation to uphold, and certain formalities to keep. He would let Aimée go, with a smile and a nod of his head, back to her papa where she belonged.

Aimée and Auguste rode home in silence. When the carriage stopped, he grabbed her arm as if afraid she might dash away and yanked her into the house. He dragged her up the stairs and tossed her through the doorway of her studio like a filthy rag.

Stumbling forward, Aimée grabbed the arm of the divan and pulled herself up. She turned to her papa with a scornful look, exactly the look she'd worn as a child. It surprised Auguste, as much now as it had then, that his daughter refused to submit to his discipline.

"Your indiscretion is unacceptable!" he shouted.

Aimée took a bold step toward him. The low hum inside her, the subtle buzz, had risen like a swarm of mosquitoes, and she felt the force of her adrenaline. "It was only a painting," she stated.

Auguste strode to the other side of the room. At the very least Aimée could feign humility. The slightest look of remorse would have made him feel better. It was outrageous, the shameless iniquities committed by the women in his house. He'd been so good to them, given them every freedom, and they'd done nothing but humiliate and betray him.

"This is done!" He made a large sweeping motion with his

arm. "Your painting, it's done. I will no longer support it. I should have known better in the first place. It's no profession for a woman."

His hair stood on end as he ran his hand through it. He knew he was acting rashly, without an intelligent plan, but his life had shattered out of his control, and he could no longer see a clear way forward. He was not a cruel man. He loved his children. He had sent Jacques away *because* he loved him. It was the only thing he could do. With Aimée it was different. He had a choice, and he was well aware he might be making the wrong one.

"Did you hear me?" he shouted, his body pitched forward, his fists clenched, but his daughter just stood defiant, with her silent, impenetrable stare.

Aimée felt the blood in her veins, and a rush in her ears. Her maman's anger all these years suddenly made sense to her, the flying, smashing objects, the ferocious screaming.

"It's for your own good." Auguste was breathing hard. "You have no sense of men's true intentions. That little situation with Édouard could only have ended one way." He latched his fists behind his back, his eyes roaming the room, the walls of paintings and shelves of books. Why couldn't Aimée see that it was no life for a woman to be shut up with her painting and nothing else? It was one thing for male artists—they were like a pack of animals, alternately ridiculing and protecting each other through the chaos and madness. Women artists lacked the camaraderie of men. They were alone in it. And, clearly, this was no life for a woman.

He gave a quick nod. "You will marry," he said, calmer now. "It may not be an ideal gentleman, but I will make sure he will have the means to care for you."

Her papa's presumptions infuriated Aimée. It was as if she should have no say in her life. "I will not marry," she said steadily.

He reeled toward her. "You will do as I say! Do you hear me?" He raised his fist as if to strike her, but Aimée didn't move or cower. In a mad rush he snatched a penknife that lay on the table, and with one swift motion he leaped to the canvas propped on the easel and slashed the knife through it.

"There," he said, immediately feeling ridiculous, petulant. This, more than anything else, seemed to get a rise out of Aimée. The expression on her face made him think she would have preferred he hit her.

A burning sensation ran from the center of Aimée's body to the top of her head as she stared at the jagged gash torn through her meticulously painted pile of books. When she looked away, the low-burning fire, the bookshelves, the tables and chairs appeared with a distinct outline, everything sharp and clear as if she'd sketched her life in around her.

She looked back at her papa. He was breathing heavily. His face was bright red, and his hair stood on end, but he no longer looked angry. There was a stillness between them, a sense of defeat on both sides. Aimée stared back at the slashed canvas and thought about how life was like a painting. There were certain rules to follow, but mostly a lot of choices to make, where to draw a line, where to add a bit of shadow, or a bit of light. And whether you followed the rules or not, whether it was beautiful or hideous, at some point you had to step back and accept what you'd created.

Auguste dropped the knife, letting it clatter to the table. "You will marry," he said, his voice stripped of bravado. "You have no choice."

Turning, he strode from the room.

Madame Savaray witnessed the entire thing from the hallway. She'd been in the parlor reading the last chapter of Balzac's

Le Père Goriot, when the front door slammed. Putting her book down, she'd risen from her chair—a simple movement of the legs that was getting more and more difficult—and stepped into the hallway just in time to catch Auguste dragging Aimée up the stairs.

She didn't trust her son any more than she trusted Colette these days, and she did not feel the least bit guilty spying outside the studio door, especially not after witnessing his outrageous behavior. Destroying a perfectly good piece of artwork in a moment of passion was a dramatic gesture she would have expected from Colette, but not from her son, and she had a mind to tell him so.

She waited at the top of the stairs, wondering, as she watched Auguste slam the door, if all the worst characteristics of Colette had rubbed off on him.

"It's childish to slam doors," she said, moving in front of him. "Not to mention it alerts the servants and sets them gossiping. And I'd say they don't need any more of that right now."

"What do you want?" Auguste was in no mood for a scolding from his maman.

"That was atrocious." She gave a quick nod at the studio door.

"Why are you skulking around anyway?" He went to step around her, but his maman stepped with him.

"I would not make accusations where they are not warranted. I do not skulk. And I may be the only woman left in this house willing to speak with you. I believe it is in your best interest to listen."

Auguste crossed his arms and slumped forward. His body ached in more places than he cared to admit, and the solid, reasonable way his maman was looking at him made him want to bury his face in his hands. "What is it then?" he asked.

Madame Savaray could see her son's exhaustion and pain, and

a well of sadness pooled down where she'd once carried him, now a grown man with graying hair. "You had better think this through." Her voice was firm, but with a wisp of softness. "We're all suffering over the loss of Jacques. But I am well aware that there was nothing else you could have done. The boy was not your son. No one would have expected you to pretend otherwise."

Auguste pulled his arms apart and held a hand to his forehead. He did not want to be reminded of Jacques. He wanted to go to his room.

"Now this business with Aimée, on that I cannot agree with you. Her painting is an asset to all of us." Madame Savaray rested a hand on her son's arm. "My dear boy, marrying her off will solve nothing. She does not have the spirit to withstand a loveless marriage. It will destroy her."

Auguste drew his hand over his eyes and down his face, pulling at his rough, unshaven chin. "She was posing nude for Édouard. What exactly do you suggest I do about that?"

One of the kitchen maids had told Auguste. A rosy thing who said she didn't mean to be disrespectful, but he ought to know her sister had gone to sit for Édouard and she had seen Aimée posing, *in the flesh*. Her sister—this maid reassured Auguste—would *not* be taking her clothes off, so he needn't worry about any indecency there.

For some reason, Madame Savaray was not surprised. It was unacceptable, yes, but a misstep easily put behind them. Certainly not worth all the fuss Auguste was making.

"I daresay, it's not Édouard's fault," Auguste continued. "It's all a woman's meant for in that business. I don't know why I ever thought otherwise."

Madame Savaray shook her head. "There are perfectly respectable women artists."

"Well, Aimée is not one of them." He put a hand on his maman's shoulder and gently moved her aside. "My mind is made up," he said, and he trudged heavily down the stairs.

When Madame Savaray went into the studio, Aimée was kneeling on the floor, her dress pooled out as if the fabric had melted around her. She looked childlike, sitting like that, Madame Savaray thought, sighing deeply as she arranged herself in a chair. The tragedy of everything seemed impossible to get past and made her feel weaker than usual.

"Your papa won't do it," she said, "keep you from painting; he can't."

Aimée twirled a paintbrush between her thumb and finger. "Of course he can," she said. "And he will." When her papa ruined her painting she realized it was not an empty threat like the ones he often screamed at her maman. Something in his voice was different. This one he'd keep. "He wants me as bored and idle as Maman. I imagine he thinks I'll be begging him to marry me off then."

Madame Savaray did not like Aimée's tone. The very least her *petite-fille* could do was show a little humility. "Marriage isn't the worst idea," she said. "Getting out of this house might be your only chance at a normal life. A decent husband, even if you don't love him, can work out. I didn't love your *grand-père,* and he certainly never loved me. Not in the way one would expect from a husband, but we respected each other."

Between her fingers, the bristles of Aimée's brush felt as soft and damp as the nose of a kitten. "I can't marry," she said, her voice thin. "I'm pregnant."

Madame Savaray clasped her hands and her pulse quickened as if her heart understood it had come upon a crisis before her mind could catch up. She felt the emotional vigilance she'd kept up through the loss of Jacques give way to crippling sorrow. Looking at Aimée's delicate, curved back and her long, white neck, the disgrace Madame Savaray should have felt for her *petite-fille* turned to hopeless disappointment. There was no use standing up for the girl now. If there had been a chance of turning Auguste around, it was gone. This was a transgression he would never forgive.

"Get off your knees," she said, quiet but firm. "You will sit up properly and tell me exactly how this happened."

Aimée released her fingers, and the brush rolled and dropped to the carpet. She stood up, light-headed and very thirsty. She walked feebly to the table along the far wall and poured a glass of water from the pitcher. The water slipped cold and clean down her throat, and the chill of it spread through her chest. She imagined it spreading all the way to her womb and chilling this thing inside her that had so suddenly shifted her strength to impotence—a strength she was beginning to wonder if she'd ever had in the first place. She walked to the divan, feeling as if she'd left a piece of herself trailing behind, like a loose thread. Maybe, if she kept walking, she would unravel into nothing.

Aimée—her voice neutral and flat—told her *grand-mère* how she found Henri, how they painted Leonie together. It seemed a long time ago now. She told her what happened the day she went to his apartment unexpectedly. Madame Savaray listened with tightly clasped hands, her knuckles white, her lips a straight, disapproving line.

It was not until Aimée got to the part about Édouard that Madame Savaray stood up. She did not sit back down. She had been certain the child was Henri's. Madame Savaray gripped the back of the chair and looked at the hollows under Aimée's eyes, like darkened half moons. The girl deserved a harangue of reproof, but all Madame Savaray could muster was, "A married man, of all things!"

A knot tightened along Aimée's shoulder blades. She hadn't felt guilty about that. Not one bit.

Madame Savaray released her grip on the chair, shifting her eyes over the paintings on the wall: a wide, gray river, a hunched old man, a stone building, blue skies, clouds, water. It made no difference now which paintings were entered into the Salon de Paris, or whether Aimée got a new commission, or if there was any interest from dealers. None of it made any difference.

It unnerved Aimée, watching her *grand-mère* gumming her lips and twisting her hands with a look of full-blown panic. She had always imagined her *grand-mère* as having an endless reserve of calm endurance.

Aimée went to her and took her hand. It was soft and rippled with veins. "Sit down," she said, smoothing her fingers over the frail bones.

"No, no. I need to move. I feel very unsettled." Madame Savaray pulled out of Aimée's grasp and walked the length of the room.

Until now, Aimée had blamed Henri for throwing her into Édouard's arms, Édouard for abandoning her, and now her papa for ruining her life. But watching her solid, honorable *grand-mère,* Aimée realized this was her own doing. She hadn't turned out like her *grand-mère;* she was more like Colette, a sinful, self-indulgent woman.

Pausing at the far wall, Madame Savaray stared ahead for a minute. *This will end badly,* she thought. *There's no way around it.* Gathering herself, she turned, sharply, standing as she used to when dealing with her husband on matters of great importance. "How long have you been in this condition?"

Aimée tugged on her shoulder, digging her fingers into the taut, wiry muscles. "A couple of months."

"Can you be certain?"

"Yes."

"Then we have a little time yet."

"Time for what?"

"To figure out exactly what we are to do."

"I don't see that there is anything we can do."

"One can always do something. The thing we will not do is *tell* anyone."

"You won't tell Papa or Maman then?"

"Of course not." Madame Savaray gave a sharp gesture with her arms as if pushing away the air in front of her. "We will go down to dinner," she said, as if hitting on a solution. "It's imperative we maintain some semblance of order. We will sit and eat as if nothing were out of the ordinary."

She went to the door and held it open, giving Aimée a measured look, a look of warning, as her *petite-fille* walked obediently out of the room.

Both were unaware that it would be years before Aimée entered her studio again.

Chapter 20

There were no more Thursday-night soirées. People heard there was a falling out between the Savarays and the Manets, but there were often disagreements between families. That was no reason to shut up one's house. So it was concluded that the real reason must lie with the boy, Jacques, who had so curiously disappeared. Colette was notoriously flirtatious. It wouldn't have surprised anyone if the child had not been Auguste's. And this was the conclusion most people drew in the end.

Aspersions were cast on the morality of the family. Social engagements circled around the Savarays, only they were not at the center anymore, and they declined more invitations than they accepted.

Auguste stuck to his threat. He had the servants clear out Aimée's studio, her paints, easels, palettes, knives, and brushes. He sold her paintings to a dealer, a skinny man with a craggy face who paid one thousand francs for all of them. It wasn't until the man's oily fingers hooked around the gilt frame of a rather exceptional landscape that Auguste felt a pinch of remorse. He would be the one responsible for all this wasted talent, but he was not going back on his word. He stood by as the dealer piled the paintings into a cart and rolled them away.

Aimée did not watch her work disappear down the street, or go into her empty studio. She did not miss the paintings themselves, only the ability to cocoon herself in the act of painting, to hold her emotions at bay by pretending Henri was beside her, Jacques playing happily in his bedroom, Leonie waiting to take her hand and kiss her cheek, Édouard nothing more than a family friend, her stomach a flat, seedless thing.

Boredom brought a restlessness Aimée had never known before. She became terrified of her own body. At night, she would lie on her back and dig her fingers under her hip bones where her stomach was no longer squishy and flat, but firm and gently sloped. She felt like she was growing sideways, her waist thickening in the wrong places. Hoping to bide a little time with her corset, she pulled the strings tighter than usual, imagining she was flattening the baby.

It took Madame Savaray until the end of November to come up with a plan. It was going to take a good deal of lying, but Madame Savaray was not beyond it. There were times a woman had to lie. She would take it up with God later.

Early one afternoon, she went into Aimée's room where the girl sat at her desk staring at a gathering mass of clouds. "Get your coat," Madame Savaray said. "We're going out."

Without question Aimée followed her *grand-mère* out of the room.

Clouds dark as coal billowed overhead, and a flash of lightning lit up the buildings on the rue de Calais as they stepped out of the carriage. A single drop of water hit the pavement at Aimée's feet, and then a torrent of cold, biting rain hurled from the sky. They hurried for cover, their heads down, water pelting the tops of their hats.

As they mounted the stairs to Henri's apartment—Madame Savaray leaning heavily on the banister—Aimée felt a rising anticipation at the thought of seeing Henri again. She was a jitter of nerves by the time he opened the door.

Madame Savaray was too breathless to respond to Henri's "Good afternoon," and so she nodded and walked into the apartment, leaving him with Aimée.

Instead of shifting his eyes to the floor, Henri greeted her directly. His secret was out. There was nothing left to hide. It was a brief exchange, unremarkable from the outside, but both felt unanticipated relief.

Taking Aimée's coat, Henri made way for Leonie, who put her strong arms around Aimée's shoulders and kissed her damp cheek as if nothing had ever gone wrong between them.

"What wretched weather to be out in," she said, brushing the water from their coats with a slap of her hand.

Madame Savaray sat in the chair Henri pulled out for her, feeling uncomfortably large as she shifted her buttocks on the narrow seat.

Tense and a little queasy, Aimée went to the sofa and sat down, looking around for signs of Jacques. Everything looked different. The single bed had been replaced with a double. The stove was black and polished and glowing red, the pile of ashes cleared away. Blue flowered crockery lined the cupboard shelf, and the art supplies, which had taken over before, were nowhere in sight. *Girl in the Afternoon* still hung on the wall, along with the large nude of Leonie, and a dozen more studies of her from all different angles: a hand, a bust, a shoulder blade, the curved arch of a foot. Henri had picked her apart with precision. Aimée imagined that at night, with his hands, he put her back together.

She noticed a small bed in the corner neatly made with a stuffed rabbit propped on the pillow. Next to the rabbit sat a rusted toy monkey that had once been Aimée's. In each hand he held a stiff wire. As a child she'd spent hours twisting the crank on his back, watching him lurch into motion, climb the wires, flip over the top, and make his jerky, mechanical way back down. Aimée wished she could take the monkey in her lap, twist the crank on its back, and watch it climb the wires one last time.

At the stove, Leonie poured coffee. Henri sat across from Madame Savaray, but kept his chair at an angle so he didn't have to face her head-on.

Everything felt strange, with the thunder cracking outside and the lightning streaking through the room. No one spoke. There was nothing save the occasional boom of thunder to quell the silence. Leonie set the coffee on the table with a plate of cheese and bread, prepared beforehand, and sat next to Aimée. She wanted Aimée to see that she didn't hold any grudges. Henri had told her the truth about growing up in the Savaray house, the truth about Jacques, and not for one minute did she hold him accountable. As far as Leonie was concerned, it was all Colette's fault. That vile woman had slipped into his bed in the middle of the night, in the dark, and what was Henri supposed to do? Leonie might have grown up poor, but she'd been raised decent and proper. To have a maman such as Colette, well, that was worth all the pity in the world.

Madame Savaray shifted in her chair. Her knee ached, the bottom of her dress was wet, the storm irked her, and no one, it seemed, wanted to discuss why they were here. It was clear that it would all be on her. "They have agreed to take the child," she said, looking directly at Aimée, who wasn't sure whether she should feel grateful, or outraged.

Another flash of lightning turned the sky into a sheet of white, and the room, for that split second, was brilliant.

Aimée felt the sofa shift under her as Leonie edged closer. Solid, practical Leonie—none of this would unsettle her. Aimée glanced at Henri, who kept his hands wrapped around his mug and his eyes turned away from everyone. It was humiliating to think that he knew of her condition. Looking at his profile, the curve of his narrow lips and the rise of his small nose, she felt the same pull, the same attraction and longing she'd always felt, but knowing what he had done with her maman changed it to something disturbing, repugnant.

She realized then that her image of family, of her place in society and the rules she'd been told to follow, were all lies. Lines were blurred, roles confused, rules broken and neatly covered up. Even her stalwart *grand-mère*—who Aimée imagined hadn't told a lie in her life—was sitting here, orchestrating a ruse that would go on for a lifetime.

Madame Savaray picked up her coffee, the warmth of the cup only a slight comfort. It was no wonder no one was saying anything. How could one speak of relief and sorrow in the same breath, of a child who was to come and go, and never be mentioned. She set her coffee down and reached for a piece of cheese, hoping food might take the jittery edge off her stomach.

"Where's Jacques?" Aimée asked, this sudden turn of conversation startling everyone.

"A friend took him for the afternoon," Leonie said. "We thought if he saw you and Madame Savaray it would upset him. He's only just stopped asking for his maman."

It was outrageous to Aimée to think these children would grow up as siblings, her child and her maman's, and from the tight pull of her *grand-mère*'s mouth, Aimée knew she felt the same way. Outrageous, and yet, somehow, the perfect solution.

Leonie took Aimée's hand and gave it a reassuring squeeze. Aimée looked at her. Nothing was said, but something very important passed between them—something of a deep and intimate understanding, a moment of profound gratitude and acceptance. They would never speak of it, but it was this moment that would allow for all that was to pass between them. And years later, when Leonie was much older, when memories consumed her, this was the moment she would come back to, the moment that would help her understand, no matter how painful, that she had done the right thing.

"How will we manage it?" Aimée asked.

"You can live with us," Leonie said. "Until the baby is born. Not here, of course. It's much too small."

"What will we tell my parents?"

Reaching for another piece of cheese, Madame Savaray said, "I have a friend in England—Lady Arrington. Widowed, without children. I wrote and asked if you might stay with her. She said she'd be grateful for the company. I told her you would be traveling in the late spring. It's only a matter of convincing your papa to send you abroad."

"But I won't be going abroad."

"You will, after the baby is born. So it's not entirely a lie."

Henri hadn't said a word. He looked wholly absorbed in his cup of coffee.

"We want to move anyway," Leonie said. "My *grand-tante* passed away, and she's left me a little money."

Madame Fiavre had been the only family Leonie had, and Aimée felt a stab of sympathy.

Leonie looked at Henri, trying to catch his eye, continuing when he gave no sign of disapproval. "Your papa's sent money too," she said. "He writes that he'll send it every month, for Jacques."

"I don't want his money," Henri said, hating for Aimée to think that he was taking it willingly.

"Then you're a fool." Madame Savaray slapped her hand on the table. She wished Henri would sit up straight and stop looking so desultory. "You don't have the means to provide the boy with a home he deserves. He might not be Auguste's child, but neither were you. It's selfish to be prideful. Leonie's a prudent woman, with a good head on her shoulders. You listen to her. She knows what's best for the boy. I expect you'll be marrying her now, what with these children involved. Make a proper woman of her."

Henri gave a slight smile, which Madame Savaray took as passive and noncommittal. "Well?" she said sharply.

He nodded. "One thing at a time."

Madame Savaray grimaced. "Another month and Aimée's condition will be all too obvious. The three of you can't possibly stay in this infinitesimal room. It would be highly improper, not to mention there's the risk of Colette making an unexpected visit. The sooner you get away the better."

"I know of a cottage in Thoméry that's for let," Henri said. "I plan to go out tomorrow and have a look."

"Good." Madame Savaray stood up and looked out the window. "The storm's easing up. We ought to be going."

Henri went to retrieve their coats. First he helped Madame Savaray on with hers, then he held Aimée's as she slid her arms through the sleeves. From behind, he reached up and adjusted the heavy fabric over her shoulders. Before she could move away, he drew his hands down her arms and gave an unmistakable squeeze.

Long after she and her *grand-mère* stepped back out into the cold, wet afternoon, Aimée felt the pressure of Henri's hands on her arms. Whether his quiet acknowledgment was pity, or some silent apology, Aimée accepted it, wanting to forgive him in a way she could never forgive her maman.

Chapter 21

When they returned home that night, Madame Savaray went to Auguste. Deeply concerned, she told him that Aimée needed discipline before she was to be married off. Marriage had never kept any woman in line, she said, raising her eyebrows, "But I don't need to tell *you* that. What Aimée needs," she insisted, "is to be sent away. I propose sending her to Lady Arrington. You know how the English are." Another raised eyebrow. "Far more disciplined in matters of the flesh than we." Madame Savaray stood over Auguste in her black, high-necked dress, hoping it made her look authoritative, unrelenting. She needed this plan to work.

Auguste folded his arms across his chest. "You're just trying to get her out of marriage."

"Yes," Madame Savaray said, "I am. I don't think it's the answer. What we can agree on is that she must be removed from temptation. Your solution is marriage. Mine is England. At least mine isn't permanent."

Auguste walked to his desk, drawing his chair out and making a great show of seating himself in front of his work. "I'll think it over," he said.

Madame Savaray pinched her lips together. This would not

work without his consent. "Auguste," she started in again, but he shot his hand in the air.

"I said I would think it over." He picked up his pen. "If you are quite through, I have work to do."

Madame Savaray watched her son scribble something on a piece of paper, set it aside, and pick up another. He used to be reasonable and kind. All she saw now was an irate, bitter man. She supposed anyone could get beaten down, eventually, which was how he looked, beaten down. His eyes were puffy, his skin sallow, his broad shoulders slumped and defenseless where they had once looked so formidable. Affection was what he needed, Madame Savaray thought, but there was no room for that in their relationship. There never had been.

"I'll need an answer soon," she said, mustering what authority her age and position afforded. "Lady Arrington has already agreed, and she is awaiting my reply."

"You should have consulted me first." Auguste didn't look up. "Let her wait."

What he couldn't say was that he didn't want to make any more decisions concerning Aimée right now. He regretted the ones he'd already made, and he didn't need his maman staring at him with her accusatory look while he muddled over another.

Two weeks went by, and still, nothing came from Auguste in the way of an answer.

Aimée and Madame Savaray moved through their days with increasing anxiety. Aimée did not eat as much as she should, and Madame Savaray ate more than was good for her. Neither one of them slept much.

Colette was still too wrapped up in her grief over the loss of

Jacques to notice. She rarely sat in the parlor with them, and since her Thursday-night soirées had ended, she spent little time concerned with the details of the house. The servants were left on their own, and Madame Savaray couldn't help but notice that they were taking full advantage.

But this was no time to worry about the servants. Aimée's middle was thickening. There was no rounded stomach yet, but her condition would be obvious soon. Madame Savaray worried she would compromise the baby if she kept tightening her corset. A proper, expandable corset would have to be purchased, and that would be the end of hiding anything.

Madame Savaray decided she must go to the factory, to Auguste's office where everyone could see she had come on important business. He wouldn't dare send her away, and she wouldn't leave without an answer.

Madame Savaray sat on the hard, wooden chair opposite Auguste's desk. She hadn't been to the factory in years, and as she listened to the rhythmic clank of the thin metal discs on the bobbinet machines, she remembered the feel of a perfect strand of thread between her fingers. She missed that life.

"I've booked Aimée's passage." It was a risky thing to say, but she had no other choice. Aimée had to go. "I've heard these new paddle steamers make the trip from Calais to Dover in under two hours."

For a moment, the balance of power swung between mother and son. Auguste leaned back with his hands clasped across his stomach. His maman wore a steadfast expression that he recognized from his childhood. It was the one she wore when she would tell him, in that unwavering voice, exactly how a thing was going to be. He looked out the window where a pigeon perched on the sill, cocking his head as if listening in on them. The truth was that Auguste was grateful the decision had been made for him. Sending Aimée away was the sensible thing to do; he just couldn't be the one to do it.

"Very well," he said, finally. "Have you told Colette?"

"Of course not. That's your concern." Madame Savaray stood up, clutching her reticule, so relieved it was all she could do not to circle around the desk and kiss her son's cheek.

Auguste watched his maman, smiling, her head bobbing ever so slightly to the rhythm of the machines. He remembered how huge she had seemed to him as a child, towering overhead, a deep resonance to her voice that gave her an almost brutish quality. He had found comfort in her strength. He had thought his great maman was capable of anything.

Leaning forward, he wondered if he'd missed, all these years, what an asset she was to him. "I will write to Lady Arrington myself," he said. "I will want to know how Aimée is getting on."

"Of course." Madame Savaray waved her hand over the desk. "Hand me a pen. I'll write out the address."

She had worked this part out also, with Henri. It was his idea. He said he knew a woman in England who would help them. "How well do you know this woman?" Madame Savaray had asked, and he'd said well enough. "And what makes you think she'll lie for us?" she'd demanded. "Because she's good at it," Henri had said, and they'd left it at that.

Madame Savaray wrote the address on a piece of paper, and pushed it in front of Auguste.

Aimée's departure was on a Friday. Madame Savaray had made sure of that. Auguste would have to be at the factory to inspect the week's finished products. He had given Aimée a hasty good-bye on his way out that morning, a nod, and a word of advice about obeying Lady Arrington. Colette was bothered she hadn't been consulted on any of this, but not enough to protest, and certainly not enough to mention it to Auguste. Her daughter was no different from the rest of them, her entire life subject to the decisions of a man.

In the vestibule, the trunks already loaded, Colette looked over her daughter's shoulder into the street. It surprised her how difficult it was to say good-bye.

"I never cared for the English," she said. "They're much too stiff if you ask me. Regardless, I'm sure you'll manage."

Madame Savaray hovered behind them, puffing air over her bottom lip.

"At the very least, it will be a change of scenery," Aimée said, looking out into a day that was bright and chilly and promising.

"A dreary one, but a change." Colette reached for Aimée. It wasn't her usual way, but an embrace seemed the proper thing to do when one's daughter was going abroad for an indefinite period of time.

Taken aback, Aimée leaned in and awkwardly returned the hug. It was then that Colette noticed her daughter had put on a little weight; there was some substance to her chest now. She pulled away. Aimée's complexion was rounder and rosier than she'd ever seen it. "Filling out." She gave Aimée's stomach a little pat, and Aimée winced. "Maybe you'll find an Englishman for a husband."

"I'm sure I will not." Aimée noticed the delicate spider veins running through her maman's temples, and the thin, bruised skin under her eyes. Her maman looked fragile, which was startling, and for a moment it worried Aimée to leave her.

Madame Savaray pushed her way between them, gave Aimée a vigorous hug, and turned her toward the door. "Best be getting on."

Before stepping into the carriage, Aimée looked back. Her

grand-mère and her maman stood side by side on the threshold, her *grand-mère*'s magnificent black hair turning midnight blue in the sunlight. Aimée gave her a look of deep gratitude, returned by a sharp nod from Madame Savaray. A bond of trust and secrecy had formed between them. They were in it together, that they knew. But neither knew what threatening emotions lay ahead, what helpless, intolerable pain might have to be endured. They could only hope to come through it.

After the carriage pulled away, Madame Savaray hurried inside, but Colette stayed on the doorstep watching the commotion in the street. A white-haired man with a large dog stepped into the road, a carriage halted, and the horse swished his thick mane and slapped his tail against his back. *All these people coming and going,* she thought, *lives being lived.* A shout echoed. Handcarts rattled by, filled with the last of the root vegetables, pushed by strong-armed women. Colette imagined these women enduring the hardships of life with the same relentless strength with which they pushed their carts. How simple, she thought, to throw oneself into a job. Haul something heavy. Dig potatoes. Survive.

She turned, and the sun slipped away from her face as she stepped back into the house. For a long time she stood in the dim, cool hall listening to the silence. She wanted to be young again, with all the possibilities of a future. She wanted to be going far away too.

Instead of heading to her room, Colette went into the parlor where Madame Savaray sat looking out the window. The old woman's chin was tilted up, and Colette could see the protruding muscles along her neck, and her paper-thin skin hanging under her chin. *How miserable to be old,* Colette thought, sitting on the sofa and straightening her shoulders.

"A cup of thick, warm chocolate might comfort us," Madame Savaray said.

"Yes." Colette smiled. "It might."

For a brief moment they looked at each other, and then looked away, aware that Aimée had always been the buffer between them. Without her there was a danger of things becoming too personal.

They became aware of something else too, something obvious yet profound. They were aware of how mundane and tedious their lives had become. And how neither one of them had anything of meaning, whatsoever, to do.

Chapter 22

Instead of taking a train north to Calais, and then a boat across the English Channel, Aimée took the train from Paris to the station at Fontainebleau. It was strange to go such a short distance, and travel into an entirely different life. A passage across the sea would have made it feel more believable, or at least more momentous.

Aimée sent her trunks ahead in the carriage and walked, following the Seine, weaving her way under massive oak trees, tall and ordered like sentinels along the river. A bitter wind blew off the water, but the sun was shining, and Aimée didn't mind the cold. She paid close attention to the gray-green color of the river, to the bursts of white sunlight on top, and the cool blues of the sky. Yes, this was where she would come and paint every day, as long as the weather, and her condition, permitted.

She cut through a meadow that had lost its summer luster, past rows of mud walls tangled with massive grapevines, and out onto a road where she'd been directed by the porter at the station.

A few kilometers down the road, she came to a stone cottage overgrown with Virginia creeper. When she stepped up to the door, an enormous black dog bounded out, barking uncontrollably. Leonie was right behind him, grabbing at the scruff of the dog's neck, scolding in a deep, warning voice. Then she wrapped her arm around Aimée and pulled her through the door.

"This is Laertes." The dog had calmed down, and Leonie rubbed the back of his head. "He followed Jacques and me home from the village one day. Wouldn't leave our sides, and then the butcher threw him a bone from his cart as he drove by, and this fool dog thought we were the source of food. We've been stuck with him ever since." Leonie spoke with a quiver of nerves. "I don't know where Henri and Jacques have gone to. They must be outside. Come, I'll show you the house."

Aimée followed Leonie into the drawing room, Laertes sniffing her from behind. Leonie seemed nervous, almost skittish, and Aimée found she was nervous herself.

"It's not very large," Leonie apologized, looking around as if this had just occurred to her. "But after our apartment, it feels utterly indulgent. All these rooms, and there's a view of the river from the upstairs."

Aimée smiled, and told Leonie it was lovely, which it was. *Humble,* she thought to herself, but she didn't mind that.

The rest of the house consisted of a kitchen and dining room opposite the drawing room, and two upstairs bedrooms with a dressing room adjoining them. The bigger room was Henri and Leonie's, with a bed in the corner for Jacques. The nude painting of Leonie hung—boldly, seductively—on the far wall opposite their bed.

The smaller room would be Aimée's, with a chair, a desk, a washstand, and a wardrobe. Her trunks had already been placed at the foot of the bed, and she wondered if Henri had done this for her, or if the porter had carried them up.

She walked to the window—noting the tidy landscape on the

wall opposite her bed. There was a view of the river, just as Leonie had said, and of a weedy garden with an ancient, knotty plum tree, the ground still littered with rotting fruit.

On the train ride, Aimée had felt gloriously independent, leaving home, leaving her parents. How ironic it was that her sin was what had finally gotten her out. But now that she was here, it was impossible not to accept the full truth of her situation. She was utterly dependent, and there would be no privacy in this small house. If the winter wasn't too harsh there was always the outdoors, but in her condition she wouldn't be able to go into the village. She certainly couldn't be seen at church. And her friend, who stood hovering in the doorway, was not just a friend anymore. Aimée was now beholden to Leonie; she would be the mother of her child. What a change in the roles they once held.

"Are you all right?" Leonie asked, sensing Aimée's hesitation, and wanting, very much, for her to feel at home.

Aimée nodded, but she didn't turn from the window. She'd just spotted Henri and Jacques coming up the path, both dressed in brown trousers and white shirts, Jacques's wrinkled and spotted with grass stains. The boy was dragging a stick in the dirt and holding tight to Henri's hand. They were talking excitedly, both faces lit up, smiling.

It startled Aimée to see Jacques happy. She'd imagined him scowling and lonely. It had been only a few months since he'd been taken from his home. How quickly children accept what they're given.

"I hear Henri," Leonie said. "Come, let's go down. Jacques will be so excited to see you."

She hurried down the stairs, while Aimée paused to glance at herself in the mirror, smoothing her hair, aware of the change in her body, her fuller chest and rounder face. For once, she looked almost pretty.

From the hallway, Aimée watched Leonie hold the door open for Jacques, who came skipping in with Henri right behind, Laertes leaping and wagging his tail. When Aimée stepped forward, Jacques halted at the sight of her. Then he spun around and buried his head in Henri's legs.

"Come, come," said Henri softly. "It's your *tante*."

They had decided to refer to Aimée as Jacques's *tante*. It might confuse him at first, but he was only three years old; he'd quickly forget she used to be his sister.

Aimée crouched down. "Jacques," she said in the same soft voice Henri had used. "I've missed you so very much."

Jacques pulled his head up, gave Aimée a fervent look, and buried it again in Henri's legs. Leonie pried him from Henri and picked him up. Jacques wrapped his legs around her and threw his arms around her neck. It reminded Aimée of the first time she held him, and she felt a pinch of jealousy.

"It'll just take a little time," Leonie said, stroking the boy's blond hair. "Come, let's get something to eat," she whispered in Jacques's ear and carried him into the kitchen.

It was foolish to think Jacques would come running into her arms, but the rejection still hurt. Aimée stayed crouched until she felt Henri's arm on her shoulder, his hand reaching to pull her up.

He stood quite close, and Aimée noticed that the freckle under his eye wasn't fluttering at all. His face was perfectly still, and this made her uneasy. Only it wasn't just his calmness, but also the subtle tenderness between them in the way he held her hand.

A bang came from the kitchen, possibly a pot falling to the floor. Leonie gently reprimanded Jacques, and outside the dog barked.

"Henri?" Leonie called, and he dropped Aimée's hand.

"I'm pleased you've come," he said.

Aimée folded her hand against her skirt. "I haven't decided if I'm pleased to be here." There was a lightness to her tone that did not match how fast her heart was racing. "But, of course, I'm grateful."

Henri smiled and pulled off his coat. Aimée's honesty never failed to surprise him. It's how she'd been that first day when they'd met as children, dead honest and amusing at the same time.

"Jacques will come around," he said. "Leonie's delighted you're here. As you know, I'm not always decent company. Rarely even tolerable." Henri—polite and self-deprecating—shrugged his shoulders.

"Neither am I," Aimée said lightly.

Henri had the urge to hug her. Instead he hung his coat on a peg by the door.

They walked down the hall, an ease between them that showed itself in the casual way they entered the kitchen, like old friends.

Standing over the stove, Leonie noticed this, and it pleased her. She smiled, stirring onions in a cast-iron pan with one hand and pouring milk from a pitcher with the other. Her cheeks were bright pink, and it reminded Aimée of all the times she'd watched Leonie stir chocolate over her *grand-tante*'s stove.

"Aimée, my dear, you must be famished. Please, sit, " Leonie said. "Supper's almost ready. We never eat in the dining room. I can't see the use of carrying everything that far. Besides, we were thinking of turning that room into a studio."

Aimée smiled. "A splendid notion. Although, I would love to get out of doors as much as possible before the weather turns." She smoothed her hands over her stomach, an instinctive habit she'd recently developed.

"Precisely what Henri said." Leonie laughed and set the pitcher on the counter.

Aimée noticed that even here, at the back of the house, the light coming through the windows was pure and lovely. The smell of onions browning in the pan and Jacques's adorable voice pleading to stir were comforts.

"Not now," Leonie said. "Go sit next to your *tante,* or bring the spoons to the table."

Holding the spoons tight against his chest, Jacques circled the table, setting a spoon at each place, triumphantly placing Aimée's next to her bowl, pleased enough to forget his shyness and confusion.

They gathered around the table. Leonie ladled the steaming soup while Jacques ordered his papa to guess the ingredients. With a stoic expression, Henri began listing items such as toads and tadpoles, Leonie piping in with a bird claw or a cat eye, and Jacques, laughing fitfully, asking for, "More, more."

Aimée was stunned by this familial ease and intimacy. She had an urge to laugh along, defying the restraint she'd been taught in the Savaray household. So this was family, she thought . . . *it just wasn't hers.*

As she reached for her spoon, she felt the almost indiscernible thump of a foot low down in her belly. And it was then that she understood, in a way she had not yet come to grips with, that that little foot wasn't hers either.

Chapter 23

The tight quarters and lack of privacy were new to Aimée, but she found a comfort in the small cottage, a sense of safety. Under Leonie's bustling care, the house exuded warmth, every corner filled with laughter and Jacques's bouncing enthusiasm.

For a short while, Aimée felt like a part of their intimate sweetness.

She resumed her painting, sometimes by the river, or near the mud walls, but mostly in the dining room Henri converted into a studio. Now, more than ever, she could see the influence of Édouard's instruction in her work, and she thought of him with less bitterness, remembering what he'd exposed her to that afternoon on his divan. She wondered if he'd ever know she carried his child. She would never be the one to tell him.

Aimée tried to paint Jacques, but he squirmed, hating to sit still for any length of time, so she gave that up. Leonie was still a willing subject, and Aimée found her even lovelier to paint in her own domestic setting. Aimée captured her leaning over the stove, shaping loaves of bread, and lounging on the sofa with Laertes at her feet, her eyes bright, lambent in the firelight.

Henri also painted, but he stuck to landscapes, and—when

forced indoors—passionless still lifes. He was not handling the arrangement nearly as well as the women. It confused him, all this gaiety, living with Aimée, and having Leonie in his bed at night. And the friendship between the two women, the looks, the outbursts of laughter, all that chatter, he felt somehow in the middle of it, and left out, all at the same time.

What he wasn't fully aware of, or not yet willing to admit, was how dangerous their situation felt. He cared deeply for Leonie. He didn't want to hurt her, but quietly painting beside Aimée, seeing her every morning, hearing her in the next room at night, brought an arousing intensity and risk. When Aimée looked directly at him with her slippery, gray-blue eyes, made some bold observation, or smiled absently at her own wit, it brought back feelings Henri had swept aside time and again. As children, their closeness had felt natural. When he was a teenager, it both confused and comforted him in a way that often made him feel ashamed. He loved Aimée, but he had never imagined a future with her. It would have been impossible. Only here they were, their futures tied together indefinitely, and he couldn't imagine his without her now.

As the tiresome winter days wore on, life became harder in the cottage. There was a shift in atmosphere, a subtle infusion of tension in the details of everyday life.

First there was the bathing. The tub needed to be hauled into the kitchen. The water heated, dumped out, reheated—and, of course, the uncomfortable intimacy of disrobing just behind the kitchen door. The privy, which was outside, was absolutely freezing. Aimée had to get up at least twice a night, and the creaking stairs usually woke the entire house.

Then there were the weekly letters Aimée wrote to her papa,

fabricated stories of her time abroad that were sent to England where a friend of Henri's forwarded them back to Paris with postage from London. It was overwhelming to think how much lying she'd already done. She knew very little of London, but had to be detailed enough to make it believable, which was getting harder and harder with the exhaustion of her pregnancy. Her legs were sore, her back ached, and her feet were too swollen for her slippers. Her stomach was being pressed up into her throat, and everything she ate burned her esophagus.

Leonie did what she could to help. But she was also increasingly wary of what was going on around her, especially when it came to Henri. He'd stopped reaching for her at night, darted her kisses in the morning, and when she'd slip her hand into his, his fingers hung limp as a washrag. Once, when she'd teasingly sat in his lap at the breakfast table, he'd quickly pushed her off and made some excuse to get up. Leonie reminded herself that Henri could be fickle—he'd come around. No need to let a man's mood get her down, because there was a baby coming, a fact that they were all too hesitant to mention.

Leonie had her reservations about mothering someone else's child, but she'd lain with Henri often enough to suspect something might not be right with her, and Aimée could be her only chance at a baby. Yet she and Aimée never spoke of this—not even in private—and this nagged at her. As far as Leonie was concerned, it wouldn't do any good to ignore it, much better to face these things head-on.

But Aimée wasn't prepared to face anything, head-on or otherwise. Her very state of being felt altered. Everything was messy and confusing. From the beginning she'd shied away from Henri and Leonie's kisses, trying not to notice when they held hands, or exchanged ardent, uncomplicated looks. It had been impossible to ignore the intimate sounds that came from their bedroom at night, and later on, the low, argumentative whispers.

The situation was unbearably complicated, especially because she and Henri were exchanging their own looks of private complicity. Aimée played at indifference, quietly angry at the feelings rising up in her. She'd started to direct her frustration at Henri, batting her brush in the air and hissing at him to stop distracting her.

"Nothing can distract you," he said once. "Not even me. I never could." Standing in the studio, with the cool light surrounding them, Henri reminded her of the time she made him take his shirt off. "Not even my bare chest could distract you," he said with a short laugh.

This was too much. Aimée set her brush down, said she wasn't feeling well, and went up to her room.

After that she tried to tamp down on her unspoken emotions, leaving her painting the moment that breathless feeling came up. She'd lie in her room, stretched on her side, confined and enormous, and try very hard to think of what was ahead. But tucked away in the cottage it was impossible to make the birth of a baby, or her passage to England, seem real. All she could think about was Henri, and how, in a very short time, they would be separated again.

Chapter 24

April brought the first warm day of the season.

Aimée and Henri took their paints and portable easels to the river and left Leonie and Jacques turning over dirt in the garden. Laertes followed, settling into a patch of sunny grass with his head between his paws. There had been heavy snowfall that winter, and the water was high, rushing with the force of spring. The sound was invigorating, as was the rich smell of the earth thawing under the sun.

Henri painted the swelling river, silver in the sunlight, the low banks and the muddy fields. Aimée painted Henri at his easel, and the large poplar to his left, its branches dusted with delicate, moss-green buds.

Her style had changed during her time here. It was lighter, more vibrant and alive. She was excited again by her work. She found the colors harmonious, her lines rich and authentic in their irregularity.

She enjoyed painting Henri, watching him without having to divert her eyes as she captured the winter tone of his skin, his eyes reflecting the glint off the water, his long neck, and narrow, slightly stooped shoulders.

"Do you remember the time my parents took us to Samois-sur-Seine?" she said, her voice breaking the silence that had been between them for hours.

Henri smiled. "We stole that boat."

"You didn't want to."

He looked over the top of his easel. "You would not be deterred."

"No." She smiled. "I would not."

They went back to their painting, both thinking of that day, the fun of it and the freedom. How they'd clambered past the tall pine trees growing out of the ravines, slipping, jumping from rock to rock. Aimée had spotted the boat first, and leaped into it despite Henri's protests. He'd followed, secretly loving how brave she was. They'd thrown the rope off, pushed the oars against the mud, and lain down in the bottom of the boat, side by side, staring at the scattered clouds.

"You know," Aimée said, dipping her brush, her eyes on her palette, "I only painted because you did."

"That's hardly the truth." Henri leaned close to his canvas, dabbing green on white. "You were the one always dragging me into the studio when I preferred roaming outside, keeping me at it for hours. I would never have learned the discipline if it weren't for you. You were always so determined and certain of everything."

Aimée brushed in an eyebrow, concentrating very hard. "I was never certain of anything. I just did it to be near you."

"Why did you keep at it then?"

"After you left, you mean?"

"Yes."

Henri had stopped painting, and Aimée looked at him. His eyes were a spectacular blue. "I was good at it, and I wanted to be good at something." She looked back at her canvas. She hadn't filled in Henri's eyes. Now she didn't want to. They were such a painful blue. "I painted because there was nothing else," she said, quietly.

Under the bright sun, and rushing river, Henri felt reckless and impulsive. He wanted to take Aimée into the grass and make love to her. He wanted to show her that there was so much more.

"I was wondering if anyone's bothered to ask if you *want* to give up this baby," he said.

Aimée's arms and legs tingled. The tenderness in Henri's voice, the concern, made everything feel impossible. "It doesn't matter what I want," she said.

Henri set his palette down and walked over. "I don't want you to make a decision you will come to regret." Reaching up, he slipped her paintbrush from her fingers.

Grasping for her voice, she patted the top of her enormous stomach. "It's a little late for that now."

Henri took her hand, and she wondered if his hands could make her feel what Édouard's had.

"You could stay on with us," he said.

"That's ridiculous." Aimée yanked her hand away, as furious with Henri as when she'd seen *Girl in the Afternoon* at the Salon de Paris. He had no right to keep drawing her back into his life whenever it suited him. "It would be impossible. We couldn't keep up the lie of my being in England. And when Papa finds out, there would be no more money. What would we all do then?"

"We would work it out." He took a step closer.

"It's impractical."

"It doesn't have to be."

"It is!" She flung her voice at him. "It's all of it impractical. Besides, it's impossibly hard, living together in this way."

"We could manage."

The weight of Aimée's stomach felt enormous. She pressed a

hand under the large swell that was crushing everything inside her. "It's you, Henri. It's impossibly hard living here with you."

"Oh." He looked down, his hair falling softly forward. "I see."

But he did not see. Aimée thought of their kiss in the hallway so many years ago, how excited and innocent and certain she'd been. "I am in love with you." It came out loud and defiant, and it angered her to say it. "I always have been. It doesn't matter what you do, I seem incapable of getting past it. How could I possibly go on living here?" Shouting her love at him was not the way she imagined this going, but they were long past sentiment and romance. It was, all of it, ugly and wrong.

Henri leaned in with both hands on either side of her face, and Aimée pulled away with a piercing sense of shame, tears springing to her eyes. "Kindly carry my paint box and easel home," she said, whistling for Laertes.

"Aimée?" Henri put his hand on her shoulder, and she jerked out from under it.

"Don't touch me," she said, a desperate pitch to her voice that infuriated her even more.

She walked away, her stride clipped with determination, Laertes following at her heels. The near kiss had set her pulse racing, and when Henri was out of view she leaned heavily against the trunk of an enormous oak and eased herself down to the cool, damp grass. Months ago she'd abandoned her expandable corset, and her breasts rested, heavy and large, on top of her hard stomach. Laertes lay next to her and pushed his head under her hand, whining softly.

It was painful to face how much she had wanted that kiss, but that was beside the point. It was an undeniable testament to Henri's character. She had tried to put his repulsive conduct with her maman behind her, wanting to believe he was an honorable man at heart. But he wasn't. When it came down to it, Henri took what he wanted.

Aimée remembered Leonie handing her an apron their first morning in the kitchen, saying, "It'll be good for you to feel useful," in her kind, straightforward way. Leonie had taught her how to knead bread, pushing her hand into the soft dough, showing her how to turn it, and push again and again until it sprang back.

Looking up through the pale green leaves, mottled sunlight falling on her face, the specks sharp against her eyes, Aimée thought of the satisfaction she'd felt watching everyone eat the thick bread she'd baked. In her whole life she'd never done anything as practical as bake that loaf of bread.

Over the hill, Henri squatted on the bank of the river hurling rocks into the water. He remembered a time as a child in England when he'd gone swimming in a storm. It had amazed him how instantly the rain and wind had disappeared as the water closed over his head. The whole world had become still and silent. He would have liked to feel that quiet now, except all he'd be was wet and cold when he came back up, everything still waiting for him. Throwing his last rock, he picked up the paints and easels and headed back to the cottage, trying to quell the dread of facing Aimée and Leonie.

Sitting in the grass, Aimée felt something push against her ribs, followed by a fluttering sensation low down in her belly. It was the fluttering of a little hand—Aimée knew this right away—tiny fingers testing out their strength.

Chapter 25

The screams were terrifying. Jacques wouldn't stop crying, and Laertes, who had been cast outside, sat on the doorstep howling. The midwife had come and gone. She had other deliveries to attend to. And, as she put it, "I'm not here to wipe her brow. I'll come when I'm needed."

But she wasn't there when she was needed.

Jacques, hungry and neglected, was asleep on his bed curled next to Laertes, who was finally let in. Leonie had consigned Henri to the kitchen. He'd boiled water, heated towels, reheated towels, and boiled more water. Feeling useless and exhausted, he poured a glass of brandy and was just about to sit down when he heard Leonie scream for help.

It was ghastly, Aimée on the bed, her legs splayed open, everything exposed. There was an ungodly amount of blood, and somehow, in the midst of it, a baby had slithered out and lay in a slimy mess on the sheet. Leonie hadn't let go of Aimée's hands, and she was shouting, her voice high and frantic. "Is it breathing? Henri, is the baby breathing? It hasn't made a sound!"

Henri swiped the baby up as if snatching something from a

hot fire. It was still and lifeless, the umbilical cord like a slithery, twisted snake coiling from the baby's purple stomach to the opening between Aimée's legs.

"Get a blanket. Warm it up." Leonie wouldn't let go of Aimée's hands.

Henri couldn't move. He stared at Aimée, his heart seizing. Her head was rolled to the side at an unnatural angle. Her eyes were closed, her face stark white.

And then, the slippery, inhuman creature in his hands wriggled ever so slightly.

"Don't go to sleep." Leonie shook Aimée, and her eyes shot open, looked around wildly, and dropped shut again. Her hands slackened, and Leonie reached for the baby, tucking its legs and cradling it against her chest. It let out a raspy howl, and Leonie burst into tears.

"Oh, praise God," she whispered. "Hand me the blanket. Over on the dresser."

Henri found the blanket, a cotton boutis Leonie had quilted, painstakingly stuffing the flower motifs with tiny strips of cotton batting. Next to it was a matching christening cap and booties. Tenderly, swiftly, as if she'd done it a hundred times, Leonie wrapped the baby and laid it on the only dry spot she could find on the bed.

"Hand me the scissors." Leonie's hand was shaking as she tied off the umbilical cord with a piece of string. "There." Henri passed them. She no longer sounded frantic, but firm and authoritative. "Go for help. Quickly."

Henri stared at Aimée. "What's wrong with her?"

"I don't know." Leonie snipped the umbilical cord in two. "Feel for her pulse."

Henri pressed his fingers to the inside of Aimée's warm wrist.

"I feel nothing!" he cried, pulling his hand away. "Why won't she open her eyes? Where's the midwife? It will take over an hour to get to town and back. That's much too long!" He paced from the bed to the door.

Tears were streaming down Leonie's face. She wiped them with the back of her sleeve and picked the baby up. Cradling it in one arm, she pressed a cloth to Aimée's damp forehead. "Take the lantern and go. It's the only thing to do."

Halfway out the door, Henri turned, watching Leonie sway back and forth with her head bent near the baby's, her hand wiping, either sweat or tears, from Aimée's pale, still cheeks. He felt a sudden respect for Leonie that was deeper than anything he'd ever felt before. Her decency, her care for Aimée, for this baby, for Jacques, for him—given how little he gave in return—overwhelmed him.

Rushing from the room, he dashed down the stairs and out the door. He ran down the road, the sky filled with bright flecks of stars and the sliver of a new moon. It felt exhilarating to run, to feel the pounding of his heart and the sweat beading on his forehead.

Running harder, faster, the packed-dirt road slamming beneath his feet and the air harsh in his lungs, Henri made a bargain: if Aimée lived, if the baby lived, he'd go back to England. He'd never wanted to go back, but Auguste's words haunted him—*a man must know who he is; otherwise he has no place in the world.* If Henri was going to do right by his family he must face his past, his father, and that house. He'd find out the truth about what happened to his mother. He'd take back his real name so he could give it to Jacques, to Leonie, and to this new child, realizing that in all the confusion, he'd forgotten to see if it was a boy or a girl.

. . .

The midwife was already on her way, a dark, shadowy figure hurrying along the side of the road. She let out a gasp when Henri came bolting up.

"The baby's . . . come," he panted. "Aimée's not well."

The midwife shoved her bag at him, picked up her skirt, and trotted along as quickly as the dark, rutted road would allow.

She dashed up the stairs with Henri following. With one look the midwife saw that there was no time to go for the physician.

She was not a big woman, as Henri imagined midwives should be, but neat in figure and unusually pretty. With deft, efficient hands she pulled various things from her bag, pressed smelling salts to Aimée's nose, and when that didn't work, straight vinegar.

Eventually, Aimée regained enough awareness that the midwife commanded her to push. She shot Henri a look. "This is no place for a man. Go on and make yourself useful. There's dried chamomile and meadowsweet in a jar on the counter. Pour boiling water over it, let it sit for five minutes, and then strain it and bring it up." She glanced at Leonie, who was bent over Aimée with the baby in her arms. "Did you make the nettle soup?" she said, and Leonie nodded. The midwife turned back to Henri. "Heat that up too."

In the kitchen, Henri poured hot water over the tea leaves and went outside while it steeped. It was so dark that he couldn't see his hand in front of his face. Crouching down, he ran his fingers over the heads of the violets that grew in clusters around the house, feeling for the tender stems. Back inside he arranged the delicate blue flowers in a glass jar and set them on a tray. He ladled the soup into a bowl, strained the tea into a cup—the smell of chamomile sweet and strong—and put them on the tray with the flowers. He set the tray on the floor outside the bedroom door, hoping Leonie would know the violets were for her, and that she would also know they were for Aimée, and somehow understand.

Lowering himself to the floor with his back against the wall, Henri sat and waited. He heard the sharp cry of an infant, hushed whispers, and the rustling of sheets.

An hour later the tray was still in the hall. The soup and tea were cold, the heads of the violets perky and expectant. Henri stood up. The quiet unnerved him, and he paced back and forth until he was so heavy with sleep he had no choice but to go into his room, crawl into bed next to Jacques and Laertes, and close his eyes.

It took Aimée twenty long minutes to push out the placenta. Seconds after, she went unconscious again, with a steady stream of blood pouring from between her legs.

Henri awakened to Jacques jumping on the bed and Laertes tugging the blanket to the floor.

He felt weak, his stomach pinched, tight and fearful. Perhaps it was because he hadn't eaten anything, or that Aimée lay dead in the next room. He flung an arm over his face, blocking out the sunlight, until Jacques and Laertes became impossible to ignore. Sitting up, he let Jacques take his hand and pull him out of the room. Laertes bounded ahead, pausing to sniff the untouched tray in the hallway.

Once the dog and child were fed, Henri went back upstairs and picked up the tray. He didn't care what those women were doing. He was going in.

Aimée lay on her back, her smooth white throat exposed, her closed lids lined with fine blue veins. The bloody sheets had been stripped and new ones were in their place. The midwife had gone, hours earlier, Leonie said, taking the tray from Henri and glancing briefly at the flowers. The most shocking thing was the baby propped on a pillow on Aimée's chest, suckling on her swollen breast.

Leonie set the tray down. Despite Henri's stare, she did not move to cover Aimée. After yesterday, discretion seemed pointless.

But it was not the exposed breast that disturbed Henri; it was Aimée's closed eyes, her slack body, her face the same unearthly white as the day before. He looked at Leonie in horror, and she gave a reproachful frown.

"It's not likely a woman could produce milk if she were dead," she said, shifting the pillow under the baby's head. "The midwife said it's the best thing for Aimée. It might help her regain consciousness, if her body feels it's needed. And the baby must eat."

So, it was in this way—with Leonie's support, holding the baby to Aimée's breast every two hours—that Aimée nursed her child, at first completely unconscious, and then in a confused haze as if everything were underwater. At times, Aimée woke to a sharp cry that she thought was a cat. At other times she felt soft, wrinkled skin against her stomach and her nipples being tugged. Later, a blanket tucked to her chin, warm broth spooned into her mouth. She heard hushed voices, footsteps, felt a hand on her forehead, her lips dabbed at with a moist cloth.

It took her two weeks to fully regain consciousness, and by then the baby was gone. It was this absence, the empty sag of her stomach and the painful swelling of her breasts that made Aimée sit straight up in bed one morning in a panic, fully alert, but only vaguely aware of what had taken place, her alarm having no clear reference.

Madame Savaray, who had not moved from her chair in almost three hours, leaped up as quickly as her aging body would allow. "Be easy about it," she said, propping a pillow behind Aimée's head.

"What's happened?" Aimée remembered intense pain, as fierce and reckless as a train ripping through her, and yet complete detachment, as if she'd observed the screaming, writhing woman from a safe corner of the room.

The mattress sagged as Madame Savaray sat on the edge. "You got that baby out, for one thing," she said. "Almost lost your life in the effort."

The burst of energy Aimée had bolted up with was already depleted. It was hard to hold her head up.

"I don't know the whole of it. I've only been here for a few days." Madame Savaray peeled a strand of moist hair off Aimée's cheek and tucked it behind her ear. "It's a good thing you didn't go to your grave, my dear. Your parents would never have forgiven me." She gave a quick, tender smile. "I knew you'd pull through. I told Henri, she may look itty-bitty and frail, but she's solid." She tapped a gentle finger on Aimée's chest. "More strength in there than most. What irks me is that no proper physician was called in. Something ruptured, was the diagnosis from that incompetent midwife. *Something?* How preposterous. And then you were left in the care of Leonie, who, I must say under the circumstances, did a fine job. But she is not, after all, a proper nurse. Did you know she was the only one with you when that baby was born?"

Aimée had a vacant, stupefied look on her face that worried Madame Savaray. She tucked the sheet around her *petite-fille*'s legs and pulled the blanket over her lap.

"Where's my baby?" Aimée asked, milk leaking from her nipples, soaking the front of her nightdress. The one thing she remembered clearly was the tingling sensation, the suckling and pulling, the flow of milk through her breasts that were now lumpy, hard and swollen.

"She's gone to the nurse." Madame Savaray picked up a glass of water. "Here." Aimée took a sip and handed it back.

"A girl?" Aimée closed her eyes.

"Yes."

"What's her name?"

"Jeanne." Madame Savaray set the water down with a thump. "Open your eyes," she said, and Aimée did. "Now, my dear, you are not to think of that baby." She cupped Aimée's chin, the pads of her fingers soft and wrinkled as if they'd been soaked in water. "It was a mistake having you nurse her. I doubt, very much, it was what kept you alive, even though Leonie insists upon it." Madame Savaray stood up and went to the window. She unlatched the shutters and swung them out. "Stuffy as a barn in here."

Aimée dropped her head back and shut her eyes.

Outside there was a light drizzle, and the smell of spring rain and manure reminded Madame Savaray of her childhood. "Your papa suspects nothing. Your letters were thoroughly convincing. They think I'm at an inn in Valvins for the week. I told them I needed some country air. But they don't care what I do. Auguste's rarely home anymore. Spends most of his time at the factory, or else cavorting about in cafés. Your maman hardly leaves her room."

Aimée remembered her maman lying in bed for weeks after her babies died. She understood now how distinct her pain was, how unbearable. It was the same pain that filled Aimée's womb, her breasts, ran between her legs, wrapped around her stomach, and burst open in her chest.

"Your maman's dropped all frivolity and fashion." Madame Savaray flicked a tiny black spider from the sill. "And wouldn't you know, I actually miss the old Colette? Things are pitifully dull. She rarely goes out. Hardly visits anyone. She embroiders all day. You should see the pillow covers piling up. I've tried to get her to stop, even suggested she throw one of her soirées again, and I despised those things. But she won't listen to me. We've always put each other out of countenance, and I'm afraid that hasn't changed."

What was too entangled to explain was the odd, mutual understanding that had sprung between her and Colette. Without Jacques or Aimée, without the soirées or social engagements, every day was a struggle to stave off the boredom that consumed them both.

Colette had confessed that she now understood Madame Savaray's need to wash the kitchen floors all those years ago during the war. And what Madame Savaray now understood—but still couldn't bring herself to say to Colette—was that Colette's indulgence in fashion, her elaborate soirées, came from the simple desire to be good at something, to be productive and busy. It was no different from Madame Savaray working in her husband's factory. They were just women looking to be needed.

Madame Savaray looked at her *petite-fille,* eyes shut tight against the world. "My dear," she said, softly, wishing she had done a better job of saving her. "You're going to be all right again, in time."

Aimée opened her eyes. "I'm terribly weak."

"That will pass. I've written Lady Arrington that you are unwell. We'll arrange your passage as soon as you're fit."

Aimée pressed the blanket to her chest. The milk had started a steady flow that trickled down her stomach. She wanted to cry; she felt enormous sobs welling up.

Madame Savaray could see the tears coming, and, as much as she understood, it was not something she cared to witness. It would only make things worse. "I'll send Leonie up with some tea," she said. "And Jacques is anxious to see you and give you a *pat, pat.*" Madame raised her eyebrows. "Apparently, this is what he calls a kiss? If you ask me, children ought to be taught the proper words for things, not indulged in comical nicknames."

Tears sprang the moment her *grand-mère* closed the door, with sobs so overwhelming that Aimée felt completely out of control. She clamped her hands over her breasts as if stopping the flow of milk would stem this unbearable loss. She wondered if it was the nursing that had bonded her to the baby, or if they were bonded in a way people are when they survive something together. It didn't matter now. Jeanne would soon forget the smell of Aimée's skin and the feel of her body. She would create new bonds. It was Aimée who would never be able to replace the warmth of that small body nestled against her. Over time, she told herself, she'd learn to tolerate the grief, but she was new to this sort of pain, and didn't yet fully understand the weight of it.

LONDON 1878

Chapter 26

Henri sat eating a tasteless meat pie, in a dank pub that smelled of yeast and rye and whiskey. He'd already finished two glasses of dark beer. Raising his head to the bartender, he pointed to his empty glass. "Could I trouble you for another?" He could hear the slight French accent he'd acquired.

With his own heavy brogue, the bartender said, "Not from these parts, eh?"

Henri said no, he was not. "Me brother-in-law runs an inn down the street if you're lookin' for one," the man said, refilling Henri's beer from a large pitcher. "Just ya ask for a Miss Gerty."

The inn was an airless, two-story brick building, and had the same cool, damp feel as the pub. Miss Gerty, a woman with blotchy skin and gnarled teeth, led him upstairs, gave him a fresh basin of water, set an unlit candle by his bed, and left him to his own.

Henri collapsed on the bed and pulled the thin quilt over his legs. He felt miserable, with nothing to encourage him other than the possibility of seeing Aimée again.

The last time he saw her was at the train station, three years ago. She was standing on the platform wearing a green jacket that flared over her hips. Her hat was at a tilt, and the wind had undone her hair on one side. For a moment he stood close enough to touch her, but the train whistle blew, and she said a sideways good-bye, and stepped onto the railcar. A ripple of fear had swept through Henri, and he'd reached out and caught her arm. He needed something more, a good-bye that he could hold on to. But Aimée turned to him with a look of such despair, a look that said there would be no recovering anything, that he'd dropped her arm and let her go without a word.

Henri closed his eyes against the memory, against the filthy room and the dingy light that came from the window. He had made a promise to come here, had vowed on Aimée's life, that night Jeanne was born. But he'd never wanted to do this. He'd never felt the urge to go back to his roots, dig them up, expose them. A thing died when you dug it up. Might as well leave it buried. The gallant search for truth, well, Henri just couldn't see the point.

He rolled onto his side. Laughter came through the thin floorboards, and the bed reeked of a vile odor. Henri thought of moving to another room, or another inn, but he could barely afford this wretched place, and the next was sure to be just as bad.

What he wanted was to go home, to forget the whole thing. Two weeks ago, on the fifth of May, they had celebrated Jeanne's third birthday. Henri could picture the candied violets Leonie had on the table, and the bouquet of bluebells Jacques had gathered. On the back of Jeanne's chair hung a straw hat with a blue satin ribbon. Jacques had picked out the hat from the draper in town. There was also a porcelain doll with real hair; shiny, dark ringlets just like Jeanne's. This had come in the post with no letter. Leonie set it on the table as she had with the gifts sent for Jeanne's first and second birthdays. She refused to remove it even when Jacques begged her to. He was sure the doll would take all the attention away from the hat. But when Jeanne came tumbling down the stairs, she put the hat on straightaway and wore it all through breakfast.

Picturing his family, Henri shifted onto his back and closed his eyes, trying for sleep, which was impossible with the ruckus below. He hadn't been honest with Leonie. He hadn't even been honest with himself, until now. He would have put this trip off forever, made excuses for years, because he had not really come to fulfill some bargain made long ago in the middle of the night. It was his desire to see Aimée that had driven him here.

Despite the noise downstairs, and the rank smell of the bed, Henri's breath deepened, and his eyes dropped shut again. As he sank into sleep, he felt a sense that something devastating and irretrievable had been set off, and he tried to come back up, but it was too late. He fell heavier and faster, until, finally, he slept.

The address in Henri's pocket brought him to a large house on Sussex Place. He'd been in England for two weeks, and only yesterday received an official invitation from Lady Arrington.

He felt incredibly nervous following the butler into the drawing room, and when he saw Aimée perched on the edge of her seat, pale and unacceptably thin, he froze in the doorway. It reminded him of the night Jeanne was born. Her eyes were flat, her skin chalky, and her lips white. She looked childlike, and somehow terribly old at the same time.

"I don't bite," she said, and Henri was relieved to hear a flicker of the old Aimée.

He sat across from her, wheeling the brim of his hat through his fingers and smiling stupidly.

"What brings you to London?" Aimée asked, courteous and cold, her face an eerie, emotionless mask.

"I've come to see my father."

"I see."

"Yes, well, it's an awful business. But, I suppose I've put it off long enough."

Aimée's lips twitched, but she said nothing.

"Are you unwell?" Henri scooted to the edge of his seat, longing to reach a hand out to her.

"I'm perfectly well, thank you."

"You're much too thin."

Aimée gave a sharp laugh. "The English don't take nearly as much pleasure in food as we French do."

"No, they certainly do not. The inn's served pigeon pie every night this week."

"I'm simply tired to death of meat pie. Lady Arrington's cook uses far too much clove."

"Why do you stay on?" Henri looked around the room. Clearly there were servants, and yet everything appeared coated in a fine layer of dust. The furnishings, the floral wallpaper and gilt mirrors were elaborate, but unsettling.

He looked at Aimée, whose gaze rested slightly above his head. She had not yet looked him in the eye.

"Last month," she said, her attention on the far wall, "I sold a painting for four hundred pounds and in the same week sought a commission for two hundred guineas, but then lost it to Sir Millais, who was paid over one thousand for the same project, which always enrages me, the advantage men have. And yet, it is never surprising." There was no sentiment behind her words, as if the outrage had passed and left behind a dulled complacency.

"If it's any consolation," Henri said, "I've sold nothing since you left. If it weren't for your papa's money, I don't know how we'd survive. I keep painting, but I'm as unimpressive as ever." He propped his hat on his knee. "You'll get more commissions.

It seems as if you're on your way with your art, and that's what you want, isn't it?"

"Louise Jopling's *The Modern Cinderella* will be showing at the Paris Exposition Universelle this summer. *That* is what I want," she said, and Henri saw a flicker of life still in her, "to be wildly successful." She looked, all of a sudden, very much like her maman. "You know," she stared right at him now, "that first day in the cottage at Thoméry I realized that I belonged nowhere." She flicked her hand. "I might as well stay on here. It's no worse a place than any other."

The parlor door swung open, and Lady Arrington stepped briskly into the room. She circled around, stealthy as a cat, and planted herself in front of Henri, looking at him with pale, watery eyes like she'd caught him in some wicked act.

"You're early," she said. "Was that intentional? Did you wish to find me out?"

Henri stood up, her confrontation taking him by surprise. "My deepest apologies," he said. "I've never been very good at keeping time."

Lady Arrington had an unruly cloud of white hair that Henri imagined took a great deal of effort to keep under control.

"In England," she said, her voice raspy and aged, "we observe the habits of good society, timeliness being one of them." She lifted her chin, exposing her skinny neck and the boned line of her jaw. She was as elegant as the house, and as cold as the iron gates Henri had passed through to get here. "Are you an Englishman or a Frenchman? Aimée seemed unclear on that point."

"Englishman."

"And yet you have a French surname and an atrocious accent?"

"I've been in France since I was a child."

"Yes, with the Savarays, I've heard." Lady Arrington looked at Aimée. "Have you shown Monsieur Savaray your work?"

With resignation, and a tinge of contempt, Aimée said, "No. Is that what you wish me to do?"

"What else did he come here for?"

"Tea. You invited him."

"There will be no tea today." Lady Arrington swatted her hand at them, her head bobbing on her wiry neck. "Let him view the work if that's why he's come. Why do you sit here wasting his time?"

Without a word, Aimée left the room. When Henri stepped into the hall she was already mounting the stairs, her dress a river of black silk rippling behind her. He took the stairs two at a time and followed her into a room with high windows that gave off a pure, natural light.

At first, Henri only noticed the painting to his right, a naked child with fat thighs and rolls of pink skin, sitting on the lap of a woman whose chemise had fallen over one shoulder, exposing her breast down to the nipple. It was when he scanned the rows of paintings lining the walls that he was hit with the full force of Aimée's drained pallor, her vacant wandering expression, her lack of interest in food, or anything that might sustain her. The one thing he had feared surrounded him.

He was looking at canvas upon canvas of infants. They were nursing, toddling, and bathing. There were newborns in laps and babies climbing on beds. Mothers were catching them. Washing them. Wiping hair from a brow, kissing a cheek, reading a book, picking a flower. The warmth and radiance of Aimée's longing was magnificent on canvas. It made Henri want to take her in his arms and hold her as he should have done long ago, when he'd been too afraid of what real love might do to him.

Aimée stiffened when he looked at her, warned him with a hollow stare not to come any closer. "I apologize for the tea," she said quickly. "I'm sorry if you were expecting something."

"No." Henri shook his head. "You were all I was expecting, or at least hoping for. Just you."

She winced and turned to the wall, unhooking a smock and pulling it over her shoulders.

"I was thinking"—Henri ran a hand through his hair, the idea only now forming—"that I might convince you to accompany me to my father's. He lives a fair distance outside of London, but I was hoping not to have to face him alone." What he could not face was leaving Aimée alone in this bleak house surrounded by these canvases, relics of what she'd lost.

"I don't see what use I'd be." Aimée yanked the strings of her smock and pulled them tight around her waist, looking as if she might snap in two. "If you would kindly excuse me, I have work to get back to."

"At least allow me to see you again."

"What for?" Keeping her back to him she moved in front of her easel, straightening her shoulders with a slight, corrective gesture. "It's not likely we'll resume a friendship. You'll go back to France, and I'll stay here. What would be the use?"

Henri hadn't counted on this level of abject misery. Aimée was indomitable, the gatherer of a strength that he had always counted on. He thought he'd come here and see that she was at least content, consumed with her work, and getting on with things as she always had. That was what he needed so he could return to his life with Leonie, to the children, and say it had all worked out.

Aimée picked up her brush. "Leave me, please," she said. Then, in a voice Henri had never heard before, one trembling with emotion, she whispered, "Please, Henri, I need you to go. Just go."

Not knowing what else to do, he left her.

For hours he walked under a gray English sky, a steadfast pulse of guilt like a second set of footsteps walking beside him.

Eventually, he found himself on a narrow street lined with women, their puckered mouths painted red as roses. Skirts were swept up, legs shown. Petticoats circled smooth white calves, exposing dainty ankles tucked into soft leather boots. He leaned into one girl, lured by her fleshy arms and full bust. Her lips were moist, and her tongue tasted of cinnamon. But after a moment, he pulled away, muttered an apology, and ducked down an alley.

Somehow, he made his way back to the inn. Once in his room, he splashed ice-cold water on his face.

From the moment he had met Aimée, as a bewildered boy, she had been there for him, sensitive and rigorous in her friendship. Letting him keep his silences, his secrets, but forcing him to get on with his life. He had moved forward because of her, because she'd shown him how. In return he had given her nothing. In return he'd betrayed her.

He scrubbed a rough towel over his eyes and cheeks and hands. He was not an honorable man. An honorable man would have faced what he'd done that night with Colette. Not him; no, he'd run away. And then, after abandoning Aimée without a word, she still came after him, loyal in her friendship, loving, committed. And what did he do? He went for Leonie because it was easy. It was the easy, selfish thing to do.

Snapping the towel in the air, he walked over to the bed and dropped onto his back. Not until Aimée was right in front of him at the cottage, and he couldn't have her, did he show her any feeling. And that was the cruelest thing of all, showing her what might have been, the possibilities that had come too late.

Now he had her daughter. What more could he possibly take?

He turned onto his side, feeling the tremendous expanse of Aimée's grief as if it were his own.

He could not leave her here, not like this.

Chapter 27

The house in Burford was exactly as he remembered: foreboding, but steadfast, able to withstand all manner of people inside its walls.

Low in the west, a black strip of clouds curled over the horizon, and a soft rain started. It whispered around Henri like a hushed warning as he made his way to the front door of Abbington Hall.

A tall, stern-faced butler greeted him. When Henri asked to see the master of the house the butler raised a single bushy eyebrow, gave an incredulous smile, and told Henri to wait in the library.

"I'd prefer the drawing room, if it's all the same," Henri said.

"The library's where we show people." The butler strode to the door.

Henri's chest tightened, and he could feel a line of sweat forming under the band of his hat. The windows were shut up, and it smelled of dust and age.

"Sir?" Behind him, the butler stood waiting to take his hat.

Henri handed it over, and the butler left with the hat held at arm's length, clicking the door shut behind him.

With a slow breath Henri faced the room where books lined

the walls to the ceiling, surrounding him. Somewhere, he knew, on one of these shelves were the books his father had written. Henri suddenly felt as if his lungs were collapsing. In a panic he looked toward the window, reminding himself of the sweet smell of grass, the cool rain, and the earth beneath his feet. Reminding him that past the heavy front door of this house the world still existed.

Trying for slow, shallow breaths Henri attempted to scrutinize the things around him without any particular attachment: the carpet, huge, threadbare, a floral pattern circling under his muddy boot prints, stenciled wallpaper, another floral pattern, a hunting painting—dogs and men and rifles—an English landscape of no distinguishable place.

Henri hated this room. He had tried to avoid it as a child. When his father was in a good mood, he'd make Henri sit in here and listen to him reminisce about the success of his first novel and the glorious, halcyon days before his marriage. Henri's behind would grow numb in the leather chair, and his clasped fingers would tingle with impatience. The clock would strike the dinner hour, and still his father rambled on. Henri always had the sense his father had no idea who he was talking to. But Henri preferred these outbursts to the dark days when his father shut himself in his study. Then, Henri never knew what was coming, and he had learned to be cautious, to make himself scarce.

He wondered, now, why he hadn't been more afraid for his mother. Maybe she'd seemed safe shut up in her room. He had thought she never left the house, until one morning he woke early and saw her walking over the hill. She walked swiftly, her head high, her coat flapping. He had the frightening feeling she wasn't coming back, and he didn't move from the window until her small figure emerged once more in the distance. After that, he woke every morning to watch for her return. As soon as he heard the front door he'd run downstairs with a frantic, "Good morning, Mama," holding very still as she passed, hoping for the rare pat on his head, resisting the urge to hug her when it came.

Then, one morning, only a thin fog crept over the empty hill. Henri thought maybe his mother had gone out earlier than usual and he'd just missed her, but there was a sick feeling in his stomach. For hours he stood with his hands clasped in prayer trying to will her back.

Looking around the library, Henri's gaze settled on the upholstered armchair where his mother sat those days before she disappeared, when he asked her if she would read one of his father's books out loud. She had looked at him tenderly, remorsefully, and he had stood next to that chair and put his hands on her cheeks. He had thought then that she might love him after all, despite how she was.

The enormous clock on the mantel gave a single, sharp toll as it struck one. It startled Henri, and he walked abruptly to the window. A light rain still sifted down, the wind causing it to lift and fall in irregular patterns over the hills and fields and gardens. Jonquils were in bloom, and the daisy stalks were up, their buds tight and green.

"Henri?"

A female voice came from behind, and Henri turned to find the woman who had taken him to France so long ago. She wore a dark blue dress, just as she had that day, only her hair was no longer blond, but silver, and pulled high on her head. In his memory, she was a wispy, pale beauty with a hardened face. There was still a hint of her beauty left, and her hardness defined in fierce lines on her brow. She had lived in this house Henri's entire childhood, and only now did it occur to him that she had likely been his father's mistress.

"Miss Marion Gray," he said, smiling. He hadn't thought it would be good to see her, but it was.

"You have impeccable timing." She crossed the room with a limp he'd forgotten she had. As a child, that limp was the only thing that had made her seem vulnerable.

She did not offer her hand as conventional women did, but took hold of his and held it firmly, pressing it between both of hers. "I'm sorry to tell you your father died," she said directly. "December 5. You've just missed him."

It was as if a rope had been cut around Henri's middle. The tightness let up, and he looked into Marion's misty eyes, finding himself embarrassingly light-headed, but not stricken, as one might assume. Someone else's son would have been devastated to come all this way, after all this time, only to have missed the father he had not seen in seventeen years, by a mere five months. But Henri was relieved, and it showed all over his face.

Marion smiled. "You're right." She nodded as if she could read his thoughts. "He'd only grown meaner. Fiercer. Sadder." She let go of Henri's hand, this last word spoken tenderly.

"And my mother?" he asked, and it was impossible not to hear his expectant tone, the anxious anticipation and hope.

Marion shook her head. "No, my dear. She never came home."

Henri nodded, looking at the upholstered chair, a deep, familiar regret spreading through his whole body. He had known this the moment he stepped into the library. Her absence was in the dust, in the untouched books, the empty desk and the silent, vacant air around him, and yet there was a part of him that could not let go of her.

"It's not teatime," Marion said, "but let's have some anyway, in the dining room. I despise it in here." She gave a little shiver, took hold of Henri's hand, and led him from the room.

Walking down the hall, safely away from the library, Marion said, "The servants have absolutely no respect for me, but I'm the only one they have to answer to now. If I want tea at an irregular hour, tea it is."

It was the same dining room table he'd sat at as a boy, the same sideboard and elegant-backed chairs, probably the same teacups and silver. And even though it was far from comforting, Henri found he could breathe a little easier. Unlike the library, the dining room didn't hold the faded memory of his mother. She had never once taken dinner in here with them. It had only been Marion, his demure grandmother who he remembered as a silent, wide-eyed presence, and his fickle, mercurial father, either slumped in his chair, speechless and sour, or shouting, loud and fast, spit flying.

For a while, they drank their tea in silence. Eventually, Henri asked, "Why didn't you write that my father had died?"

He swirled the dregs of sugar at the bottom of his cup, the last bit of tea rising up the sides of white porcelain and sliding back down.

Marion watched him carefully. "Why would I?" she answered, forthright. "I never knew what happened to you after I left Paris. And then, so many years later, you write asking for my help. Asking me to lie for you." She smiled, an ironic smile, showing he was quite right to assume she'd agree. "You asked not a single question in return, nothing of your father, or your mother. I assumed you'd rather not know." She reached for the teapot—a round belly of shiny silver—exposing her delicate wrist as it stretched away from her lace cuffs.

A spout of tea steamed into his cup, and Henri dropped in two lumps of sugar, watching them promptly sink to the bottom. "You were right. I didn't want to know."

Marion tilted the teapot over her cup with a finger pressed to the lid. "Why now?"

"I suppose facing my past became inevitable. I'd put it off as long as I could. I'm very good at putting things off."

She set the pot down, picked up her fork, and cut into a slice of lemon cake. "You could have put it off indefinitely. It wouldn't have been the worst thing. I left home and never returned. I lived over a draper's shop, had a drunk for a father, and sang in the opera. Left it all behind when I came here. I have no idea what happened to my pitiful father. Probably made his grave in a ditch somewhere." The cake slid into her mouth.

Henri traced the gold swirls in the cream-colored wallpaper with his eyes. "I want to know what happened to my mother," he said. "I want the truth."

Marion finished her bite and daintily dabbed the corner of her mouth. "You're a grown man." She folded her napkin and set it next to her plate. "Not much sense keeping it from you." Standing, she left the room.

When she returned, she slid a folded newspaper clipping in front of Henri and sat back down to her cake. "I don't know if it's the truth," she said. "But it's why your father sent you away."

Henri's stomach dropped. He unfolded the paper and pressed the creases down with his fingers.

EXAMINER, NOVEMBER 25, 1860

> Since the printing of our last story on the disappearance of Mrs. William Aubrey it appears the London police have found reason to suspect her husband, the acclaimed author, Mr. William Aubrey, of her murder. Chapman and Hall cannot keep enough copies of Mr. Aubrey's latest novel, THE TIDES, in print

> since the whole of London is enamored with the fictional heroine who disappears at the end of the novel, killed at the hands of her husband. The police are investigating Mr. Aubrey of having committed the crime to create sensationalism for his novel and increase its popularity. As of yet, no body had been found.

Sickened, Henri flipped the paper over, pushed his chair back, and crossed to the window. The rain had stopped, but enormous thunderheads sat on the horizon like craggy, mountainous peaks. He felt a wave of nausea. Not once, not even when the authorities kept coming, had he suspected anything this grotesque.

"I don't know whether he killed her or not," Marion said flatly. "If he did, it certainly wasn't for the reasons suspected. Evelyn was alive when she left this house that night."

Henri shot around. "How do you know?"

"Because I found her."

"What? Where?"

Marion drew herself forward, shamelessly missing the excitement she had drawn from the disaster. "She was on the North Sea, near Hartlepool. A man named Peter Emsely helped her. They'd been engaged once. She had broken it off to marry your father."

Henri folded his arms and locked his hands around his elbows. "Then this news story is just a fabrication?"

"Like I said, I don't know." Marion reached for her cake and took another bite. She often wondered if Evelyn had secretly enjoyed the scandal. What spectacular revenge, William being blamed for her murder. "Your father was a violent man," she said. "I'm sure you haven't forgotten." Henri hadn't. He could still feel the back of his father's hand. "But he never touched your mother. Did you know that? Regardless, your mother was terrified he'd force her back if he found her. She made me swear I'd never tell where she was."

"Did you?"

"No."

The room grew dark as the storm crept near. The pressure in the air was giving Henri a headache, and he pressed his fingers into his temples. "So that was it? You never saw her again?"

Marion finished her cake and ran her tongue over her teeth to make sure there was nothing unseemly stuck in them. "I never saw her again."

She thought of leaving it at that, but she had to be very careful how she played her hand here. Henri was an Aubrey, after all, and the heir. It might be to her benefit if he thought the worst of his father.

"One day in December your father left. He hadn't gone anywhere since Evelyn's disappearance. He was gone for a week, and when he came back he went into Evelyn's room and took everything—her writing, clothes, even her bedding—and burned it all. It was barbaric, frightening. I watched him shove item after item into the hearth. He didn't care who saw: not myself, or the cook, or the housemaid." Marion hesitated because this was the part that had always gotten to her. "He said, 'She's gone. She's dead.' He said this very calmly, as if certain of it."

"You never inquired further?"

"What was I to do? Your father was drawn to the dramatic. It may have just been a notion, a feeling. Maybe he'd gone to look for her, and when he couldn't find her, he decided she was dead to him. I don't know."

Marion looked away from Henri—his pale, serious face so

much like his mother's—and smoothed a wrinkle out of the fine white tablecloth with her fingertips. How ironic, that William had kept her here, in all this wealth, just as she'd planned. She remembered the day she arrived, young and beautiful and determined. This house had been her escape. Not from a man, but from a life of poverty. For a moment she considered telling Henri everything, now that she'd started; about his mother's journal, about the truth of his father's books, but she didn't. Maybe it was resentment for all she'd endured, for her internment here at Abbington Hall, for the loneliness she'd lived with. Or, maybe, it was just the deep bitterness that she'd carried around her entire life.

Whatever the reason, she decided to keep Evelyn Aubrey's secret, which was both loyalty and betrayal.

"I know nothing more," she said sharply. "A few months later, William told me I was to take you to Paris and deliver you into the hands of that family." She looked at Henri. "Your father's reputation was ruined."

"But he was never convicted."

"It was no matter. Your mother wasn't found, and people believed the worst. To your miserable father's credit, he didn't want you living with that scandal. He believed you would never have gotten away from it in England. William knew the Savarays from his travels abroad. They were wealthy, with a good reputation. Seemed the best thing for you."

"I reminded him of my mother, of what he had done. Best to do away with both of us," Henri said bitterly.

Marion walked over to him, her limp more severe now, as if it had worsened in just a few short hours. She was a small woman, and Henri looked down at her, noticing the fine lines around her clear eyes, eyes that were not as aggressive as he remembered, only terribly sad, with a hint of humility, which was not how he had ever thought of her.

"I do believe he was trying to protect you," she said. "He wasn't a good man, but he wasn't always a bad one. He may have loved you. There's always the chance of that, love being so unruly and out of one's control."

Henri shook his head. "I'm sure he did not." He gave a quick, ironic laugh. "You know I've never read *The Tides*. I tried once, but I couldn't bring myself to open it." His low voice was laced with controlled hysteria. "Could he have killed her? How does one live with that, the mere idea?"

"Henri," Marion snapped at him. "It was a rumor. One does not base one's life on rumors. Put it out of your mind. You must." She turned and drew her arm out in a sweeping gesture, slowly, as if on stage. "Because all of this is now yours."

Henri followed the sweep of Marion's arm, looking out into the cold, heartless room. This house was as extreme as his father, ostentatious enough to distract people, cover things up. Henri clamped his arms across his chest and bent his head as if bracing against a fierce wind. He didn't want Abbington Hall. He didn't want anything to do with it.

"It's late," he said. "I ought to be going."

"You mustn't travel in this weather. I insist you stay the night."

"I need to get back to London."

"Whatever it is, I'm sure it can wait."

"No, it cannot." Henri moved quickly to the door, and Marion followed.

Outside a warm wind had picked up. The sky was dark and tense, the storm brewing overhead. Marion loved a good storm. It made her feel as if something tremendous and exciting was about to happen. She looked at Henri, remembering a time when all she had to do was cast a look at a man and he'd give her anything she wanted. She was far too old for that now.

"You'll want to contact William's lawyer about the estate—Barlow Greeves, 11 Coventry Street." Marion shouted above the wind. "They didn't know where to find you."

"Why didn't you tell them?" Henri cried back.

"They didn't know I knew. I figured you'd come home when you were ready." Marion's skirts whipped around her. "Get on into that carriage. The sky looks menacing. We don't want to be out in it any longer than we have to," she said, knowing she'd stay out long after his carriage pulled away, just to enjoy the thrill of being caught up in the wind.

"The man who helped my mother, Emsley did you say? Is he still alive?" Henri shouted back.

"I don't know." Marion looked up. Clouds rushed overhead as if pushed by a current. "He had a law firm in London. If he's still alive, he shouldn't be too hard to find." Henri stepped into the carriage, and Marion caught his arm. "What's going to happen to me?" she cried. "I have nowhere to go. I have no other home."

Henri reached for her hand. "Abbington Hall is more your home than mine. You needn't worry about a thing," he said, hurrying into the carriage as the first, fierce drops of rain began to fall.

Chapter 28

On the train ride back to the city, the rain falling steadily, Henri thought of his children. He pictured Jacques as a grown man standing in the Savaray drawing room, facing Colette, his real maman. Jeanne and Jacques would want to know the truth someday. They'd dig it up, just as he had.

He put his hand to the glass and traced a stream of water with his finger. He couldn't wait to see Aimée. He wanted to tell her everything he couldn't speak of that first day when they were children, when she sat in his room, curious, wanting to know all about him.

The rhythmic rocking of the train and the steady noise of the churning pistons made him drowsy, and Henri leaned his head back and closed his eyes. He wouldn't go to Aimée empty-handed this time. He'd put everything in order first. He wondered how it would go over when Lady Arrington found out he was Henry Aubrey, if she'd know the name, the history. He'd have to face that now. It took on a new meaning with his father gone, now that he and Jacques were the only Aubreys left.

. . .

Finding Mr. Emsley's office was easy. His name had hung outside the same door for the past thirty-seven years. All Henri had to do was ask around.

The building was small and dark. Inside it smelled of leather and old wood. Henri stepped toward the man hunched behind a large desk.

"Pardon me," he said. "I'm looking for Mr. Peter Emsley."

The man didn't look up. He dipped his quill pen, slowly, his hands as old and leathery as the place smelled. "Who might you be?" he said, his voice rough as bark.

"Henri . . . I mean *Henry* William Aubrey."

The man was completely still other than his eyes, which shot up. "I don't know what you're after," he said as if defending against accusations already made. "I have no information to give you."

"Not according to Miss Marion Gray," Henri answered.

The tip of the man's pen rested on the page of an open ledger, but he did not make a mark; instead he dropped the pen back into the inkwell. He pulled his head up and looked at Henri with bloodshot eyes that peered from behind thin, wire-framed spectacles. The man was tall and paunchy with a thick white beard that ran up the sides of his face and blended into the scruffy line of hair cresting his bald head.

"I used to wonder if you'd come," the man finally said, pulling off his spectacles and letting them hang from a silver chain around his neck. "After a time, I stopped wondering. I suppose, with your father's death, I should have prepared myself. Please, I have been impolite. Won't you have a seat?"

"Thank you, kindly." Henri pulled up a chair. The office was pleasant, sparse, but neatly furnished and clean. "I apologize, Mr. Emsley, if my presence is troubling to you in any way."

"Please, call me Peter," Mr. Emsley said, and there was kindness in his dark, inquisitive eyes. "You, my boy, are not what troubles me. It is your mother who has always troubled me. You are just a reminder."

The tick of the large clock filled the silence as Mr. Emsley sat with his hands crossed over the top of his prominent belly, trying to sum up Henri. He pulled open his desk drawer. "I need to wet my whistle. Care for a drink, son?"

Two tumblers and a dark-green bottle came out. There was a loud pop of the cork, followed by a pungent, smoky odor. Mr. Emsley poured Henri a glass and scooted it across the desk, then drank his in a single gulp. "Ahhh." He shook his head, twirling the empty glass between his hands. "I suppose you've come to ask about your mother, and you have every right. She came to me the night she went missing. She needed my help. In the end, I failed her."

Henri took a cautious sip of his drink. The alcohol burned his throat and gave off a fierce sting to his nostrils.

"She didn't love me, but it was no matter. I had always loved her. I would have done anything she asked."

It was hard for Henri to believe this man had ever been young and in love with the mother in his memories.

Mr. Emsley poured another drink. Again, he drank it in a single swig, running his tongue over his top lip and then drawing it back in his mouth. "I hid her in the town where my mother lived. My mother was not right in the mind. She was quite mad, actually. I promised Evelyn it would only be for a short while, that I'd come for her." It had grown dark, not completely, but enough so that the objects in the room lost their definition. "But I never did. My father found a letter I'd written to Evelyn. He was a nosy man, my father, and a vicious one, a man who would not have his name tarnished with scandal. When he understood I was hiding Evelyn, he threatened to put my mother in an asylum. For years he'd wanted to lock her away, and he would have, if I didn't agree to stop contact with Evelyn. He wrote a letter to Evelyn—in the hand of my partner—saying I was dead."

Henri took another careful sip from his glass. Something in the story, in the dark room and stale air, unnerved him.

"I was going to go back for her." Mr. Emsely whistled through his teeth. "I swear it. As soon as my father eased off, but it took months, and by that time, she was gone." He held up his hand, turned it back and forth in the dim light as if checking his own existence. "My mother was so thoroughly convinced I was dead that when I arrived she thought my ghost had come to call. She thought it was very kind of me to take the time, and asked how I was getting on in heaven. She wanted to know if I was having a decent go of it up there with the angels." He gave a long, guttural laugh and wiped his eyes. "Oh, my. She's what I was left with in the end. A demented old woman who outlived everyone but me."

Henri set his drink on the desk and leaned forward with his hands pressed over the tops of his knees. "You went back and my mother was just gone? No letter? No one saw her leave?"

Mr. Emsley shook his head. "Nothing, my boy."

The room went quiet. For a while the two men sat in the dark, and then, softly, Mr. Emsley said, "She didn't take her coat."

"What?"

"Her coat. Left the house in the middle of winter without her coat. That's always gotten to me." Mr. Emsley stood up and went to the shelf for some matches, fumbling and knocking a few to the floor. "I looked for her." He lit the lamp, drawing the wick down, a warm, circle of light softening the room. "Workhouses, brothels, factories. Places I was sure she'd never go. I looked anyway. Searched the city over." His words were slightly slurred. "I still do. Not every week like I used to, but periodically, just to be sure."

Reaching down, he pulled open the bottom drawer of his desk and took out a bulky object. "Her coat. I never had the heart to get rid of it."

Henri touched the soft, brown wool. It was the same coat she'd worn walking in the hills those mornings when he watched for her return.

Mr. Emsley sank into his chair, his watery eyes glinting behind the glare of the lamp. "Take the coat," he said. "And be so good as to leave me, please. There's nothing more I can tell you."

Henri scooted the coat back across the desk. "I'm much obliged, but it's yours." From his breast pocket Henri pulled a worn piece of paper and held it out. Mr. Emsley hesitated.

"It's a sonnet," Henri said. "My mother wrote it. I found it under my pillow the day she disappeared. I think you should read it."

Mr. Emsley tugged at the chain around his neck, his spectacles jumping up and down. "Can't read a thing in this light, not even with these." It wasn't true; he just knew he wouldn't be able to get through it without making a fool of himself.

Henri held the piece of paper under the lamp. He remembered Colette standing in his apartment the day she found it, taunting him. Colette had thought it was a love poem, and when Henri had reread it he realized his mother's words weren't fraught, but hopeful and eager, like a woman in love. Now he understood why.

Henri cleared his throat.

DEAR CHILD, DEAR BOY

Dear child, dear boy, one whom I call my own
Whose first affections thou showed to me

Before ever I, could show it to thee
Entwine all of thyself in the unknown
Then you will tremble not when truths awake
The tempted soul to find, not grief but strength
In wakened hearts that go to many lengths
To seek the love we tried so hard to break
From slumber deep I wake to take my flight
In haste I flee for new fledged hope is near
Grieve not when I have gone away, my dear
As colors wane and darkness takes the light
Look to find sweetness in the passing
For something tells me love is everlasting

"I never fully made sense of it until now," Henri said quietly. "The second quatrain was most certainly written for you."

When he looked up, Mr. Emsley was smiling, and there were tears in his eyes. "Thank you. Thank you for that, my boy," he said.

And Henri could see that he meant it, and that those words made all the difference.

That night, Henri slept deeply without any dreams and woke refreshed and confident, ready to head into the busy street to find his father's lawyers.

It was simpler than he'd imagined. His name had never been officially changed. Legally he was, and always had been, Henry Aubrey. After obtaining a certified copy of his birth entry from the General Register Office and signing his English name on a number of crisp, white documents, Abbington Hall was his. He was also bequeathed a large sum of money, some from royalties from his father's books, but mostly from an estate in Essex that had been sold off years before.

As Henri walked away from the lawyer's, navigating the curving streets, swept up in the current of foot traffic, he felt strangely giddy. He wasn't concerned with the money, or the estates. He wasn't thinking about Leonie or the children and what it would mean for them. All he could think of was how he could now help Aimée. He could take her from that dreadful house and bring her to Abbington Hall. He could support her. She could paint freely. She wouldn't be dependent on Lady Arrington anymore, or her papa.

But when Henri arrived at Sussex Place and pushed his way through the tall iron gates of Lady Arrington's, he found the house dark, the windows shuttered, and the curtains pulled closed. Three times he rang the bell, but no one came. He waited, pacing the street in front of the menacing black gates for over two hours. Eventually, he became so discouraged that he trudged back to the inn.

Every day, for the next two weeks, he went to the house on Sussex Place, but it remained shut up. He wondered if they'd gone away to the country, or the seaside. Lady Arrington did not strike him as someone who ventured off to fresher climates, but if they had gone away, he would have no way of finding them.

He drank, night after night, in the same dingy pub down the street from his inn. Single men huddled over tables, sometimes in twos, but never in great, lively groups like in the Parisian cafés. There was no banter, no uproar of laughter or outbreak of accusation, just a melancholy exhaustion, as if these men had no energy for the most menial of conversations.

One night, Henri sat in his room, thoroughly drunk and yet

strangely lucid, all of his jumbled thoughts of the past few months condensed into a sharp picture.

He saw Aimée's pale, shadowy figure wandering the rooms of his monstrous, foreboding childhood home. He thought of her paintings, of all those babies, and he realized then that she'd be just as miserable at Abbington Hall with Marion Gray as she was with Lady Arrington. The truth was—she'd said so much herself—that Aimée didn't care where she lived. It wouldn't make any difference at all.

This was when Henri realized the truth of what he had to do, but it was too troublesome to dwell on, so he swept past it, brushing it off so quickly that he wouldn't think of it again for months. And when he did think of it again, it would feel as if he was coming upon it for the first time.

PARIS 1878

Chapter 29

Things were dismal in the Savaray household. That first year after Jeanne was born, Madame Savaray held on to the hope that Aimée would return the following spring as planned. But Aimée did not, and her letters, over the years, had grown short and indifferent. The last one had read: *Doing splendidly, dear Grand-mère. Painting away and keeping to myself. Regards to the family, Aimée.*

Splendidly? Madame Savaray didn't believe a word. And Lady Arrington's letters were just as vague and formal, with absolutely no real information to speak of. Something was terribly wrong, Madame Savaray could feel it, and if it weren't for her useless knees, she would have gotten on a boat and gone directly over the English Channel to find her *petite-fille*.

As it was, Madame Savaray could hardly walk anymore. She managed without too much trouble around the house, but a simple outing, a short walk in the park, would do her in and she'd have to keep to bed for hours.

When she took her yearly trip to Thoméry in May, her right knee swelled to three times its normal size. She'd gone every year since Jeanne's birth, on a Sunday morning when the family would be at church. There was a wooden bench in the square with a perfect view of the church steps where Madame Savaray could sit in her black dress and veiled hat. No one took any notice of an old woman enjoying a nice, spring morning. That was one benefit to being old. People rarely noticed you were there at all.

The first year, Jeanne had been a fat, happy one-year-old propped on Leonie's hip. The next year she was an adorable, toddling thing in a white dress with a shiny, lemon-colored ribbon around her waist. And this last year, well, Jeanne just couldn't get any prettier with those dark, bouncing curls and plump, rosy cheeks.

From her bench, Madame Savaray leaned forward and tilted her sunshade back so she could watch Jeanne skip up and down the church steps. The little girl kept stroking the blue satin streamer on her straw hat, causing the hat to tilt lopsided on her head. Jacques, wearing pink-and-white-striped trousers and a blue blouse, reached up and set the hat right before taking his sister's hand and leading her carefully down the stairs.

He was six years old now, and a serious, resolute-looking child. Madame Savaray could see Colette in him, the part that balanced the sensitive, diffident side of Henri. It was a determination in Jacques's walk, in his expression, and this strength pleased Madame Savaray. It was so much more acceptable in a man, for better or for worse. It would serve him well in life.

All of this she observed from her bench, watching as the family made their way down the church steps, lingering outside to speak with friends before waving good-bye and starting down the road toward home.

Long after they'd gone, Madame Savaray sat on, filled with a longing so painful it made her think she'd rather lie down in that church graveyard than return home.

When the sun was high in the sky, Madame Savaray set out

on the long road to the station, scolding herself for wallowing in loneliness and trying to ignore the explosions of pain going off in her knee. She refused to hire a carriage. It was a small town, and she would be more conspicuous in an open carriage. She didn't want to draw attention to herself, and she certainly didn't want Leonie and Henri to think she was checking up on them. Though that was precisely what she was doing.

It amazed Colette that Aimée had been gone for over three years, and that Jacques had been gone even longer.

For a time she thought things might go back to the way they were. She imagined that Henri would be unable to care for the child, and he would bring Jacques home. Once their son returned, Auguste would forgive her. He would call her back into his room. She would throw her soirées again, and Aimée would come home.

None of this happened. After a time, Colette understood she would never come back from the loss of Jacques. His absence had sprung the memories of her other lost children wide open. Now all four boys—the two who died in infancy, and precious little Léon and Jacques—blended together, and she no longer tried to sort out one from another. She remembered little hands and feet, the arc of a rounded head in her palm, a forehead soft as milkweed, a pitiful whimper, small gurgles, and piercing cries.

At times Colette tried to dig up her anger, thinking she might revive herself, but it was as if her rage had collapsed into a heap of self-deprecation intent on tormenting her. And Colette was vigilant about this torment, reminding herself of all she'd done to deserve it, thus preserving her hard edges and biting personality.

She gave up embroidery and took up the piano. She had

always played, but not well. She hired a young, eager teacher whom she took to her room on their second lesson. That lasted a few months, and then she gave him up as easily as she'd given up embroidery. There had been no one else since. She hadn't even enjoyed it. It was just something to do.

She considered learning to draw, but she feared that would remind her too much of Aimée—whom Colette missed more than she'd admit—so she decided against it and kept at the piano. She didn't need a teacher anymore, as she was playing very well. At all hours of the day, the house was filled with her music. Sorrowful, delightful, maddening, intimate. The sounds of an emotional life she no longer lived. She'd be flushed when she finished, vibrant, exhilarated, with a feeling of excitement as if there were a roomful of people waiting to applaud her.

Sometimes she caught Auguste listening in the doorway with that look of inflamed desire that their arguments used to ignite. A few words might pass between them, formal, polite, nothing of the truth. Nothing of the torment Auguste was going through, the regret and misery, the loneliness. Nothing of Colette's collapse, of the anger she'd turned inward, and how it was eating at the very core of her being. A nod, a reluctant smile from one or the other, maybe a question about supper, or how the new maid was getting on, trivial things that made no difference.

Then they would part, and one of them might feel the urge to turn back, but neither would.

It was in the spring of 1878—the spring Henri went to England and the Exposition Universelle came to Paris—that things changed.

Colette had no intention of going to the Exposition. Everywhere, grand, elaborate parties were being held. She'd heard Édouard Manet's was going to be especially magnificent, and this roused something in her, but she had not received an invitation. The Savarays were rarely invited anywhere anymore—after so many refusals people had given up—and Colette did not care to step out and be snubbed by the society that had once relished her company.

Madame Savaray told her she was being foolish. "I'm not going to let you sit around bemoaning not being invited to some garish party." She slapped her hands together. "We're going to see the exhibits. It's the event of the year." She turned to Auguste, who happened, on this occasion, to be in the room. "And you are coming with us. We will step out together. We're still a family, after all, and if I am willing to throw myself into the crowds with my bad knees, the two of you can stand a little snubbing from people you never cared for anyway."

So they went, Auguste taking Colette's arm and leading her through the swollen streets, past musicians and dancers and acrobats, flags flying from windows by the thousands, bodies pressing and knocking into them on all sides. The thunderous commotion was overwhelming and thrilling at the same time.

Swept up, Auguste and Colette allowed themselves to fall back into a time when they'd been a part of the social community, when this was what had been important. They stood a little straighter, smiled a little wider, and nodded to everyone they passed, the long feathers on Colette's hat bobbing forward, Auguste tipping the edge of his hat with his fingers.

Seeing the art exhibit brought back particular memories. Colette remembered the dress she'd worn the year Aimée was in the Salon de Paris, the tight bodice and all that trim. She'd felt grand that day, spectacularly important.

Auguste also thought of Aimée, but with a good deal of remorse, which he worked through by reminding himself—standing in front of a painting of a quiet sea—that sending her abroad had been the right thing to do.

Taking in a vivid Japanese painting, Madame Savaray imagined how their lives would be different if Aimée had never seen Henri's painting at the Salon de Paris all those years ago. What if Aimée had simply passed it by? Walked out into the garden and never looked back? Henri might never have been found. He might have stayed lost to them forever, and in this way they wouldn't have lost Aimée. They most certainly wouldn't have lost Jacques.

Looking at her son, tall, thinner than he used to be, but still strong and self-possessed, Madame Savaray felt proud. She watched him take Colette's arm and whisper something in her ear. Despite his fickle nature, he was loyal.

She turned back to the painting, thinking how much she liked these Japanese artists. Their work was clean, simple, and delicate, with meticulous lines and clear, vibrant colors. She wished life were that clean and simple, that radiant without the frills. She shook her head. The Savarays had never had a chance at a life like that. It wouldn't have mattered if Henri had stayed lost, or if her son had married a simpler woman, chaos would have found its way in.

Things shifted between Auguste and Colette after the Exposition. There was no weeping or forgiving, just a subtle warming and acceptance on both sides.

For Auguste, it was something about being out together, having the weight of Colette on his arm, her gloved hand resting on top of his. It made him feel as if she still belonged to him.

He held on to her all day, guiding her through the crowds. When they stopped in a café he ordered for her, and she looked at him gratefully, as if his care and protection was exactly what she wanted.

It was true that Colette missed the attention of a man. Not the physical attention—she had no desire for that anymore—but she did miss being held on to, supported.

So they slipped into a quiet affection that was different from anything they'd had before. There was no fighting, no passionate tossing about in bed, just a walk in the park, a light discussion in the parlor after dinner, a smile or two of coquetry, as if they were coming into something for the first time that made them both a bit shy.

Colette still slept in her own room, and neither spoke of changing this arrangement. Once, Auguste kissed her before going up to bed, a deep, longing kiss, but it led to nothing more.

One morning, in the parlor, a square of early sunlight slanting across the shiny wood floor, Auguste folded down the edge of his newspaper and looked at Colette over the top of it.

"I met an American man last week, a Robert Cassatt."

"Oh?" Colette looked up from her book.

"Retired stockbroker and real estate man. Very prominent. They have an apartment on L'avenue Trudaine," he said, the fashionable side of Pigalle an indication of the family's propriety and prosperity.

"How nice." Colette went back to her reading, uninterested in new acquaintances.

Auguste snapped his newspaper straight and cast his eyes over it. After a minute he said, "They have a daughter. A fine painter, I hear. Her papa told me she had a small piece in the Exposition."

Colette shut her book and placed it in her lap. "This is about Aimée then? Your regret?"

From behind his newspaper, Auguste said, "I was merely thinking it might be time for Aimée to come home."

"Come home to paint, you mean?"

Auguste turned a page, looked it over. "I suppose so, yes."

"Auguste," Colette said gently. "Put down the paper."

Auguste folded the paper in two and set it on the table beside him. Sunlight had crept over the floor and pooled in Colette's lap, covering her smooth, white hands.

"This daughter of his has her own studio," Auguste said, "outside the home. She is allowed to keep it as long as it supports itself."

Colette nodded. "A fine idea."

"Precisely what I was thinking, a fine idea."

"Then you'll write to Aimée? Ask her to come home?"

Auguste rubbed the underside of his chin. "I'd say it's high time, wouldn't you?"

"Yes, yes, I would."

Chapter 30

So Auguste fully intended to write that letter, but in early July Colette fell ill. The doctor said it was only a nasty cold, and that she should keep to her bed. In her feverish state, Colette was convinced she was dying. Every limb ached, her head throbbed, and it hurt to swallow. Once, she didn't make it to her chamber pot, and a humiliating mess had to be cleaned from the floor. A persistent cough developed, along with a few nosebleeds, and the doctor was called again. And again, he insisted there was nothing to worry about; the fever would go down, and her symptoms would pass.

Aimée was forgotten for the time being by everyone other than Madame Savaray, who had not received a letter from England in three months. She'd written several, all of which had gone unanswered.

She wrote again, telling Aimée that Colette was dying, and that she must return home immediately. Of course, Madame Savaray did not believe for one minute that this was true, but she would have said anything to bring Aimée home, and the illness was as good an excuse as any.

There was no doubt Colette was seriously ill, and that she was taking full advantage, acting up as usual and vying for attention, especially from Auguste, who was beside himself. He wouldn't leave her side. He screamed at the doctor. Called him an imbecile. Insisted he wasn't doing enough.

The doctor, used to hysterical husbands, took it graciously. "Well," he said, snapping his bag shut and picking up his hat, anxious to be done with his now daily exams of Colette. "Her fever is down from yesterday, just as I predicted. As I said before, it is my professional opinion—and, mind you, I have been in this profession for thirty-five years—that your wife will make a full recovery."

At that moment Colette moaned, rolled her flushed face over the edge of the bed, and vomited into a large ceramic basin.

Auguste dashed over and pulled her hair out of her face. "Does this look like a woman who is recovering?"

At the door, the doctor said, "These things take time," and left.

Colette's forehead burned against Auguste's palm, and she looked at him with wild eyes. "I must see my son!" she cried. "If I am dying, I must see him. Please. It's all I ask of you. Please, let me see Jacques one last time." She collapsed over Auguste's arm in a fit of coughing. Auguste patted her thin, frail back, her spine a brittle, bumpy line under her dressing gown.

"I'll send for the boy," he said, propping her against the pillow, smoothing the hair away from her hot, moist cheeks.

Colette began to cry.

Auguste pressed a hand to her chest. "Stop, my love, you mustn't. You'll make yourself worse. Please stop." He wiped the tears from her cheeks. "You're going to be well again," he said. "It's nonsense, all this talk of dying. I will not permit it. You'll be fit in no time, the doctor said so."

"I cannot help myself," Colette sobbed. "I must see my son."

"I know, my love, I know. I'll send for the boy. But no more talk of dying. Do you hear me?"

Colette's sobs were overtaken by another gruesome coughing fit. When she had control of her breathing, she sank down in bed, exhausted. "I'm terribly cold," she said.

Pulling back the covers, Auguste climbed in next to her. Colette lifted her head from the pillow and rested it on his chest, a button on his shirt making a small, circular indent on her cheek. He wrapped his arm around her, feeling the feverish warmth of her body against his.

There was no walking from the train station this time. Madame Savaray had the carriage pull right up to the door of the little cottage in Thoméry.

Leonie greeted her with an uncomfortable smile and led her into the house, apologizing for the children's mess; rocks dropped like crumbs down the hall and into the parlor where an elaborate stone house had been built in the middle of the braided rug.

Madame Savaray cocked an eyebrow with a look of asperity that Leonie chose to ignore. As far as Leonie was concerned, she'd let the children do as she saw fit. She was alone here, and no one was going to come in and tell her how to raise her children now.

Wordlessly, she watched Madame Savaray scan the sparse room, her eyes narrow and accusing as they roamed over the faded sofa, the single end table, and the two cane chairs—one with a small hole in the seat.

Stepping deliberately around the children's stonework, Madame Savaray sat down in the chair nearest the cold hearth and propped her walking stick against the curved armrest.

Leonie hovered in the doorway, nervous, shifting her arms first down at her sides, then across her chest. "Can I offer you a cup of tea? Chocolate?"

"Cognac if you have it, or wine will do." Madame Savaray glanced out the open window, the brown muslin curtains shifting in the breeze. She could smell drying wheat, and hear the faint rush of the river.

"I'll only be a moment," Leonie said, and went down the hall to the kitchen.

She had been in the bedroom tucking in the sheets—still warm and stiff from the sun—when she'd heard the clomping of horses' hooves and the crunch of carriage wheels. She'd dropped the sheet and flown down the stairs, certain it was Henri.

Seeing Madame Savaray hobbling over the stones, Leonie was hit with stunning disappointment. Until that moment she hadn't let herself feel how much she missed Henri, how painful it was that he hadn't written, or how frightening the thought that he might not return. It was no comfort that he had promised to marry her. He'd promised this many times over the years. *It's best for the children* was what he had said. England was for "the children" too. He was going to reclaim his rightful name so he could give it to them. None of it was for her.

Leonie arranged the glasses on the tray, a thin streak of flour appearing across her middle as she leaned into the counter. A quick, cold fear ran through her, and she bowed her head. Over the years she had tried, very hard, not to imagine the day a Savaray came to claim Jeanne, but she'd feared it all the same.

Carrying the tray back to the parlor, Leonie set it on the end table and handed Madame Savaray a glass. She did not take a glass for herself, but sat across from her with purpose, prepared to meet this head-on, fight with all her might if need be.

It was obvious how uncomfortable Leonie was, but for some reason Madame Savaray didn't make the slightest effort to put her at ease. Instead, she asked after Henri, and learned, much to her shock, that he was in England.

"Has he seen Aimée?" she demanded, Aimée's silence suddenly becoming clearer to her. Of course Henri was behind it. Always Henri.

"I don't know. I've not heard a word from him."

Madame Savaray gave her a measured look of accusation. "Why did he go?"

"To find his father."

"How long has he been gone?"

"Almost three months."

That was exactly when Aimée stopped writing. Madame Savaray tapped the edge of her glass with her fingernail. A small chiming sound rang out. "Do you expect his return?"

Leonie's face darkened. "Of course I expect his return."

"Why, then, would he not write to you?"

"Madame," Leonie pulled herself to the edge of the sofa, perched, Madame Savaray thought, like a flighty bird. "Why have you come? Clearly, it has nothing to do with Henri's being in England."

Madame Savaray snapped her head to the left and looked at a poorly rendered painting of Jacques with baby Jeanne on his lap. "One ought not tilt on the edge of her seat. Sit or stand. It's unbecoming to hover in between. It makes you appear agitated."

"I am agitated," Leonie responded, and Madame Savaray couldn't help thinking how much she admired this reasonable, straightforward woman.

"Where are the children?"

"Out in the field."

"Running wild? Unsupervised?"

It wasn't Madame Savaray's intention to be hard on Leonie; she was just tense, and fighting off the despondency she'd felt the moment she'd stepped into this house.

She set down her wineglass. She had not taken a single sip. "I've only come to make an outrageous request that you can, by all means, refuse."

Tears sprang to Leonie's eyes, and she pressed a hand to her chest, shaking her head in embarrassment. "My apologies."

"What did you think? That I was here to reclaim those unruly children?" Madame Savaray slapped at the front of her dress as if they were climbing all over her. "Stones in the drawing room," she muttered.

Truthfully, seeing this messy bit of youth reminded her of the joy that could be found in a stone, and she was overcome by the same longing she'd felt watching the children on the church steps. It was a longing to be a part of something delightfully young again, even if just for a moment.

"Colette is terribly ill," Madame Savaray said. "She believes she's going to her grave, and her last, unequivocal request is to see Jacques. I, for one, think it's senseless. But, there you have it."

Leonie was silent as she wiped the tears from under her eyes. After a minute she asked, "Is Colette to be trusted?"

"I couldn't say."

Leonie shook her head. "I don't think it's a good idea."

Madame Savaray took hold of her walking stick and gave it a thump. "I told Auguste, if he was going to be so fainthearted as to send me on this errand, that I would not insist, or even make a good argument. Besides, the doctor says Colette will make a full recovery. I'd be surprised if something as incidental as a fever did her in. I'm not convinced she hasn't brought the illness on for a bit of excitement."

"But there's a chance she's dying?"

"We're all dying; it's just a matter of when."

A worrisome thought had crept into Leonie's mind. "If I said *yes,* how would we manage it? What would we tell Jacques?"

Madame Savaray gave a throaty scoff. "He's a child. Tell him anything you like. Tell him a distant relative wants to see him. It won't mean anything to a child."

"Do the Savarays know nothing of Jeanne?"

"Nothing."

"What if Jacques says something about his sister?"

"They'll think she's yours. They have no reason not to."

"You want to take him today?"

"I'll bring him back tomorrow on the earliest train."

Leonie looked out the window. She couldn't see the children. They'd probably gone down to the river. Jeanne had never spent a night without her brother. She'd be beside herself.

"All right." Leonie was reluctant, and yet she felt fairly certain that refusing a dying mother's request to see her only son was not something easily forgiven by God. And if not God, Leonie didn't see how she could forgive herself. "You must promise to look after Jacques yourself, and stay in the room the entire time he's with Colette."

Holding tight to her walking stick, Madame Savaray heaved herself from the chair. "He'll be fine," she said. Then, with cold authority, "Best not to disillusion yourself that you're his maman. Jacques will find out the truth one day, whether you want him to or not. They always do."

Leonie stood up with a flash of anger. "Well, today is not that day."

"Of course not. You needn't look so alarmed. I'm only saying it for your own good. Things hurt, that's all, mostly the truth, and it comes to light eventually, as much as we don't want it to. I'm only suggesting you prepare yourself in advance, so you're not entirely undone by it."

Leonie had spent a lot of time warding off this very thought, and she was not prepared to face it now, when she was about to say good-bye to her son.

"I'll call in the children," she said. Then she gave Madame Savaray a steely look. "I'm trusting you."

Madame Savaray nodded. "As you should," she said, even though they both knew it was not really up to her.

Chapter 31

Auguste sat at a café staring at his dinner, unshaven, pale, and thin. He'd hardly slept or eaten since Colette had fallen ill.

He stared into his stew, pushing around bits of fish and floating leeks. Jacques would have arrived at the house already. Colette would have seen him. He would have eaten his dinner. He might even be in bed.

Auguste lifted his head. The oil lamps on the tables were as bright as torches, and they made his eyes ache. The yellow tiles on the walls swam under the glare as he waved the tavern maid over.

He told the girl to take the food away and bring another absinthe.

By the time he left, Auguste was thoroughly drunk. A clock chimed as he climbed the steps to his house, but he didn't count the tolls, and he'd forgotten to wind his watch, so he had no idea what time he finally made it through the front door. He propped himself against the wall, breathing heavily. When no one came he tossed his hat onto the floor and groped his way up the stairs.

Opening the door to Aimée's old bedroom, he crept stealthily, stumbling into the bedside table. An object went flying, making a soft thud as it hit the rug. Jacques stirred.

Moonlight fell in a wide strip across the bed. Normally, the curtains were pulled shut, and as Auguste eased himself down on the edge of the mattress, he thought perhaps they had been left open because Jacques was afraid of the dark.

He gently touched the boy's hand, realizing this was all he would ever have, this image of Jacques's soft hair splayed across the pillow, his parted lips, one arm flung over his head as his eyelids fluttered, darting around his dreams.

The loneliness of the last four years hit Auguste, and he wanted to take Jacques in his arms and hold on to him. He couldn't imagine reliving those years. But he couldn't see a way out. He'd lost so much. He wished he could blame Henri, but it wasn't Henri's fault. A small crack in his life began the moment he lost his first child, one that had only widened and spread with time. Henri was just a chink along the way, the loss of Jacques the final shattering.

Perhaps, Auguste thought, it wasn't too late to take Jacques back. Maybe, with the return of his boy, the fissures of his cracked life would recede and he'd be whole again. He would offer Henri money. Pay him off. What struggling artist would choose a troublesome child over money? The boy must be a burden. He would be relieved to be rid of him. Auguste stood up. Colette would have something to live for if she had her boy back. She'd fight harder. She'd stay alive.

Just then Jacques's eyes flew open. Auguste jumped back from the bed, stumbled to the door, and rushed from the room.

Back in his own room, he slammed the door and dropped onto the bed. Clutching his throbbing head he fell into a swirling, drunken slumber.

By the time he rose, stiff and achy, fully dressed with boots still laced and drool crusted on the side of his cheek, it was nearly ten o'clock and Jacques and Madame Savaray were already on the train back to Thoméry.

Auguste changed his clothes, splashed cold water on his face, and rubbed his wet hands through hair that still reeked of stale cigar smoke. *What a mad fool.*

He entered Colette's room, with its sour smell of sickness and curtains pulled shut against the bright morning. But when he looked at his wife, he saw that she was sitting up, her back pressed against the carved headboard and her hair brushed neatly over the shoulders of her white dressing gown. Her face was no longer blotchy, but smooth and even toned, her eyes bright and clear.

"My dear." She smiled as she untangled a weak hand from the crumpled bedclothes and reached out to him.

A thin rod of sunlight escaped through a crack in the curtain. It looked like a gold scepter lying across the wooden floorboards. Auguste stepped across and took her hand, her fingers thin and delicate under his grip.

"I saw Jacques," she said, her voice light and natural, the pitch of hysteria she'd carried for weeks swept away. "I saw our boy. He is beautiful. He spoke to me. He was very polite." She smiled, as proud as any maman could be.

Auguste sank to his knees at the edge of the bed. She had said *our boy.* It didn't matter that it wasn't true. It left him feeling that he could finally forgive her.

"Yes," he said. "I saw him too."

"I'm glad," she said. "I'm glad you had the strength to see him." And she pulled Auguste's hand to her lips and kissed it.

Chapter 32

By the time Aimée stepped off the train, the sun had already sunk behind the shadows of the buildings. A heavy fog crept over the city, and when the carriage stopped at the front door on the rue l'Ampère, the street was completely dark. Not a glimmer of light came from a single window as she made her way to the carriage entrance around back. She'd sent no notice of her arrival, so she hoped a kitchen maid might still be up, or Marie, whose bedroom overlooked the courtyard.

The last letter from her *grand-mère* had been at the post office for over a month before she received it, along with an earlier letter postmarked in May, and another from June. Apparently, Lady Arrington had not thought it necessary to have the post forwarded to Brighton, where they had spent the summer.

Her *grand-mère* had written of Colette's illness, but no letter followed, which meant her health had most likely improved and there was no need for Aimée's sudden return. Yet when she'd read her *grand-mère*'s letters she had felt a tremendous longing for home. It wasn't her family she longed for, or the house, or the familiar streets of Paris; it was simply a desire to step back into a life she recognized.

Aimée moved along the dark courtyard, with a hand out in front of her, bumping into the arm of a shadowy figure.

"Gracious!" she cried, and a girl stepped forward.

"I beg your pardon," she mumbled.

"It was entirely my fault," Aimée said. "Are you all right?"

"Fine, mademoiselle."

"Are you employed here?"

"Yes," the girl answered.

"If you'd be so kind as to let me in, it's Mademoiselle Savaray."

The girl peered at Aimée for a moment. "Right away, mademoiselle."

They went in the back door, and the girl took a candle from the table, leading Aimée down the hall and up the ground floor stairs to the parlor.

"Should I wake someone for you?" the girl asked, lowering her candle to the wick of a lamp.

"No, thank you," Aimée said. "I would be grateful in the morning if you would send someone to fetch my trunks at the station."

The girl curtsied. "Yes, mademoiselle."

"That will be all."

The girl backed out of the room, quick footsteps echoing behind her. Realizing she hadn't asked after her maman, Aimée stepped after her, but the girl was gone.

The stairs loomed on Aimée's right, and she reached up and smoothed her hand along the banister, remembering how Jacques used to hold on when he jumped from step to step. He went so fast she was sure one day he'd go crashing down. But he never did. He had always been so quick and sure of himself.

Aimée walked back into the parlor, wondering how big Jacques was now. She sat on the sofa, rubbing her forehead with one hand, trying to wipe out any thoughts of Jeanne before they crept in. She would not picture Jeanne. How could she? She didn't even know the color of her daughter's hair, or if it was curly or straight. She didn't know if she was a wispy, delicate child, or plump and round. No, Aimée would not think of her. It would be no use. And whatever happened, she vowed not to go out to Thoméry to have a look.

The familiarity of this house was what she had missed, and Aimée tried to absorb everything around her. Things taken for granted, like the musty smell of the rug and the faded, blue tint of the fabric on the arm of the sofa. It was strange to have everything exactly where she'd left it; the sofa enduring the passage of time with nothing lost other than a slight fade of color.

Aimée closed her eyes and rested her head on the cushion, smoothing her hand over the firm velvet seat. She realized all of her memories were now separated into the time before Jeanne, and the time after. Home was the time before, and she found this surprisingly comforting.

The house was deathly silent as Madame Savaray made her way slowly down the stairs and into the parlor. She hadn't been able to sleep, so she'd come down to retrieve a book she'd left on the console.

Aimée's figure—her dark dress flared to the ground, her tilted head, her pale throat exposed and skeletal—frightened Madame Savaray. For the split second before Aimée's hand moved, Madame Savaray thought she was having a vision of her *petite-fille*'s death.

"Aimée," she whispered. The flame of her candle quivered, small flickers of light leaping over her spare, lined face.

Aimée's eyes flew open. "*Grand-mère,*" she said, standing quickly.

They stared at each other. Aimée felt as if decades had passed.

Her *grand-mère* was almost unrecognizable. Solid gray patches of hair brushed upward from her temples and ran into the thick braid down her back. Her robust chest was caved in and shapeless, her cheeks sunken, her robe tied tight around her withered middle. In her right hand she gripped a walking stick, leaning into it exactly as Aimée remembered her papa doing when he'd wounded his foot in the war—tentative, reluctant, as if the need for support were a failure, a weakness they hated to admit.

Tears flooded Madame Savaray's eyes, and she blinked them away. Setting her candle on the console, she hobbled over to Aimée and grasped her hand.

"You look miserable," she said, patting her *petite-fille*'s hand over and over. "Simply miserable. Was it a tremendous mistake sending you away? I've worried every day over that."

A lump swelled in Aimée's throat. It had been a long time since anyone had touched her. "Of course not. Why would you waste a moment's worry? I wrote you that everything was all right."

"I never believed a word of it."

Hearing those simple, honest words, Aimée felt her bitter resolve slip away, leaving her as weak as a child. "You're right." She laughed, a harsh, shaky sound. "It was miserable."

Madame Savaray lowered herself onto the sofa, holding her walking stick out in front of her and smoothing the ivory tip as if working a ball of clay. Aimée sat next to her. Her *grand-mère* even smelled old, sour, and musty, her breath pungent.

Looking straight ahead, Madame Savaray said, "My dear, there is no delicate way to put this. I must tell you straight out that your maman has died."

The room felt suddenly very warm. Wrapping a hand around her wrist, Aimée rubbed the hard outer bone of her forearm and looked toward the door, half expecting her maman to walk through and prove her *grand-mère* wrong. Her maman was too spirited to die, indestructible, a force beyond the power of nature.

"Why did you not write to me?"

"I couldn't tell you in a letter." Madame Savaray dug a handkerchief out of her pocket. "I didn't believe she was dying. I thought she'd brought it on just to see Jacques."

There was a stab in Aimée's ribs. "She saw Jacques?"

"Yes."

"Papa agreed?"

"He would have agreed to anything in the end. Colette behaved herself with the boy, asked pointed questions, his likes and dislikes, that sort of thing. Jacques was very polite. It was only when she reached her hand to him that the poor boy faltered." Madame Savaray looked into a dark corner of the room, remembering Jacques's pale face. "He seemed frightened, at first, then something shifted, a sudden recognition, and he stepped up and took Colette's hand. He held on to it until she fell asleep. The next day your maman seemed fully recovered. Even your papa was convinced she'd brought it on herself. But a few days later the fever returned. She died quite quickly. Influenza, the doctor said."

Aimée walked toward the door. It felt as if the fog outside had crept in and was smothering her. "I can't do this," she said suddenly, and buried her face in her hands.

Hoisting herself from the sofa, Madame Savaray abandoned her walking stick and braced herself against the pain to go to Aimée.

Aimée flinched as her *grand-mère* placed a shaky hand on the bare skin just below her neck, the sensation tender and painful.

"It's not easy, coming home," Madame Savaray said. "Things are different, and yet too much the same. You will settle, in time.

Your coming home means everything to your papa. You're all he has left."

"I'm the last one he wants." Aimée straightened, and Madame Savaray's hand slipped from her neck.

"Nonsense. He fully restocked your studio," Madame Savaray said as if this made up for everything.

"Why did he not write to me?"

"Your papa doesn't apologize. And he's never wrong."

Just then a searing flash of pain bore through Madame Savaray's knee, and it buckled under her. *Pathetic,* she thought as she crumpled to the floor. *Useless.*

Aimée dropped down beside her. "*Grand-mere!* Are you all right? Should I call someone?"

Madame Savaray was sprawled like a child, her legs straight out, her exposed calves thick and shapeless like hunks of white marble above her stockings that were bunched down around her swollen ankles. She looked into Aimée's stricken face and burst out laughing so hard tears came to her eyes. Startled, Aimée let out her own distorted laugh, and sank down next to her *grand-mère.* They both gave way to the absurdity.

"How preposterous," Madame Savaray said, wiping tears from her cheeks. "Help me up before I am utterly humiliated."

Madame Savaray held her arms out as her *petite-fille* stood up and lifted her to her feet. She felt feeble and old, but happy.

"Come," she said, the laughter already a thing of the past. "It's time we were in our beds. You'll be a surprise for your papa in the morning."

Aimée slipped her arm inside her *grand-mère*'s, and together they walked from the room, grateful, each of them, for the support.

Chapter 33

The next morning Aimée stood in her papa's bedroom. The curtains were pulled back and the windows wide open. The fog had burned off, and the air was warm and clear. A steady rumble came from the street.

Her papa sat on the edge of his bed, fully dressed, his black cravat stiff under his neck, his olive-green morning coat buttoned, his shoes shined and buckled. It was encouraging that he had not shut himself up, mourning in the dark as Aimée imagined. She had been afraid he'd be as aged as her *grand-mère,* but he looked as she remembered, thinner, but still broad shouldered with a full head of dark hair, his confident chin jutting from a wide, cleanly shaven jawbone.

He stood slowly, looking at her without surprise. "When did you get in?" he asked.

"Last night."

"I'm sorry I wasn't awake to greet you."

"It's no matter. I wasn't expected."

"You could have woken me."

"There was no need," she said.

Auguste nodded, plunging his hands into his trouser pockets. *Of course there wasn't.* Looking away he said, "I'm afraid I missed breakfast. The new housemaid was good enough to send up my coffee." He pointed to the tray. "She's even brought two cups. She must have forgotten I'm only one now. Won't you take some with me? I could send for chocolate, if you like, or tea?" He gave Aimée a bemused smile. He'd never noticed what she drank before, or bothered to ask. "I'm afraid I don't know what you prefer."

"Coffee will do," Aimée said. "Thank you."

She walked to the nearest chair and sat down. Her papa poured the coffee with an unsteady hand. The cup clanked against the saucer, and a bit of coffee splashed over the side as he handed it to her.

Aimée held the cup in her lap, the rich, earthy scent mingling with the smell of stale cigar smoke. It was her maman's favorite tea set—bone china edged in gold—brought out only for dinner parties. Aimée wondered if her maman had ordered the best set to be used every day, or if the new housemaid simply didn't know any better.

Her papa sat across from her without taking a cup for himself. Things were drastically different; they both felt this right away. Perhaps this meant they could start anew, an encouraging thought, if not a little frightening.

Aimée took a small sip. Her papa had not asked if she wanted cream or sugar, and the coffee was strong and bitter. In the past, her maman had somehow been tied to all of Aimée's interactions with her papa. Without her, Aimée had no idea where to begin.

Shifting uncomfortably in his chair, Auguste cleared his throat, but said nothing.

For a week after Colette's death he hadn't gotten out of bed. He'd stared at the bedroom walls until the repeating pattern of dogs and deer had blurred into his dreams. He longed for sleep, for the temporary peace it allowed before he woke in the middle of the night, startled, with a sense of dread he couldn't quite place until Colette's absence hit fast and hard, the pain fresh and gut-wrenching every time.

It was on one of those nights when Auguste's mistakes became very clear to him.

The next day he was able to get out of bed, the stillness in the house profound, but the stillness in himself even more acute, as if a great storm had blown over, one that had trampled his heart, but left a glimmer on its surface.

Watching Aimée, sitting straight-backed in her chair, carefully sipping her coffee, he felt the weight of his mistakes in her, and this made him terribly sad.

"How did you fare with Lady Arrington?" he asked.

"Wretchedly."

Auguste smiled, his daughter's forward nature still catching him by surprise. "I see."

"No use professing otherwise. *Grand-mère* would tell you soon enough. She has a way of getting the absolute truth out of me."

"Out of everyone, although she'd never admit it. She fancies herself someone who stays out of other people's affairs."

Aimée laughed. "Yes, yes, she does."

"Ah." Auguste slapped his hand on his knee and stood. "I have something for you." He went to the writing table under the window, dug around in the top drawer, and brought back a slim weekly journal.

He handed it to Aimée.

"What is it?" She read the title, *L'Impressionniste*.

"It's those artists you used to speak of, les Indépendantes; they call themselves L'Impressionniste now. Your maman and I went to one of their exhibits a few years back."

"Did you?" Aimée peered at the small print. "I read about it in London's *Art Monthly Review*. What did you think of it? Was it absolutely as appalling and fantastic as the Salon des Refusés in '74?"

"It frightened me. All these revolutionaries, men seeking change. The last time men felt the need to rise up and change the way things had been done for hundreds of years there was war and bloodshed. And, in the end, very little change."

Aimée looked into her papa's open face. Never had she heard him admit fear.

"I had no intention of going to the exhibit," he went on. "Why would I want to see paintings of laundry women or soot-covered trains? It was entirely your maman's idea. I thought she'd suddenly taken a fancy to these artists, but when I asked her she said, 'Not in the slightest. They're laughable.'"

Aimée could hear her maman's amused impatience, as if waiting for the rest of the world to catch up to what she'd already figured out.

"Your maman's exact words were, 'I was hoping to find something of Aimée in them.'"

A heavy presence came over Aimée, and her throat felt pinched and dry.

Auguste tapped the journal with his finger, his cuticle a perfect half moon at the bottom of his neatly trimmed nail.

"I've underlined a few bits." He craned his neck, running his finger along the thin, black line of his pen. "It says here, 'Where can we find more grandeur, more truth, and more poetry than in these beautiful landscapes?' The journalist even has the gall to compare the paintings to the prose of Victor Hugo. Here, 'The same epic dignity, the same force, simply in its solemnity.'" Auguste raised his fist in the air and thumped back to his chair. "Now, Victor Hugo is a man to revere. I don't claim to understand L'Impressionnistes any better than the first time I was exposed to them, but that journalist makes a good argument in support of them."

Whether her papa understood, or not, didn't matter. That he and her maman had tried to understand at all made Aimée feel recognized in a way she'd craved her whole life.

"Would you be so kind as to read it aloud?" Auguste crossed his hands in his lap and settled back. "I'd like to hear it again."

It took Aimée a minute to find her voice, but her papa was in no hurry. She was conscious of his eyes on her as she read, of the quiet nod of his head, but mostly of the way he listened, earnestly, and with purpose.

Chapter 34

Despite the waves of heat that rose off the tracks, Henri waited until the train was out of sight, until the last piercing whistle could no longer be heard. Only then did he grab his suitcase and head down the dusty road toward the cottage.

The sun was high in the sky. His skin tingled under the glare, and beads of sweat formed on his forehead. Blackberry bushes grew thick along the road, and the thorns snagged the sleeves of his coat. It made Henri smile, this bit of nature holding on to him. London had been awful, all that noise and filth. The fetid smell of the inn had only gotten worse in the summer heat, and he hadn't had a decent night's sleep in weeks.

The hum of the river felt like a blessing. The smell of wheat drying in the sun, its golden stalks bowing and rippling in the wind, the clusters of thick, purple grapes hanging heavy on the vine walls were like small gifts.

Jeanne was the first to see him, crouched in the grass with her skirt hiked over her knees. She was diligently poking a beetle that kept rolling over and playing dead.

"Papa!" she cried, and Leonie and Jacques looked over from where they were picking pole beans in the garden.

Jacques came running. Laertes bounded from under a shady bush and let out a sharp, excited bark. And then children and dog were flinging themselves at Henri, who, finding it impossible to keep his balance, came down on his knees in the road. Jeanne smothered him in kisses, and Jacques, as if he weren't almost a boy of seven, wrapped his arms around Henri's neck and buried his face in his chest.

Laughing, Henri stood up with the children clinging to his legs. Leonie was standing under the plum tree brushing dirt from her hands. Thin strands of hair scattered across her face. The branches hung low around her, heavy with fruit, filtering the sunlight that flecked the top of her bare head. Her sleeves were rolled, and her arms and chest were a rosy pink. Henri had forgotten how lovely she was.

He walked over and put his hands on her round hips and kissed her. She resisted, pulling back with a tight purse of her lips, but when Henri slipped a firm hand to the small of her back and pulled her in, her whole body softened.

Leonie had seen him from a distance, relief choking her up. She'd wanted to run into the house and make herself presentable, but her anger had kept her rooted.

When he pulled away, she was crying. "I thought you weren't coming home," she said, slapping a gentle hand against his chest.

He wrapped his arms around her. "Nonsense," he said, kissing the top of her head.

They stayed up very late that night. The children hadn't wanted to go to bed, and when they finally fell asleep, Leonie and Henri hardly made it to their room before their clothes dropped to the floor.

Henri desperately gripped Leonie's fleshy bottom as he thrust into her, her body supple and forgiving. She rose up, tightening her legs around him and his hip bones dug into her inner thighs.

She draped her arms around his neck, her breasts heavy against his chest, the hard tip of her tongue flicking to the roof of his mouth. Henri tried to slow himself, but he couldn't, and he shuddered and moaned and fell on top of her.

"Forgive me," he said, rolling to the side, hot and breathless, holding an arm across Leonie's damp stomach, a hand on her breast.

"It's to be expected." Leonie wove her fingers through the fine chest hairs that grew in a line from Henri's belly button to the top of his groin. "You're home now," she said. "You'll have plenty of time to make up for it." But there was no confidence in her voice. She wanted him to say it, or at least concur.

Instead, Henri smiled and closed his eyes, sleepy, the air still and moist, the murmur of the river, the chorus of the frogs and crickets, peaceful and soothing.

As his breath deepened, Leonie made a sharp noise in her throat, wiggled out from under his arm, and sat up, pulling the sheet over her lap, her breasts heavy and free. "Don't for one minute think we're done here."

Henri blinked and looked up at her. Cool moonlight lit the room. Leonie's bare chest and the bloom on her skin reminded him of the times she'd modeled for him and then they'd gone directly to bed. "You're beautiful," he said.

Leonie laughed and pinched his arm. "You're trying to excuse yourself. What with that ridiculous kiss in front of the children, and this?" She swooped her hand over the bed.

Henri smiled. "I'm apologizing," he said, pulling himself up next to her.

"And I accept." Leonie offered a noble nod of her head. "But that does not excuse the fact that you did not show me the courtesy of a single letter, which means you have a lot of explaining to do. I want to hear every detail of your trip."

"Right now?"

"Right now."

Scooting back down, Leonie settled her head in his lap. Henri pulled the sheet over her hip, running his finger down the dip in her waist and up her side, cupping his palm over her shoulder.

It came out willingly, but, as Leonie expected, without emotion, just the bare facts, about his father's death, Abbington Hall, the money, and the lawyers. Not once did he mention Aimée, but Leonie had expected that too.

"We don't have to leave France." Henri stroked Leonie's hair. "We can sell Abbington Hall. Buy something of our own here."

Leonie was quiet. She'd expected a family to contend with, parents, possibly siblings, not an estate. Not once had Henri mentioned that he came from wealth.

She rolled onto her back and propped her knees up, the top of Henri's thigh round and firm under her head. "I certainly don't want to leave France," she said. "But I don't want to leave this home either. It's perfectly suitable, and the children are happy here. Although the money is exciting, isn't it?" She reached up and touched Henri's cheek. "I can order that silk from the draper's Jeanne begged me for. What do you think Jacques would like? Perhaps a new fishing pole? *You* can finally buy me a proper engagement ring," she said, pausing for a response. Henri only smiled at her. "More importantly," she added, "we can finally stop taking money from Auguste Savaray."

Henri nodded, but it made him sorry. He couldn't tell Leonie that he saw those monthly installments as small symbols of forgiveness, reminders that Auguste still cared for him and Jacques.

"Henri." Leonie's voice turned grave.

"Yes?"

"I must tell you something."

She kneeled in front of him with her hand flat against his chest, and told him about Colette.

Chapter 35

Being home was harder than Aimée imagined, everything familiar, and at the same time different.

That first day back, she went into her maman's bedroom. The sun had stretched and settled into the day, and Aimée moved through the bright clarity, past her maman's neatly made bed, the untouched pillows and the tightly tucked covers. She stood in front of the dressing table and looked at the crystal perfume bottles lined in a row at the base of the mirror.

There was a particularly pretty bottle with gold leaves pressed into the glass. Aimée lifted the stopper and brought it to her nose. It did not smell like the maman of her childhood; it was a newer scent, the one her maman wore the day she hugged Aimée good-bye.

She ran her fingers over a glass jewelry box, touched a cluster of pink roses painted on a pot of rouge. From a silver hairbrush she pulled a strand of dark hair, thick as thread, and curled it around her finger as she walked to the armoire and opened the doors.

She expected to find her maman's many magnificent dresses hanging as they used to. But there were only two, a solid blue and a striped pink with sprigs of flowers in ruched fabric. Both dresses were shoved aside to make room for a mound of neatly folded cloth. Aimée lifted a piece of white muslin. The material hadn't been hemmed, and the edges were frayed around a border of embroidered yellow roses. In the center rose a great, black bird with a bright red beak. Aimée laid the fabric at her feet. Taking the stack from the armoire, she unfolded each piece and spread them on the floor, covering the room from end to end in her maman's brilliant embroidery of flowers, dragonflies, and exotic plumed birds.

Kneeling down, she spread the last piece across her lap. The bird stretched its colorful wings over her thighs and looked up at her with a single beady eye.

Her maman's desires—her rage and passion and need and longing—were in every stitch, in each fantastic, lustrous color. It seemed to Aimée that the air pulsed with the beat of a hundred wings, and from it her maman rose, glorious and free, having found a way out.

A week later, Aimée stood above Colette's grave, dressed in mourning with a veil over her eyes. She found the fresh mound of unsettled dirt thoroughly disturbing. It was foolish to have expected a tidy, comfortable patch of grass, but Aimée had.

She wanted to hurry away, but she forced herself to stay. She placed her palm on her maman's gravestone and said a short prayer. Just to the side was Léon's tiny headstone. Aimée hadn't thought of him in so long. She hardly remembered the day they buried him. Only that she had cried because she couldn't lie next to him and hold his hand. Reaching down she wove her fingers into the cool blades of grass over his grave. Eventually, the grass would spread. Leon's grave would blend into his maman's, just as his grave blended with his baby brother's on the other side.

Over time, Aimée thought, her maman would be as settled here as her children.

A gust of wind scattered a handful of leaves over the ground, and Aimée bowed her head. These children weren't alone anymore. They had their maman, and her maman finally had her sons back.

Aimée yanked a clump of grass and sprinkled the blades in her lap, green against black. She had not yet cried, and for a moment she let herself believe the tears she shed behind her veil were for her maman. But it was Jeanne she was thinking of. The last time Aimée had walked the streets of Paris, Jeanne was nothing more than a mystery growing in her womb. How frightened Aimée had been. And yet, in that uncertainty and fear there had been room for hope and possibility. Nothing had been decided yet. Now, everything was fixed. She would grow old with her papa; and then she would be alone. Not even in death would she be reunited with her daughter. They would never know each other. Their graves would never touch.

Chapter 36

Standing in front of his old home on the rue de Passy, Henri realized he'd made the silliest mistake. The Savarays did not live here anymore. They hadn't lived here since the war, and yet this was where he had come.

The sun was mild, the day slightly cool. Henri stood with his hands in his pockets, thinking of the first time he saw Aimée, a thin girl with a determined look as she peered at him from the doorway of the parlor, slapping at her dress as if to beat the pleats into submission. It was in this house where he had first felt Auguste's firm hand on the top of his head, and wished that he were his real papa. Where Colette had so lovingly tucked him into bed at night and kissed his forehead, filling the place inside him that desired a mother's love.

Henri turned from the house, knowing that it would be for the last time.

He took a cab to the rue l'Ampère, where he'd originally intended to go. That day he'd confessed to Auguste, he'd been too fearful and tongue-tied to offer a real apology. At the very least, he owed him that.

It was Marie who answered the door. Henri was glad to see her shock of red hair, now flecked with silver. Her eyes widened in surprise, and her lips curled into a smile. She'd always liked Henri.

In the parlor, she took a lemon candy from her apron pocket. "For Jacques," she whispered. "You sit tight. I'll be back directly."

Henri smiled and thanked her, slipping the candy into his pocket.

It was very quiet, and he waited, nervous.

He heard footsteps first, light and quick, and when she rounded the corner Henri stared, stunned. All he'd dared hope was that Aimée was safe somewhere in the depths of Lady Arrington's lair, but she was here, right in front of him. She had not disappeared. She had simply come home.

The window was open, and a breeze sent Aimée's curls scattering across her forehead. Attempting indifference, she reached up and brushed them back into place. Henri's presence could still, after all this time, affect her so deeply.

This was the reason she had not wanted to see him again in England. Her first year there—her stomach soft and folded from childbirth, her insides torn up—she'd piled all of her memories into a neat corner of her mind and covered them up with grief. When Henri had shown up at Lady Arrington's, full of compassion and apology, she'd felt a stirring, a coming back to life, and she hadn't wanted to come back to life, not without Jeanne.

"My apologies; Papa is not at home." She rounded the back of the divan and sat down.

Henri sat across from her, unable to wipe the shock from his face. She was as thin as the last time he'd seen her, but healthy, her skin above the line of her dress flushed with color. "I came to offer my condolences," he said.

Of course, Aimée thought. Of course he had come about her

maman. "That is exceedingly kind of you." There was a small lifting in the corner of her mouth, a near smile.

"I suppose it's best for Auguste to be out. I'm not sure he'd be inclined to receive me."

"I believe he'd find the gesture thoughtful, nonetheless. I will be sure to pass on your sympathies. It can't be easy for you to come."

"No, it's not, but necessary."

The tenderness in Henri's eyes sent a familiar ache through Aimée. She turned her head away. "Would you care for something to drink?"

"Thank you, kindly, but no. I hadn't planned on staying."

On the table next to Aimée's chair sat Colette's thimble, which the maid had found between the couch cushions earlier that morning. Aimée looked at the tiny gold mushroom dome, indented with miniature holes, and the scroll of flowers carved along the bottom. It seemed her maman had just set it down and stepped out of the room, that at any moment now she was going come back in to retrieve it.

"I feel utterly out of sorts." Aimée gave a little laugh. "Sad, and yet grateful to see you."

Henri stood up. For one brief afternoon, he wanted nothing to have gone wrong between them. "It would be a great pleasure, Mademoiselle Savaray"—he extended his hand to her—"if you would walk with me. It's a fine day for it."

Aimée's hands tightened in her lap. "I don't believe that's a good idea."

Reaching down, Henri pulled her hands apart and took hold of one. "I beg you? Walk out of doors with me. Point things out like you used to, colors and light. Tell me I'm a fool not to see it the way you do."

"You don't know what you're saying."

Henri held her hand and waited, watching as her face shifted from resistance, to reluctance, to consent.

"Very well," she said.

In the Tuileries Garden, they strolled side by side and said nothing. It was five o'clock, and the light was beautiful. But Aimée did not point this out. They didn't talk about the breeze, or how the tops of the great chestnuts made a sound like rushing water. Neither mentioned that Aimée's dress kept blowing into Henri's legs, or that he did not step aside to avoid it.

It was as painful as Aimée imagined, walking in the park at twilight with Henri, the surreal beauty of it, the feeling that he wanted something from her, and the anger she felt toward him for wanting it too late. It was the same set of tangled emotions she'd felt that day in Thoméry by the river, when he'd tried to kiss her. Then, Henri's desire had seemed like an apology. Today, it felt like his need to make up for everything they'd lost. Couldn't he see that it was impossible to make up for the past, that there would never be any reconciliation or understanding? Aimée had realized this, fully, with the death of her maman. That you could hate someone and love them and wish they were here and be grateful they were gone, all in the same instant.

"All I want," Henri said suddenly, "is to know that you are happy." He stopped walking and looked at her. "Are you at least a little happy?"

They were on a small footbridge. Aimée turned her back and looked into the water. It was a mere trickle bumping over the stones, nothing like the rushing river that day in Thoméry.

"No," she said. "But I am not miserable anymore either. I am coming into contentment, I think." What she wanted, more than anything, was to ask after Jeanne, but she didn't dare. She was sure if she spoke the name she'd come apart in front of him.

Henri put his hands on her shoulders. "I'm sorry," he said

delicately, leaning his head near her ear, the softness of his breath on her cheek. Aimée thought he was going to say he was sorry about Jeanne, but instead he said, "I'm sorry I left you."

She turned around and looked at him, and it was not a look of gratitude or forgiveness, but one of crushing, insurmountable pain, and it was then Henri knew, for certain, what he had to do. He'd known since England, but hadn't been able to face it until now.

Taking Aimée's hand, he pulled her off the path into a grove of English hawthorn. Standing there, his shoes crushing the bright red berries that had fallen to the ground, he put his arms around her. Aimée did not resist. She sank into the warmth of his body, slid her hands into his, and let him kiss her. All of the things they couldn't say passed between them. It was an acknowledgment, a memory, an apology, and, finally, a pulling away, and a good-bye.

Henri did love her, Aimée thought. It was just a useless love. A love that had never been able to find a way out.

"Thank you," she whispered.

Then she turned and walked away, unaware that those were the last words she would ever speak to Henri, and that they would turn out to be the perfect thing to say.

Chapter 37

Leonie fought hard. But, in the end, after weeping and pleading, she gave in; there was nothing else she could do.

"Not tonight," she begged. "Give me one more day."

Henri agreed, holding her in his arms, promising they would be all right, while in his own heart he felt a shattering of regret. This was the exact undoing he had been afraid of in England.

The next day, the family did nothing exceptional. Except, Leonie let Jeanne grate the chocolate into the pan over the hot stove, which she'd never allowed before, and she let her spread an extra layer of plum jelly on her breakfast roll. Later, in the garden, Jeanne was allowed to dig all she liked. Leonie watched her from behind the clothesline, pinning up the sheets, as she always did on Saturdays, not once scolding Jeanne for getting her dress dirty.

Henri stayed close to Leonie all day. He took her hand whenever she was near, gave her shoulder a pat, her waist a squeeze. Their contact was desperate and reassuring.

They had a picnic lunch by the river under the shade of a huge oak tree. Henri and Leonie watched Jacques and Jeanne slip down the muddy bank and splash each other in the water.

That night, Leonie made blackberry pie and cream for dessert. Then, despite Jacques's moaning, she gave the children their baths, which usually only happened on Sunday mornings. This, on top of the leniency and second helpings, did not go unnoticed by Jacques.

At bedtime he asked, "What's happening, Maman?"

Tucking the covers to his chin and kissing the top of his head, Leonie said, "Nothing, my dear," wondering what lie she was going to come up with in the morning, and knowing that no matter what it was, Jacques would never understand. All she could hope was that he would forgive her, but she imagined that was far too much to ask.

Going around to Jeanne's side of the bed, Leonie smoothed her hand over her daughter's small forehead and sang her to sleep, remembering Jeanne as a wiggly baby who never wanted to be put down. She thought of the first time Jeanne said, *I love you, Maman,* and of all the times she had said it since, offering up her love so willingly, so innocently.

Not until Jeanne and Jacques were safely asleep did she let herself weep into her daughter's hair, rocking and humming. At three years old, Jeanne was the same age Jacques had been when he came to them. He had been too young to remember his previous life. Jeanne would forget too. As much as Leonie wanted to be remembered, it was a comfort to think that someday Jeanne would not miss her, that Jeanne might be spared that pain.

Henri had to pull Leonie away, undress her like a child, and tuck her into bed. He smoothed her hair, as she had done Jeanne's, and held her until she fell asleep.

Standing over his children, he had second thoughts. They

were curled together. Jeanne's head was buried in Jacques's chest, and Jacques had his arm around her. Protecting her, even in sleep, thought Henri, as he pulled Jeanne away.

She slept on his shoulder as he walked down the dark road. The dry leaves crunched so loudly under his shoes he worried it might wake her. But her small body stayed limp, one arm thumping him softly in the back. It was cold, and he was glad he'd managed to get Jeanne's coat on even if he hadn't been so successful with her boots. Henri had no idea how he was supposed to get those tiny things on her feet, not to mention lace them up, so he'd just shoved them into the top of her suitcase and tucked Jeanne's stockinged feet inside his coat.

On the train, Henri stowed the bag along with Jeanne's hatbox with the birthday hat from Jacques. Henri shifted the sleeping girl from his shoulder to his lap where she curled up with her feet on the empty seat next to him. He brushed his hand over her hair and watched dark objects rush past, his heart tied up in knots.

When the train stopped Jeanne sat up, her eyes wide and startled. "Where are we, Papa?" she asked, and Henri told her to shush, everything was all right.

He carried her off the train, certain she'd be fully awake now with all the banging and screeching, but as he walked through the bright, gas-lit streets, her head fell forward on his shoulder, and she slept again.

It was a little past ten o'clock when Henri arrived at the Savaray home. Marie answered the door, anxious because of the hour, but even more so when she saw the child.

"Please, monsieur, come in. That little one will catch her death of cold," she said.

"I'll wait here." Henri cupped the back of Jeanne's head. "I'd be grateful if you'd fetch Auguste, straightaway."

Auguste was about to climb into bed but instead found himself standing on the doorstep in robe and slippers, the gas lamp casting Henri's long, dark shadow in front of him.

The child in Henri's arms was startling. "You must bring that child in. The wind is biting," Auguste said, holding his robe closed with both hands.

Henri shifted Jeanne off his shoulder and held her like a baby against his chest, her small body curled into a ball. "This is Aimée's child, your *petite-fille,* Jeanne Savaray."

The wind lifted Auguste's hair, and he felt the cold against his scalp. "She is yours?" he said, astounded.

"No," Henri answered. "Monsieur Manet's, but he knows nothing of her."

How could this be? Auguste tried to calculate the child's age, ready to deny any responsibility, but then it hit him; Aimée, naked in Édouard's studio, his maman coming to him at the factory insisting on Aimée's departure. He put a hand to his head. This was why she'd gone to England. How idiotic of him not to suspect.

"You took the child?" he said, not accusing, but awed. "You've raised her?"

"Yes."

The irony of this, Henri standing with this child just as Auguste had stood with Jacques, did not go unnoticed by either of them. Nor did the coincidence of each of them having raised a child that did not rightfully belong to him. They looked at each other as if to say, *Yes, I know how painful it is, how intimate and fragile a man's relationship with his child can be, and how little say we have in the end.*

Henri passed Jeanne to Auguste, who held the sleeping girl effortlessly in his large arms.

That moment of letting go, the sudden weightlessness in

Henri's arms, was disorienting and made him feel strangely unburdened, cleared of shame.

He pulled his coat closed. "I went back to England. My father is dead." The wind settled, and a shudder went through the trees, a soft rustle, and then silence. "It's a wretched thing to admit, but I was grateful. I didn't want to face him."

Auguste stepped forward with the child directly between them. "I must confess something to you." He leaned closer to Henri. "A few years after you came to us—you were twelve, I believe—your father wrote and asked for you to come home."

Henri could smell the cigar on Auguste's breath. He remembered walking into the Savaray dining room one night as a boy, long after he should have been in bed, to find Auguste sitting alone at the table, a glass of red wine in one hand and a cigar in the other. Instead of scolding him, Auguste had said, *Pull up a chair, my boy, and keep me company.*

Henri took Jeanne's hand and let her fist curl around his finger. The strength in that small hand was remarkable. "Why didn't you send me home?" Henri knew the answer, but he wanted to hear it from Auguste.

"I simply couldn't let you go."

Wetness touched Henri's cheeks, and he looked down, embarrassed, peeling his finger out of Jeanne's grip. He looked at the shadow of his legs, two dark shapes against the flat stone, cut off at the knees by Auguste's slippers, the pointy, upward tilt of the toes like the bow of a canoe. Below his robe, Auguste's ankles were bare. Henri wondered if he was supposed to feel some sort of comfort, or gratitude, knowing his father wanted him after all, but he only felt a deep sadness. It made no difference now. He didn't have his father then, and he didn't have the man he used to call *Papa* now.

"I suppose I wouldn't have gone back," he said.

"You might have. The point is I never gave you the chance to decide."

"I only went back to England because of what you said the night you brought Jacques to me, about giving him his rightful name, about his needing a place in the world."

"Then he is an Aubrey now."

"We both are."

"That is good," Auguste said, but what he felt was the definitive sting of loss that no son would carry his name.

Jeanne stirred, and Auguste looked at her. Here was a new life. A beginning. He could tell by the weight of her that she was as hearty a child as Aimée had been, and he felt a surge of joy.

For a few minutes the two men stood in silence. Each thought of reaching out and shaking a hand, but neither did.

Aimée was asleep when her papa entered her bedroom, and she did not wake up when the sheets were pulled back and her child placed next to her.

Auguste was careful to tuck the blankets back up so neither one of them would get cold. For a few minutes he stood and watched them sleep. Jeanne looked very much like Aimée, lying on her pillow of dark curls, but Auguste could also see Colette, something about the almond shape of Jeanne's closed lids. He imagined, when she opened them, there would be gold flecks in her eyes.

When he closed the door, Aimée rolled over. She did not fully wake, but lingered in that space between sleep and dream. She heard the sound of Jeanne's breath and felt the warmth of her small body, and it seemed the most natural thing in the world, dreaming her daughter beside her.

Jeanne stirred and whimpered, and Aimée pulled her against her soft stomach. Deep down they both felt a familiarity, a remembering of those first two weeks together.

Later, when Aimée woke, the sky a thin, shifting gray like her eyes, she would weep silently, not wanting to wake the sleeping child, not wanting to wake herself.

Aimée wandered over the bridge to the Île Saint-Louis and down the narrow street that runs along the Seine, the shutterless windows of the ancient houses reflecting the glinting water in their glass. Great river barges floated by, large and languid, loaded with sacks and barrels. There was a shout from a laundry boat and a reply from the shore, a man jumping and waving his arms from the narrow embankment, a quarrel breaking out behind her, and the laughter of children coming from ahead.

September had always been Aimée's favorite month, when the heat eased and a hint of cooler weather was in the air, a reminder of winter, but nothing too pressing, as if there was still time for something more.

Aimée thought of Édouard Manet. A year ago she heard he was painting fog. Apparently, he managed to have all the trains delayed at the Saint-Lazare, and the engines stuffed with coal so that when they started the air would be thick with steam. At the time Aimée had thought, *How arrogant of him. How pretentious.* Édouard getting whatever he wanted. Stopping trains for his own convenience when there were people who actually needed to get somewhere. But now, with the dank, familiar smell of the river, and the cool fresh air in her face, old sensations came back, and Aimée thought that it was equally inventive of him, resourceful and confident.

She looked across the water at a wide strip of beach where lean boats snaked to the shore, women and children, ankle deep in sand, unloading baskets.

For years, all Aimée had ever been able to see was what Édouard had taken from her. Now, thinking of her time in England, of all her hours spent painting, exhausting herself beyond reason, but finding a thrill in it, she was able to see that Édouard had given her exactly what she needed to find freedom in her work. She had come to love the deceptively warm one-dimensional lives she created. *Paint entirely from within yourself,* Édouard had said. And she had. These past few years that was all she'd done.

Back at the house, Aimée went to her studio for the first time since the day her papa slashed that penknife through her painting. It smelled stale, like plaster and old books.

Through the open door she could hear Jeanne talking to Madame Savaray who was laid up in bed in the next room. Jeanne had spent the first weeks in her new home crying for her maman. Now she wouldn't stop talking. With an earnest, slightly desperate expression she talked about her home, describing the fields and the river and garden, telling them all about her maman and papa. Only once did she speak of her brother. "He's waiting for me," she said with a nod. "He always waits for me, even when I'm slow."

Now, Jeanne's small voice drifted down the hall, and Aimée imagined her *grand-mère* grimacing and trying to hide a satisfied smile.

Aimée walked to a blank canvas that stood on an easel in the middle of the room. Propping her hands on her hips in exactly the way her *grand-mère* would have, she tried to see what was waiting in the empty space.

She remembered an article she'd read by Mallarmé in London's *Art Monthly Review* touting Manet as the leader of this new "school," these "impressionists." The article said that truth for the modern painter was to see nature and reproduce her, freely, without restraint.

Gathering her old portable paint box and easel, Aimée headed back outside to the Île Saint-Louis. She set up her easel in the middle of the Pont Saint-Louis where she could see the smooth stone walls rising out of the water on either side of the bridge. Édouard had taught her to paint the changing light, to capture a moment and let it go, to remember, always, that nothing is fixed or absolute.

Arranging her hat so the sharp slant of sun wasn't in her eyes, she picked up a piece of charcoal and looked over the white peaks rising and falling in the rushing gray-green water below.

She understood now that Édouard's words were about so much more than painting. *Seek the truth,* he had said. *And love it when it is found.*

ENGLAND 1878

Epilogue

H It is gray here, and it rains a lot. I don't mind. It fits how I feel inside, and I like the raindrops pattering on my head.

I like being out of doors better than in, but I have always liked this, so at least not everything has changed. I do wonder if I am the same person that I was before. Most of the time I don't feel the same, but then I get distracted, looking up into the trees, or watching the birds, and for a moment, I feel like my old self. I feel just the way I used to when standing at the edge of the Seine looking up into the trees and watching the birds.

I found a family of mice in the bottom drawer of my dresser this morning. There are six tiny, pink babies.

I am not going to tell anyone because someone will clean them up. It is very important here that everything is clean, and the house is so big it takes many people to keep it that way. Any of them might sweep away my mice.

I will have to be very careful, and secretive, and protect them.

I brought the maman mouse a few oats and a snitch of cheese from the kitchen. The kitchen is a long way from my bedroom, and I had to hide the food in my pocket because Cook is mean.

It doesn't seem at all practical that the kitchen is so far away from everything.

When I asked why we couldn't eat in the kitchen like we used to, Maman said, "This is not France. It's just the way it's done here. We will simply have to get used to everything being so far away from everything else."

She says *this is not France* about almost everything.

The worst is at night, when it gets dark. I am not used to sleeping by myself, and I feel afraid. I want Maman and Papa to sleep in the next room like they used to. But they are far away also.

At least I have my mice.

The baby mice are no longer pink. They have ever so much gray fur, and they eat right out of my hand. I put one of my stockings in the drawer for them to crawl inside of because it is getting cold.

Maman will be angry when she finds my stocking missing. I will know she is angry because she will bite her lower lip and get that line between her eyebrows, but she won't scold me. She never scolds me anymore.

Because of this I realize there are a good many, naughty things I could get away with, but I do not want Maman to be unhappy, so I am trying very hard to be good, even if I did ruin a perfectly decent stocking.

Maman was not mad about the stocking. She smiled when I showed her the nest the mice made inside of it with ripped-up bits of paper. She promised to keep them a secret. She said,

"You're entirely right about the cleaning; far too much of it going on in this house. I'd say we could use a few mice around the place. Remind us of home, yes?"

This made me feel how much I love my maman.

And then the sad feeling came because it made me think how much Jeanne would love the mice too, and how Maman and I would tell her to keep them a secret, and Jeanne would hold her little finger up to her lips and close her eyes, as if she was shutting the secret up inside her.

Whenever the sad feeling comes, I pretend Jeanne is with me.

After Maman leaves I tell Jeanne she can't pick the mice up because she is too little and she will squish them. Then I show her how to put the oats in the palm of her hand and lay her hand flat so the mice can climb up and nibble on them. Then I tell her to hold very still.

I pretend the quiet in the room is because she's doing exactly as I tell her and keeping very still. In my heart I know the quiet is because she isn't really here, and this makes me want to cry. I don't, because I am seven years old now and much too big to cry, but I feel the feeling of crying inside even if I don't let the tears out.

Papa keeps trying to make Maman and me happy.

He tells us of all the things he did as a boy at Abbington Hall, shows us the places in his memories. But he does it in a loud, cheerful voice, and I know he is pretending because Papa is not loud, nor particularly cheerful.

I can see in his face that he is as sad as I am, and I know that he is just making up the good memories because I heard him tell Maman when he was a boy he hated it here. Maman told him we would make new memories. But, later, I heard her crying when she thought no one was around.

I guess we are all pretending not to be sad for each other.

My mice are gone. I am not worried for them. It's spring, and they will be warm outside.

I feel lonelier than ever without them, but hopeful. Hopeful because Maman laughed today, and Papa kissed her afterward.

Jeanne's birthday is in four days.

I remember how we used to pick the blossoms of wild honeysuckle, deep orange in color, and crush them between our fingers. I remember how we used to pull small saplings to the ground and let them go like catapults. I remember how Jeanne used to giggle and put her hands to her mouth, then pull them away and put them over mine.

Remembering is all I have of her now.

I have stopped pretending to talk to her because I don't know what she looks like anymore, and I don't know how she sounds. Four years old is a lot different from three years old, and I do not want to imagine her at three years old forever. I want to imagine her as she really is.

On her birthday I am going to pick flowers for her and put them on the table. I am going to buy a hat with a blue satin streamer and hang it on the back of a chair. I will ask Maman to find candy violets, even though I am not sure if violets grow in Burford as they did in Thoméry.

I am sure this will make Maman cry. I will tell her it's going to be okay, but that it's very important we do this every year.

It is important because someday I am going to find my little sister.

It will be hard because she will grow up, and I will grow up, and we won't know what the other one looks like even if we've imagined it.

But when she sees me, and I see her, it won't matter.

Our hearts will know each other.

Of this, I am certain.

ACKNOWLEDGMENTS

It is a joy to be able to thank all of those whose support, guidance, friendship, and love have helped me on this journey.

Immense gratitude and appreciation to Heide Lange, Rachael Dillon Fried, and the staff at Sanford J. Greenburger Associates, Inc., for believing in my work and seeing the possibilities from the beginning. Thank you to Stefanie Diaz for landing such early book deals abroad, and a huge thank-you to my outstanding agent, Stephanie Delman, for her indefatigable encouragement, dedication, and excitement. I couldn't have done any of this without my editor Laura Chasen's meticulous notes and spot-on insight, not to mention utter faith in me. Thank you to my wonderful new editor Alicia Clancy for stepping in and seeing this through to the end. Thank you to my copy editors Sarah and Chris at Script Acuity Studio, to my production editor, Emily Walters, to my marketing team, Brant Janeway, Angie Giammarino, and Katie Bassel, and everyone at St. Martin's Press who had a hand in getting this book out into the world.

I am deeply grateful for the wealth of information I gathered from others. Books I relied on included *The Private Lives of the Impressionists* by Sue Roe; *Growing Up with the Impressionists: The Diary of Julie Manet*; *I Am the Most Interesting Book of All: The Diary of Marie Bashkirtseff*, translated by Phyllis Howard Kernberger; *The Belly of Paris*, by Émile Zola, translated by Mark Kurlansky; *The*

Masterpiece, by Émile Zola, edited by Roger Pearson and translated by Thomas Walton; *Édouard Manet: Rebel in a Frock Coat*, by Beth Archer Brombert.

Thank you to my readers for trudging through first drafts with kind and honest critique: Ariane Goodwin, Stephen Muzzy, Heather Fulton, Sarah Heinemann, Michelle King, Robert Burdick, Isaiah Weiss, Lilia Teal, Nicole Cusano, and Bob Sekula.

A bursting, heartfelt thank-you to the mentors who supported my writing in all phases: my first teachers, Michael and Rebecca Muir-Harmony, who published my work at the ripe age of six at Full Circle School's Rumbling Raisin Press and encouraged my garrulous personality and brimming imagination; June Kuzmeskus for letting me bust through the conventional box of high school and create my own writing curriculum; and to Roni Natov for her inspiring classes at Brooklyn College and for guiding me through a thesis that led to the beginnings of my first novel.

There aren't words enough to thank my mother, who painstakingly read every version of this novel. Suffice to say I wouldn't be here if it weren't for her scrupulous, pitch-perfect edits and, of course, her loving, motherly support. Thanks to my dad, who cried tears of joy when hearing of my book deal, who loves books more than anyone I know, and who would carve a spot in gold on his bookshelf for this one if he could.

This book is dedicated to my sister, a masterful artist and my inspiration. A thank-you pales to all she has given me.

To my children, Silas and Rowan, for sacrificing their mom to many a writing weekend and for filling my days with adventure and my heart to the brim.

Finally, to Stephen, my husband, for his unwavering love and patience, for believing we would get here one day, and for giving me a life that has allowed for all of this to be.